THE  THIN

"This inventive and exciting tale ha͏_____ges—
and I loved every minute! Get ready_____ dangerous ride that
crackles with pure awesomeness."

—*Carolyn Crane*, USA Today *bestselling author*

"Engaging, old-school urban fantasy. Will appeal to readers hungering for
spirited supernatural action with a dash of forbidden romance."

—*Jenn Bennett, author of the* Arcadia Bell *series*

"A fast-paced, engaging book. A nice blend of horror and paranormal.
Dale Highland is totally my spirit animal."

—*Joe Alfano, Wicked Little Pixie*

"I greatly enjoyed *The Demon Within*, and I look forward to continuing the
books in the series. Dale feels dynamic, whole, and despite her demonic side,
completely and utterly human. I long to see her grow into her powers and
become at home in her own skin since, like many geeks, I know the struggles
of finding my place and my people. In many ways, Dale's journey is a metaphor
for anyone who has longed to find somewhere he or she can be themselves and
be fully understood."

—*Jodi Scaife, Fanboy Comics*

A
DALE
HIGHLAND
NOVEL

A CALIFORNIA COLDBLOOD BOOK
RARE BIRD BOOKS
LOS ANGELES, CALIF.

{DEMON within}

BETH WOODWARD

THIS IS A GENUINE CALIFORNIA COLDBOOD BOOK

A California Coldblood Book | Rare Bird Books

453 South Spring Street, Suite 302

Los Angeles, CA 90013

rarebirdbooks.com

californiacoldblood.com

Set in Minion

Cover design by Leonard Philbrick

Credits: Katalinks, Oleksandr Kovalchuk, Jovannig, EnishiEnya

Printed in the United States

Distributed by Publishers Group West

Publisher's Cataloging-in-Publication data

Names: Woodward, Beth.

Title: The Demon within / by Beth Woodward.

Description: Dale Highland Series | Trade Paperback Original | Los Angeles [California] : California Coldblood, an imprint of Rare Bird Books, 2016.

Identifiers: ISBN 978-1-942600-42-8.

Subjects: LCSH Angels—Fiction. | Demons—Fiction. | Fantasy—Fiction. | Paranormal fiction. | Paranormal romance. | BISAC FICTION / Fantasy / Paranormal. | FICTION / Fantasy / Romantic. | FICTION / Fantasy / Urban.

Classification: LCC PS3623.O6832 D46 2016 DDC 813.6—dc23

DEDICATION

In memory of my mom, Diane Woodward.
The first one was always going to be for you.
I wish you were here to see it.

{DEMON}
The
within

PROLOGUE

I WOKE UP BEFORE DAWN ON the floor, naked, covered in blood, a santoku knife in my hand. Less than a foot from me was a body, its head no longer attached to its neck. My hands shook, and I felt nauseated.

No, not again...

It had happened before, me waking up with a body next to me and no idea how I got there.

I called them Rages.

The first time, I was seventeen, and I murdered my best friend's prom date. Julie had been so excited when Brad Kinnard, the class president and most popular guy in school, took her to the prom. But after we were there, I found out he'd slipped something in her drink and taken her to a hotel room. When I found them, Julie was unconscious, her blue dress pushed up over her head, her torn pantyhose on the floor. He was on top of her, red and sweaty, making low-pitched grunting noises. The room smelled like industrial-strength pine cleaner. To this day, that smell makes me sick.

The last memory I have is just one thought: I want to kill him. In that moment, a red haze bled over my eyes, and my blood turned to lava. A voice whispered in my mind: *give in to it.*

So I did.

When I came to, Brad was dead, purple finger-shaped bruises around his neck, and Julie was still out cold. I had two choices: stay and get arrested, or run.

So I ran.

It had been ten years since then, and I'd had six more Rages. Every time it happened, there had been a trigger. Every time it happened, I was defending myself or someone else. Every time it happened, I left a body or two behind. And every time it happened, I could always remember what set me off. I could remember that moment of snapping from sanity to the red-filled Rage.

I'd always had a reason. Always.

But this changed everything. I'd killed, but I couldn't remember why. Sitting there, in a modern-style condominium with a skylight and an open floor plan and a carpet soaked through with blood…I couldn't remember anything at all.

The back of his head now faced me. He was male, maybe in his mid-thirties. Andrew, I remembered suddenly, his name was Andrew Seymour. And we had gone out on our first date the night before.

He'd picked me up at my apartment, his blue shirt contrasting nicely with his olive skin. At dinner, we had talked about the little things that mean everything: how we both loved the Beatles but he thought John Lennon's solo work was pretentious; how we both thought *Citizen Kane* was vastly overrated; how he could eat Chinese take-out every day; and how I could barely walk by a Panda Express without feeling queasy. We had laughed a lot. I liked him.

The last thing I remembered, we were sitting at the restaurant waiting for our dessert. I had a glass of wine in front of me. How much had I drank? I knew better than that. He had smiled at me and said, "I like you."

And I had smiled back and said, "I like you, too."

But it didn't matter. That was before. Now, I'd had another Rage, and now it was time to run.

Again.

I struggled to my feet, fighting against the heaviness that always settled in my limbs after a Rage. Rage, rage—rags. Rags, I needed rags, something to clean up any trace I might have left behind. I found some dish towels in the kitchen. I started wiping all the hard surfaces, trying to get rid of any fingerprints.

I looked at Andrew's body. What had he done to deserve this? Please tell me he did something to deserve this. Because if he didn't, if I killed an innocent person, then that means I'm...

A bell clanged. I jumped and spun around.

A clock chimed on the wall, playing "Ode to Joy." The face opened up, and little figurines danced inside. It was already 4:00 a.m. The sun would be up soon, and so would Andrew's neighbors. I had to get out of here, and fast, before anyone saw me.

I wiped everything I could, but I still wasn't satisfied. Bleach would help. I found Andrew's laundry room, and a memory crashed into me. We had come in through the back door, through this room. We were kissing. His fingers tangled in my long blonde hair, seeking the zipper of my dress. His eyes asked a question, and I whispered the answer into his mouth: yes. He unzipped my dress, and then...

And then? But there was only blackness.

I pulled the bleach down from a shelf above the washer, making sure to cover my hand with a towel first. I poured some over Andrew's body. Would it work? I wasn't going to wait to find out.

I showered quickly and bleached down the tub when I was done. Then I raced around the living room, gathering up my clothes and putting them on. They looked clean, at least.

I checked the time. Almost 4:30. Time to go.

Andrew's car keys were on the counter. I grabbed them and went outside, forcing myself to close the door slowly. I walked down his front walkway stinking of bleach. I pressed the unlock button on the key, and a black Camry flashed in response. Before I got into the car, I lingered a moment, looking at the stillness I'd left behind. "I'm sorry," I said, hoping somehow he could hear me.

And then I ran, again.

I WAS WORRIED ABOUT THE police finding me and connecting me to my other crimes. What I didn't know is that they were the least of my problems.

Twenty minutes after I left, a man pulled up to the condo. He came because he had a feeling. He'd been doing his job for a long time, and he trusted his intuition. If any of the neighbors saw him, they probably would have described him as "nondescript." He wasn't—he could never be that—but he was very good at pretending he was, when he needed to be.

He entered the condo silently, making sure the lock showed no signs of his tampering. He looked at the body, the blood, the hastily cleaned condo. He didn't take any pictures; he didn't need any. He only stayed for five minutes, but he gleaned more in that time than the cops would in their entire investigation. But he didn't care about Andrew, about how he died, or why. He only cared about one thing, and he was closer to it than ever before.

Me.

As I DROVE TOWARD THE sunrise that morning, I thought about what I'd done, about what I was. It occurred to me that a religious person might pray at a time like this, but I didn't believe in God.

I didn't believe in anything, really.

All that would change a few months later when the man finally found me.

CHAPTER

I T'S HARD TO KNOW IF you're going crazy when you were never sure of your sanity in the first place.

It had been seven months since I'd come to New York City. Seven months since I'd fled Raleigh in the middle of the night. Seven months since Andrew Seymour…but no, I wasn't going to think about that. I couldn't think about that, not while I was at work, surrounded by people. So I shoved it into a box and pushed it into the back of my mind. Not that it ever went far.

I was working at Ivanov's Books, a small store on Sixth Avenue that specialized in hard-to-find books. I loved it because it had a cool literary vibe without being too trendy—creaky hardwood floors, pictures of knights and dragons on the walls, and soft pillows lining the aisles because they were too small to fit chairs—and because Mr. Ivanov had no problem paying me in cash. The store was always quiet, despite the prime location near NYU, and had a strict twenty-five dollar minimum credit card purchase policy. I had a theory that Mr. Ivanov was an underground Russian intelligence agent, or maybe that the bookstore was a front for

the mafia, because otherwise I couldn't understand how he could possibly afford Greenwich Village rents.

Frankly, I didn't care whether Mr. Ivanov worked with the remnants of the KGB or laundered money in his spare time. He gave me a thirty-minute lunch break, and he always paid me on time, which is more than I could say about some of my former employers.

But ever since I'd started working at the store, I sometimes had the uneasy feeling of being watched. And it had been happening more often as the months wore on.

On this morning in early June as I was entering inventory into the store's spreadsheet, the skin prickled on the back of my neck. I looked up from the laptop to see if anyone was waiting at the register.

Nobody.

I stepped out from behind the counter and walked through the aisles to see if someone had come in without my knowledge. (Though even that would be a strange thing, since there was a bell hanging over the door that rang every time it opened.) But the store appeared to be empty.

In one of the aisles, there was a book on the floor—a Pennsylvania travel guide. Pennsylvania had been my home state once upon a time, but I was a different girl then. Literally. I picked it up and reshelved it. For a second, I could swear I *felt* someone right behind me. I spun around, but once again, the aisle was empty.

The telephone rang, nearly causing me to jump out of my skin. I rushed back to the counter to answer it, trying to calm my heart to a reasonable rate. "Ivanov's Books, this is Dale speaking."

The voice of my roommate, Nicole Cohen, filled the line. "Would you mind not coming home right after work? I'm bringing Devlin home with me tonight, and we'd like some alone time."

Who was Devlin again? Male or female? First, last, or middle name? I could never keep track with Nik. "Sure, no problem."

"Dale…are you all right? You don't sound like yourself."

"Yeah, I'm fine. It's just…" I hesitated. "Do you believe in ghosts?"

Nik was silent for a long time before she answered. "I think that, when people die, the essence of who they are—their *soul*, if you want to call it that—is absorbed into the fabric of the universe. And I think that maybe sometimes, you can *feel* that essence near you, that maybe it gravitates to the love it felt during life. Does that make sense?"

Hmmm. Somehow, I didn't think "universal essences" explained what I had been feeling. "No. I mean real ghosts. Like *The Sixth Sense* or something."

"Oh. Then no."

Of course not. "Yeah, me neither. I'll see you later tonight, okay?"

"Dale, are you *sure* you're all right? I can give Devlin a rain check and we can have a girls' night, if you need to talk."

"No, don't worry about it. Have fun with Devlin. I'll see you later tonight."

After I hung up the phone, Mr. Ivanov, a seventies-ish man with wispy gray hair and Buddy Holly glasses, approached me and shook his head. "She asked you to come home late again?" His Russian accent made the words sound clipped.

"It's not a big deal. It's just a few hours."

"I don't like you staying out so late on your own. You should ask someone to come pick you up."

"I don't know anyone with a car, and you know it'll cost an arm and a leg to get a cab out to Brooklyn."

"You need to be careful. It's dangerous for a young girl by herself out there."

If only he knew. But his concern made sense, given what I'd told him about myself. I'd told him that I'd just gotten out of a relationship that had become violent—true enough, but probably not in the way he assumed. I also said I was twenty-two, an age that still seemed young and vulnerable, which made people more willing to help you out. I wondered how much longer I'd be able to pull off the youthful act; at twenty-seven, I was already five years older than I was pretending to be. But no one had questioned me on it so far, so I didn't worry about it much.

I smiled at him. "I'll be careful, Mr. Ivanov, I promise. You don't have to worry about me." That much, at least, was true.

SEVERAL HOURS LATER, AFTER THE bookstore closed, I went over to an Internet café in Chinatown that was open late and accepted cash. The owner knew me now, and she waved as I sat in my usual spot and plugged my headphones into the port. I searched through the Raleigh-Durham newspapers to see if anything else had been said about Andrew's death. I knew there was probably no reason to be so careful; there are millions of people in New York, many of them transplants from other places, so it's not surprising that someone might be looking at North Carolina newspapers. On the other hand, just in case Big Brother really is watching, I don't want my Internet searches to flag me as suspicious.

But the results were the same as the last time I had checked ten days earlier: *Andrew Seymour, age thirty-four, brutally decapitated in his own home.* Six months after Andrew's death, it was no longer big news, and the latest updates were merely blurbs on the crime blotter about how police had no new leads. Only one item interested me: police were still seeking a young woman named Crystal Truman for questioning. She had apparently

disappeared around the time of Andrew's death. She was described as average height and build with green eyes and long, bleached-blond hair.

But Crystal Truman didn't exist anymore, and the woman I had become didn't look anything like her. My new name was Dale Highland. I had discarded the green contact lenses in favor of my natural blue eyes. I'd cut my hair into a short, choppy style and dyed it to an auburn shade closer to my natural color. Crystal had been big into bronzer; it was part of the California chic look she favored. But Dale was a low-maintenance, jeans and T-shirt kind of girl, and faux sun just didn't work for her. She would hate the pretentiousness of trying to feign a tan on her pale skin. Plus, I was sick of putting all that crap on my face all the time.

My stomach muscles clenched when I clicked on the link for the earliest article, the one that had run in the newspaper the day after Andrew's death. It had his bright, smiling portrait up front, followed by a picture of his condo door sealed off with police tape. The article described his death in blunt detail, stating that he was decapitated and that someone had attempted to clean the scene with bleach. I hated reading it, but I always did, like picking off a scab. I might not have looked like Crystal Truman anymore, but I knew who and what I really was.

A few weeks after Andrew's death, I sent a hundred-dollar donation in Andrew's name to the Humane Society, the charity listed in his obituary. It was more than I could afford. It wasn't nearly enough.

There was a video with the article, some talking heads discussing the violence and brutality of the death. They speculated that it might have been a gang hit, but they couldn't find any connection between Andrew Seymour and any known gangs.

But this wasn't really the video I wanted to see. I opened a new tab and did a quick search. Months earlier, I discovered someone had leaked a video of the crime scene. Somehow, it still hadn't been pulled down,

probably because most of the viewers assumed it was fake, teaser footage for some upcoming horror movie or something. If I hadn't known better, I might have assumed the same thing. Andrew's living room was still splattered with blood, despite my best efforts to clean it up. Discolored patches covered the carpet where the bleach had splashed. The santoku knife was where I had left it on the living room floor, tagged with a yellow number "3." Andrew's body had been removed by the time the video was recorded. I don't know if I could have taken seeing it again.

I watched it over and over again, until my eyes teared up and my stomach was roiling. Then I watched it some more.

Seven months later, Andrew's death made no more sense to me than it had the night he died—the night I killed him. The Rages had never come without a reason. I always remembered the extreme, violent fury that took over me, the way it consumed me entirely—berserker rage, like the legendary Norse warriors I had read about as a teenager when I was trying to figure out what was wrong with me. But with Andrew, there was nothing. One minute, I'm out on a date, and the next thing I remember, I'm next to his dead body. I'd gone as far as to search Andrew's public records online to see if I could find anything suspicious. Nothing. I couldn't track down so much as a speeding ticket. I'd met Boy Scouts with more checkered histories.

After I'd killed Brad Kinnard on prom night, the media had dubbed me the "Schoolhouse Strangler." They had a field day; it was exactly the kind of salacious story that played well on cable news. Brad's parents were rich and influential, and they went onto every TV show they could find and painted him as a cross between Einstein and Mother Teresa, saying I had killed Brad because I was jealous he asked Julie to the prom and not me. Julie never commented publicly. I couldn't blame her. Everyone knew the story they wanted to believe, and saying anything else would have only made

things worse for her. Every story has to have a villain, right? I've been the villain for a very long time now.

After I finished replaying the video, I paid my balance and left the store. It was dark by then. I needed some time to collect myself before I could go home, so I started walking up Broadway, letting the sights and sounds of the city take over and block out everything else going on in my head. I had thought New York City would be loud enough and frenetic enough to silence the accusations my brain kept screaming at me: that I was a murderer, that I had killed an innocent man, that I was evil. It wasn't. It was only enough to cover them up sometimes.

It was 10:00 before I finally made it onto the subway, feeling entirely too much like the girl who had run away from murder charges after the senior prom ten years earlier. I closed my eyes and concentrated. *I am Dale Highland. I am twenty-two years old. I grew up in Cleveland. My mother is a waitress. My father is a truck driver. I like strawberry milkshakes and Creedence Clearwater Revival and the smell of roses after it rains. I dislike cats and spiders and Adam Sandler movies.* I had long since discovered it was the little details that make a person. By the time the L train crossed into Brooklyn, my mask had slipped firmly back into place.

Only a few other people exited the train at my stop. The neighborhood where I lived still had a largely industrial feel and was still just on the wrong side of gentrification. By the time I had walked a couple of blocks away from the station, I was alone with nothing but the sounds of window-unit air conditioners and faraway firetruck sirens to keep me company. Suddenly, when I was about a block away from my apartment, I felt that strange prickling sensation on the back of my neck again. I circled around, but I didn't see anyone. "Hello?" I called. "Is someone there?"

No one answered.

CHAPTER

A FEW DAYS LATER WHEN I was off from work, I sat on the floor of my Bushwick apartment with the metal draw-down door open, my legs dangling off the ledge, my cheap laptop computer resting on my thighs. I was reading another news story about Andrew. Police said they had found his car, a 2009 black Toyota Camry, abandoned at a rest stop off of I-95. When I left it there and hitched a ride north, I figured they'd find it eventually. I was surprised it had taken them this long. They were searching the car now for clues. I'd vacuumed and wiped it down thoroughly before I left. They wouldn't find so much as a speck of dust in that vehicle.

I was so engrossed in the story that I didn't hear Nik come into the apartment. When she cleared her throat behind me, I jumped and had to grab on to the edge to keep myself from losing my balance. "Aren't you afraid you're going to fall off?" Nik asked.

I looked down at the ground, which was three stories below. "No," I answered honestly.

Nik snorted. "Yeah, if you say so." She went into the bathroom and shut the door.

Six months ago, Nik had advertised for a roommate on Craigslist. When I met her in person, I knew immediately I would like her. She was in her early twenties, about my height, and kept most of her tattoos discreetly hidden underneath her clothes. She wore her dark brown hair in Bob Marley-style dreadlocks, an odd look for a Jewish girl from Connecticut, but somehow she made it work. She was a senior in NYU's art program, and her paintings adorned the walls. She was always busy going somewhere or doing something, so I'd go days without seeing her sometimes. She also allowed me to pay in cash; most of my previous landlords had required me to buy money orders since I wasn't using checks.

Plus, I *loved* the apartment. The building had once been used for shipping and freight, which explained the now-useless draw-down door—which we weren't *really* supposed to open, but it kept the pigeons from nesting there—and the fact that what they called a "kitchen" was nothing more than a refrigerator and a hot plate. On the other hand, we had high ceilings, a hardwood floor, and enough room to roller skate in even though it was a studio with two people living in it. Nik slept on a loft bed near the back of the apartment, and I slept on the futon by the TV.

When Nik came out of the bathroom, she sat down behind me—safely away from the door. "It's time for you to join the real world."

When I didn't respond, she reached over and shut my laptop. "Hey, I was using that!" I told her.

"That's my whole point. You've been here since December, and so far, all I've seen you do is go to work, read, and look at that stupid computer of yours. Do you even have any friends in New York besides me?"

"Of course I do!" I totally didn't.

"Look, I get that you're kind of an introvert, and I respect that. I also get that maybe something happened before you came here, something

that you don't really want to talk about, and that's why you keep yourself so isolated."

Damn her. Nik was too perceptive for her own good—or for mine, at least. I kept silent.

After a moment, Nik began speaking again. "It's been six months, Dale. It's not good for you to be alone up here all the time. I worry about you."

I sighed. I had no desire to socialize, no desire to expose myself to the world beyond Mr. Ivanov's cozy shop and the apartment. But Nik had always been kind, and I didn't want her to worry. "You're right. I'm sorry. I'll try to do better."

"Great!" She pulled a purple flier out of her purse and handed it to me. It was an advertisement for something called a "warehouse party" in Red Hook that night. She grinned at me, and I realized I had been played.

"So...what is a warehouse party, exactly?" I was picturing a roomful of people dancing around in welding masks, like *Flashdance* or something.

Nik rolled her eyes. "It's a *party* at a *warehouse*. They have music and dancing and all kinds of stuff. Don't worry, though—these things always have a very mellow vibe. It's a sci-fi theme, so that'll be crazy awesome. And my friends are great. It'll be a chance for you to get to know some more people in the city."

Spending the night partying with a bunch of drunken twenty-two-year-olds didn't exactly sound like my idea of a good time. Alcohol had always affected me strongly, but after what happened with Andrew I wouldn't risk it at all anymore. But Dale was supposed to *be* twenty-two, and a big part of blending in was fitting in. "All right."

Nik bounced up and down on her feet. "Awesome. We need to leave by eleven. I want to get there around midnight."

Midnight? Seriously? "The party starts that late?"

"No, the party starts at ten, but most people don't show up until at least midnight. Why, is that a problem?"

I hesitated, worried that a long night out might be enough to trigger a Rage. But exhaustion had never set me off before, and I hadn't come close to a Rage since I moved to New York. Besides, it was only lunchtime, so I had plenty of time to eat and rest before I had to get ready. "No, it's no problem." I hoped I was right.

I OPENED MY EYES, AND Andrew was lying next to me on the futon, expressionless, staring at me with his deep brown eyes. "I'm so sorry," I told him.

His voice was flat. "Why did you kill me?"

"I don't remember. The others were always bad. They hurt other people, or they tried to hurt me."

"Was I...*bad*? Did I hurt you?" He could barely get the words out.

"I don't remember."

"What about the others? They were 'bad.' Does that help you sleep better at night?"

"No, it doesn't."

He turned away from me. I put my hand on his arm, but he flung it away. "Go to hell," he said.

I woke up drenched in sweat. I took a shaky breath, then several more until my pulse started to slow. Nik emerged from the bathroom with a towel wrapped around her. "Is everything all right? You were really tossing and turning there."

"Nightmare," I replied. My throat felt scratchy, as if I'd been crying out in my sleep.

"Must have been one hell of a nightmare. I thought you were having a seizure there for a minute."

"You have no idea."

Nik looked at me strangely. "Well, it's almost ten. You should start getting ready for the party...if you're still up for it, that is."

She was giving me an easy out. Part of me wanted to take it. But another part of me wanted to pretend to be a normal girl who did normal things like dance and drink and flirt. But more than that, I wanted to go somewhere I could escape the ghost of Andrew Seymour, somewhere loud enough to drown out the voices in my head. "I'm good."

When I emerged from the bathroom forty-five minutes later, I had changed into a pair of dark jeans that hugged my legs nicely and a plain black tank top. Not exactly party clothes, but they were the best I could manage given that my nicest wardrobe pieces came from the discount rack at K-mart. Nik immediately zeroed in on my shoes. "Sneakers? Seriously?"

I shrugged. "I don't have any other shoes. Besides, I'll be more comfortable on the dance floor."

She rolled her eyes. "You're about a size eight, right?"

I nodded, and she pulled a pair of black stiletto heels from the closet. The last time I had worn shoes like that, one of them had ended the evening wedged into a man's eye socket. "No heels."

"You have a great body, but no one is ever gonna notice it if you're dressed like you're going to the gym."

Sheesh. Nik never usually dressed up. Who knew she was a closet fashionista? Of course, I shouldn't have been surprised; she wore a navy blue halter top that barely covered her breasts and a pair of skintight PVC pants. Her dreads were tied away from her face with a scarf. Her makeup was brightly colored, and she had what looked like star tattoos underneath her right ear, filled in pink, purple, and blue. I hadn't noticed them before,

but Nik got new tattoos the way other people got new socks. Anyone else would have looked stupid or slutty. Nik looked hot. Still, I had to put my foot down somewhere, especially when she was trying to adorn it in a fuck-me shoe. "Absolutely not."

"Fine." Her lip jutted out, just a little, before she caught herself and pulled it back in. Nik set the heels down and pulled another pair of shoes out of the closet, a pair of red ballet flats. Before I could say anything, Nik started again. "They're not heels, and they've got a little bit of cushioning in the soles, so you'll be comfortable dancing in them all night long. They'll look amazing."

"All right, fine."

Nik grinned, and we were ready to go.

An hour later, we were getting off the subway and walking toward the party. It wasn't the best place to be walking around at night. It looked like an old industrial area, and unlike most other areas of the city I'd seen, there didn't seem to be any restaurants or neighborhood bodegas around. The few people we saw looked like they were heading toward the same party we were.

When Nik had said that the party was being held "at a warehouse," she wasn't kidding. It was four stories high with a weathered brick façade, and several of the windows were broken or missing. But it wasn't empty— not that night, anyway. Even from half a block away, I could hear music blasting and see multi-colored lights dancing in the windows.

Nik's friends were already waiting for us in the line. Megan, a tiny Asian girl, wore a metallic tube top over black leggings. Chaz had gorgeous caramel-colored skin and expressive brown eyes, and he wore a black tank top, skinny jeans, and Ziggy Stardust-esque makeup. His dark hair was spiked up, and pieces of it were dyed candy-apple red. He wrapped his arms around Nik and kissed her on the cheek. "I'm so glad you made it. It's never a dull night with you around."

"We thought maybe you weren't coming," Megan said. "We've been waiting here forever."

"Meg, dear, *you* thought they weren't coming. I knew they would. And we've only been waiting about fifteen minutes, so chill." Chaz turned to me. "Nik's new roommate-slash-project, I presume? I understand this is your first underground party. Didn't anyone tell you that tonight was a sci-fi theme?"

I looked around, and I noticed that I was one of the few people in line who wasn't dressed like an alien, a space traveler, or something resembling a character from *Jem and the Holograms.* I looked at Chaz and shrugged. "I'm a nonconformist."

Chaz laughed, a deeper sound than I expected. "Well, Nik's roommate-slash-project, don't worry. You'll be just fine." He wrapped his arm around me affectionately as we headed toward the entrance.

It was a twenty-dollar cover to get inside, a figure I balked at, but Nik, Chaz, and Megan paid without hesitation. Welcome to New York. I gave the guy a bill from my pocket, and he stamped my hand.

The party was up on the fourth floor, and the place was even bigger than it looked on the outside. The room was the size of several gymnasiums, and the ceilings thirty feet high. Multi-colored spotlights and strobes dangled from the exposed beams. Nik and Megan immediately detached themselves from the group, leaving Chaz and me surrounded by chaos.

Over on one side of the room, a scruffy-looking man and a woman with oversized glasses used a stationary bike and a plastic tray to create splatter paintings. On the other, people sat in a kiddie pool filled with rose petals, throwing them up into the air with glee. Out of the corner of my eye, I saw a guy run by completely naked. "Don't things like this get busted on *Law and Order* all the time? Usually because somebody gets drugged, raped, and murdered in the Porta Potty?" I whispered to Chaz.

Chaz laughed. "Nah. That's just what they tell you in school to get you to get a nice, boring job where you wear a suit and work for fifty hours a week until you die. Blah, blah, blah. Who would want that when there's all this amazingness in the world?" Chaz strolled over to the pool of rose petals, picked up a handful, and tossed them over his head. "Whee!"

I gave Chaz a weak smile. I liked his effusiveness, envied it, but in my experience having this many people in a room together often ended up with someone getting dead—usually by my hand. He went toward the crowd at the center of the room to dance, motioning for me to come along. I shook my head.

I retreated to a corner of the room and wished I had thought to bring a book with me. Instead, I had to be content with watching the lights dancing around the room. *Oooh, pretty. Yawn.*

I don't know how long I was standing there before Nik came over to me. She put her arms around me and leaned her head against my shoulder. "Aren't you having fun?" she asked with a wobble in her voice.

I patted her back stiffly. "I'm fine. Don't worry about me. I'm just a little tired tonight."

"You know what you need?" She pointed to the wall opposite us, where Megan was talking to a man dressed in bright orange phat pants covered in reflective tape. "Megan's friend Sammy always gets the best stuff for us. Just a teeny little bit of ecstasy, and you'll be more relaxed, and everyone will be your best friend."

I looked at the two of them. Megan, who had seemed so stiff and uptight when we were in line for the party, was now leaning into Sammy, her arms around his neck, laughing at something he said. On the other side of the room, Chaz was in the middle of the throng, his arms in the air, dancing with no regard to the music or beat. They both looked so happy and free. Envy surged through me. In my adult life, I'd never felt like that. I

had to think about everything I said, watch everything I did, fight to keep my Rages at bay. The dreadlocked woman standing next to me was the closest thing I'd had to a friend since high school, and she didn't even know my real name. "No, thank you, Nik," I said to her, "ecstasy's not really my thing."

She frowned. "Are you sure? I've done it plenty of times, and it's completely safe, I promise."

"Yeah. Drugs tend to have a weird effect on me." That much was true, at least. Any sort of drug or chemical was likely to have strange effects on my body. Caffeine was about the strongest thing I could take, but even that left me twitchy if I had too much at once. Even children's Tylenol made me loopy. "I'm just going to go and have a drink. You get back to your friends."

"All right. If you say so." Nik gave me a sad smile, but she left and went over to a group of people who were waving at her from the other side of the room, glancing back at me as she walked.

I sighed and forced myself to walk away from my wall perch over to the bar—really, just a couple of card tables with Solo cups stacked on top and bottles of booze behind them, Nik probably believed I was going to get something alcoholic. Oh, well. Just one more way that I couldn't be like a normal person.

A half-sized bottle of water was four dollars. I hated spending that much money, but I didn't trust that a soda wouldn't come spiked with something. I downed it in one chug and threw the empty bottle into the trashcan. As I was walking away, I bumped into a blond man in a blue plaid shirt. "Oh, sorry," I said.

"No, it was my fault. Can I…"

But I didn't hear the rest of what he said. I was already focused on something else.

Chaz was on the edge of the dance floor, facing another man, his arms folded across his chest. The other man was in his forties—giving him a good decade on most of the people here. He wore a polo shirt and cargo shorts and had the build of an ex-football player slowly going to seed. His Solo cup jittered in his hand, beer sloshing on the floor. The man laughed, obviously finding himself very funny. Chaz shook his head and tried to walk away, but the man grabbed his arm and yanked him back.

Oh, *hell* no.

I pushed across the floor until I stood in front of them. "Is everything all right here?"

Chaz spoke through clenched teeth. "Everything's fine, Dale. Just leave."

"Yeah, everything's fine, sweetheart. I was just asking your friend here if he thought I was pretty enough to stick my dick up his asshole."

The man wrapped his arms around Chaz's shoulders and started making kissing noises. Chaz shoved him away roughly. "Fuck you."

The man let out another drunken laugh. "No, fuck *you*. Just give me ten minutes with your ass, and I bet I can make a *real* man out of you!"

Chaz lunged. I jumped in front of him and held him back. "Just leave it alone, Chaz. He's not worth it."

"Oh, I see how it is." The man gestured toward us, sloshing beer on my shirt. "You let your beard do your fighting for you. That's all right, man. I get it. Don't want to break your fingernails. Tell you what, I'll fuck you *and* her at the same time!"

Chaz pushed against me, but I didn't let him go. I turned my head and glared at the man. "You need to go away."

"But baby, we were just getting started."

He stroked my cheek. I slapped his fingers away. "Get. The Fuck. Away. From us."

It felt like something snapped inside my head. The man's eyes seemed to glaze over, and he backed away from us rapidly, ignoring the indignant shouts of the people he collided with. When he was about twenty-five feet from us, his feet became tangled in the power cords leading to the DJ's booth. He fell, pulling the cords out of the outlet with him. The music stopped abruptly, and everyone turned to look at him. The man kept lobster-crawling backward until he hit the wall, hard. A trail of blood dripped from his ear.

The room was completely silent.

A couple of people went over to the man. He scrambled to his feet, waving off their offers of assistance. He shook his head, like a dog trying to clear water from his ears. Then he broke into a run, making a beeline for the stairs and leaving without another word.

I stared, my mouth hanging open. Chaz looked at me. "Can someone tell me what just happened?"

"Damned if I know."

"It was almost like…" Chaz paused, "like you scared him off or something."

I snorted. "Yeah. It must have been my mad guns." I patted my biceps— or lack thereof. "He was just some drunk asshole. He probably sobered up enough to realize what a douche he was being." I frowned. "Are you all right, Chaz?"

Chaz shrugged. "I've been dealing with morons like that since I was twelve. I could have handled it myself." He smiled slightly. "But thanks for the intervention. I might have hit him otherwise, and spending the night in jail would have sucked."

"Yes, and you would have spent the night. I don't have the money to bail you out."

Chaz grinned this time. "Fair enough. I'm gonna try to find a bathroom and try to wash his stank off. That man reeked of cirrhosis and Axe Body Spray. I'll catch up with you later, all right?"

Chaz walked away, leaving me alone again. I glanced around, but I didn't see Nik or Megan, so I decided to retreat back to my corner hiding spot. An unfamiliar voice startled me. "That was some scene."

I turned, and I almost fell over.

The man I had bumped into by the bar was standing right next to me, angled in such a way that the spotlight above him created a halo around his body. He was tall, maybe six foot two, with dishwater blond hair and golden brown eyes. His blue plaid button-down was open, revealing a white T-shirt underneath. The thin cotton gave me a great view of the muscles in his arms and chest and his wide shoulders. And his face? All angles and edges, with lengthy stubble suggesting he hadn't shaved in a few days.

He was totally, utterly masculine, in a way that sent my hormones into the stratosphere. In that one second frozen in time, I wanted to kiss him or lick him or maybe just take a picture of him to look at on cold winter nights. But I managed, with every ounce of self-control I had, not to do any of those things. I just hoped I didn't drool.

"So what happened?" he asked. "I thought your friend was going to fight that man, but then he just…" his voice trailed off.

Yeah. He just…something. Much as I'd tried to brush it off with Chaz, the man's sudden, unexplained retreat had unsettled me. Not to mention the fact that it felt like a pressure-release valve had suddenly opened up in my brain, and I was fighting the ridiculous feeling that all my neurons were disappearing into the atmosphere. I walked up to the card table and asked for another bottle of water, just so I could have something to do with my hands. The blond man followed, putting a five dollar bill on the table before I could even reach into my pocket. "Thank you," I said.

"You're welcome." He smiled, and I almost melted. "So now you have to tell me. It must be some story."

One of the tricks to being a good liar is knowing when to tell the truth. "He was just some drunk, homophobic asshole who was giving my friend problems. I asked him to leave, and he did."

He raised his eyebrows. "That's all?"

I shrugged. "I guess I was convincing."

"You must have been."

The DJ finally got his cords untangled and switched the music back on, launching into a techno remix of "The Safety Dance." The blond man shook his head. "You know, half the people in this room weren't even born when 'The Safety Dance' came out. Were *you* even born when it came out?"

That was a complicated question. There was a more than five-year difference between my birthday and Dale's. Plus, I didn't know exactly when "The Safety Dance" had come out. I went with the safe answer. "I'm not sure."

"Probably not. You look young."

This guy didn't look like he could be more than few years older than me—"real" me or "Dale" me. "Wait a minute...were *you* even born when it came out?"

He chuckled. "Yes, I was definitely born."

"Well then you know it's time for a revival."

He gave me a small smile, his eyes sparkling. "Maybe it is."

We stood there silently for a few seconds. He was so close I could smell him, man and sex and butterscotch. I took a big chug of my water, trying to fight off the dryness that had suddenly overtaken my mouth. When "The Safety Dance" seamlessly transitioned to "Smooth Criminal," he leaned toward me and spoke again. "I'm John."

"Dale."

"You from around here, Dale?"

I raised an eyebrow. "Oh, have we entered the small talk portion of the evening already? Should I tell you that I'm a Scorpio, my favorite color is green, and I like long walks on the beach?"

"Is that true?"

"No." They were part of my Dale identity, though. But the hell with it. I was never going to see him again, anyway.

"Then don't tell me those things." He grinned at me. He had a dimple in his right cheek. God, I was such a sucker for dimples. I knew I should just walk away, join Chaz on the dance floor in time to walk like an Egyptian or whatever. But I couldn't bring myself to. Just as I was about to speak again, he opened his mouth. "Are you from Pittsburgh?" he asked.

"What?" The music was loud, pulsing through the room, practically drowning out my voice. He *couldn't* have asked...

"Are you from Pittsburgh? I knew a girl from there once, and she talked a lot like you."

My heart raced. I hadn't been back to Pittsburgh in ten years, hadn't been anywhere *near* the city. I had spent the last decade removing all traces of the accent from my voice, eliminating all the "dahntahns" and "jagoffs" that marked my blue-collar Steel City upbringing. I would have sworn it was gone. "I'm from Columbus. It's only a few hours from Pittsburgh. I guess the accents are similar."

"Yeah, that makes sense."

I stared at him, partly wanting to run away and partly unwilling to go. One way or another, I needed to deflect the attention away from me. "So this Pittsburgh girl...who was she? Long lost love or something?"

He chuckled. "No, nothing like that. More like the one who got away." He shifted his gaze away from me. "I still hope I find her. But sometimes I think if I do, she'll be nothing like I thought."

"Ah, well…nobody's ever like you think they'll be. That's why we have storybooks: so we can escape to a world that's as good as the one we imagine."

"That's an awfully cynical point of view."

"It's a realistic one. If you forget that life's not a fairy tale, then it'll beat you down real fast."

We fell silent. There didn't seem to be anything more to say. "Love Shack" was playing, the shrill, repetitive notes buzzing in my ears, and the smell of alcohol and sweat was becoming stronger. It was all giving me a headache. "Well…I'm gonna go find my friends and let them know that I'm going home early. It was nice to meet you, John."

I spotted Nik on the other side of the room and began to walk toward her. "Wait!" I heard John's voice from behind me. I turned back toward him. "Would you like to go for a walk or something?"

"I don't know…" It was a terrible idea. If I'd been a normal girl, I would have been worried that he might rape me or murder me or do any of the other things parents warn their kids about. As it was, I worried what I might do to *him*.

"I'm not trying to get fresh with you or anything, I swear. I just…I don't want to stop talking to you. Just for tonight, I don't want to stop talking to you."

There was something in his eyes, something raw and deep and pained. And I understood it, because I didn't want to stop talking to him either. I wanted to be the kind of girl who spent the night wandering aimlessly around the city, flirting with the most gorgeous guy she'd ever seen—if only for that one night. But of course, I couldn't tell him all that. "Does anyone really say 'fresh' anymore?" I asked instead.

He shrugged. "I have a thing for the classics."

"The fifties called. They want their slang back."

"They've been waiting sixty years. They can wait a few more hours." He gestured toward the exit with his shoulder. "You coming?"

It was a stupid idea, however you looked at it. But I didn't feel like I was anywhere near a Rage, nothing close to the tight, burning sensation that usually preceded one. And if he tried to hurt me...well, I had the means to protect myself. I just wanted one stolen night with him. And even normal girls made stupid decisions sometimes. "Yeah, I'm coming."

We walked along silently for several blocks, the pulsing music from the party fading into nothingness. It had cooled down since the afternoon, and it no longer had the muggy, oppressive feel of a city summer day. Cars would pass us occasionally, although it was edging into 3:00 a.m., and we saw a few people wandering along like we were or making out in an alleyway. Even in Red Hook, this was still the city that never slept.

John kept a comfortable distance away from me, digging his hands into his pockets, never touching me. He was being courteous, I realized, not trying to pressure me into something I didn't want to do. A gentleman. But now, I kind of wished he *wouldn't* be such a gentleman. "Do you want to walk down toward the water?" he asked me.

"Sure."

At the next light, we crossed the street and began to head in the direction of the waterfront. Most of the buildings we saw were similar to the one we'd just left: old, industrial, brown bricks, and broken windows. A few run-down apartment buildings broke up the landscape. It was a clear night, and I looked up at the sky: flat, black, and endless. "I'll never get used to that," I told him. "Even all the way out here, there are no stars."

He shrugged. "Light pollution. It's the price of progress."

"I know. I just miss them sometimes. Other cities I've been in, you could at least see some stars. But not here."

"No, not here."

We kept walking. We passed some garbage bags sitting on the curb waiting for pickup. They smelled like rotten eggs and vomit. Something rustled, and then a small black shape skittered in front of us. John reached toward me, as if to protect me from the big, bad rodent. When he realized I hadn't flinched, he pulled his hand away. "Rats don't bother you?"

"Why should they?" He stared at me incredulously. "What? I mean, it's not as if I'd invite one for dinner or anything. *Here, have a side of bubonic plague with your risotto.* But they have as much right to be here as we do. Maybe more." I paused. "On the other hand, if we see one of those gigantic cockroaches, I'm screaming and running in the other direction."

John chuckled. "Fair enough."

We crossed the next street. For a guy who claimed he had wanted to talk to me some more, John was oddly quiet. Once I noticed the silence, it made me nervous. "So...have you lived in New York long?" I asked.

He raised his eyebrows. "Oh. Have we entered the small talk portion of the evening?"

"Funny."

"I thought so." He ran his fingers through his hair. It only made it look better, like it was artfully disarrayed instead of just messy. "No, I haven't been here long. I work as a consultant, so I bounce around from place to place as they send me to do their dirty work. But I've been in New York many times before. I'm sure I'll be here again."

"Wow. That sounds impressive." Not that I was exactly sure what a consultant did, but it did sound impressive. "I'm beginning to feel a little inadequate about being just a bookstore clerk."

"Nah. Don't feel inadequate about that. Bookstores are some of the best places in the world. I just hope they don't get swallowed up now, with everyone reading books on their telephones." He paused for a moment. "That's one of the things I don't like about the city. It keeps changing, keeps moving under my feet so much that I never feel like I can get a solid foundation. Take this, for example." He gestured to the rows of beat-up buildings that surrounded us. "It doesn't matter how old or run-down this place looks now. In a few years, it'll all be condos. *For only five million, you, too, can experience the wonder of living in a drafty loft with an hour and a half commute into Manhattan.*"

We had reached the water—though it wasn't really a waterfront, per se, so much as a rickety wooden pier that seemed to drift into the Hudson River. If boats had ever docked here, it had been quite some time ago, because it didn't look like it could hold a dingy now.

I stomped my foot on the pier, testing its stability, before I walked out on it and sat down on the edge. John followed me. A warm breeze blew through the air, smelling like fish and sewage. I took off my shoes; Nik's ballet flats were not the best for walking around downtown Brooklyn. Tempting though it was, I would *not* stick my feet in the water. God only knew what kinds of bacteria lurked just underneath the surface. John sat about a foot away from me, close enough that I could feel the heat radiating from his skin. "I don't know," I told him. "One of the things I like about New York is how there seems to be this constancy to it, no matter what else happens. Like a few weeks ago, I was walking through the Financial District, and I saw a church. It's beautiful, with this brown stone and these pointed towers and this weathered, old cemetery—and completely out of place. I go into the churchyard and take a look around, and I almost trip over it: the gravestone of Alexander Hamilton."

John nodded. "Trinity Church. I've been there."

"Yeah, but by your logic, it should have been torn down a long time ago. It's completely out of place in the middle of all those shiny Wall Street high rises and expensive hotels. But there it stands, right in the middle of Manhattan. The grave of a Founding Father. History."

He shook his head. "That's just one thing. Washington Square Park used to be a potter's field. It's where they dumped all the people who died of yellow fever so they wouldn't spread it to the rest of the city. How do you think those people would feel, knowing their final resting place is where all the beatniks go to play guitar and smoke pot?"

I shrugged. "Maybe they'd be happy that there was so much life going on all around them."

I met his eyes. They were an unusual color: light brown, with a ring of gold fire around the pupil. It was so intense that I had to look away. "Maybe it's silly of me. But I think it's kind of nice to know that, in some small way, we'll still be part of the world once we're gone."

He didn't say anything, and for a long moment I thought I had done something incredibly stupid and scared him away. But when I looked up he was staring at me, his eyes filled with an emotion I couldn't name. Before I could say anything, he leaned in and kissed me.

I felt a surge of electricity course through me—not the normal, hot-and-heavy kiss kind of electricity, but more like "this is what it must be like to make out with a lightning bolt." The initial jolt filled my eyes with tears, but within seconds my body adjusted and I realized that it didn't hurt at all. No, it was amazing and exhilarating. His lips were warm and felt like a battery zinging through me. I pulled myself closer to him, running my fingers through his spiky blond hair, parting his lips with my tongue. He still smelled like butterscotch, and I wanted to lick him all over, see if he tasted as good as he smelled.

He pushed me away abruptly. He was breathing heavily. "Dale. I'm sorry."

I wiped sweat away from my forehead. "For what? I didn't exactly ask you to stop."

John began pacing along the pier, cursing under his breath. "Wasn't supposed to happen this way," I heard him say.

I stood up. "Look, if I really objected to you 'getting fresh' with me, I wouldn't have come out here with you. I'm not exactly naïve about these things."

John turned and stopped in front of me. He reached out as if to touch my face again, but paused before he did. "You're different than I thought you would be."

"What are you..." Just then, there was a loud *bang* and a flash of light to the left of me. I turned toward the noise, thinking someone had set off fireworks nearby. I didn't see anything.

When I turned back, John was gone.

CHAPTER

JOHN HAUNTED ME.

I couldn't get him out of my head: the kiss that had jolted every cell in my body, the way he'd apologized afterward, his sudden disappearance. It had gotten so bad that I'd think I saw him out of the corner of my eye as I waited on customers at the bookstore, catch a flash of him as a reflection in the window of the pizza place where I often got my lunch, glimpse him holding onto a poll a few feet away from me on the subway. But when I would look, he was gone.

I'd see him in my dreams. Every detail had been burned into my psyche: the hard lines of his face, the way his blond hair had spiked up from his forehead, the way the party lights shined on his bronze skin. The way he touched me, feral and dangerous. God, I had been seconds away from begging him to fuck me right then and there on the pier.

I told myself that I would never see him again, that he was just some strange guy I had met at a party.

And then one Tuesday about three weeks later, he showed up.

It was muggy that day, even early in the morning, and people had been coming into the store just to get out of the heat. Luckily, Mr. Ivanov always made sure the temperature in the store was kept at a perfect seventy-two degrees *(better for the books,* he said), because even the short walk from the subway to the store was oppressive.

I went for a break around 10:00 and bought two bagels and two bottles of water from a street vendor a few blocks away. There was a homeless man sitting in front of the store, where he could feel the air conditioning whenever someone opened the door. I'd seen him before, wandering around near the subway station and talking to himself. Judging by his rotten teeth and matted, overgrown hair, he had been on the street for quite some time. I gave him one of the bagels and a water bottle. He looked at me strangely. "It's hot."

"I know. That's why I brought you the water."

"No, your light. I can feel your light."

What the hell? "You should really eat something, sir, and keep hydrated. It's supposed to be over a hundred degrees today."

The man reached out as if he was going to touch me, but jerked away about six inches from my body. His eyes widened, and he began to hyperventilate. "It burns! Get away! It burns!"

I rushed inside and slammed the door behind me. It wasn't the first time I'd had a strange encounter with a homeless person in the city, but it never failed to unsettle me.

Mr. Ivanov was standing beside the counter with his arms folded across his chest. "Why did you feed that bum? He'll never leave that corner now, and he'll scare away all the customers."

"This is New York City. If you're scared of homeless people, you'll never leave your apartment."

"Still, it is not good for business. And it's dangerous for a young girl like you. You don't understand..."

"No, I *do* understand! I was..." I said, but stopped myself from going further. The months I had spent on the street when I was seventeen, the horrible homeless shelter where people were packed onto wall-to-wall cots with dingy gray sheets, the smell of garbage and hopelessness clinging to my clothes—those were my memories, not Dale's. Dale was an average twenty-two-year-old whose biggest problem was an abusive asshole of an ex-boyfriend who lived in another state. I wished I could be Dale. "I just feel sorry for him, Mr. Ivanov."

"I know." He patted my shoulder. "You are a nice girl, Dale. But you do stupid things sometimes."

Around 11:00 the door opened, and there he was: the man who had been lurking in the shadows of my mind for three weeks. He was wearing a blue-and-white plaid shirt and khaki pants. He seemed almost totally unaffected by the heat; the only way you could tell that it was warm outside was by the way the humidity had caused his hair to curl slightly around his ears.

The sight of him was enough to make me drop the books I had been stocking on the shelves. Mr. Ivanov shook his head, and I crouched down, struggling to pick them up as quickly as I could—which wasn't very fast, since being freaked out and totally aroused at the same time had apparently caused me to lose all sense of hand-eye coordination. I kept my eyes on the floor. I wouldn't look up, *couldn't* look up.

Then a hand invaded my field of vision, holding one of the books I had dropped. I took it and let my eyes drift up slowly, lingering on his tanned skin so I wouldn't have to see his eyes. "This fell behind the shelf. You should really be more careful."

I couldn't help it. I had to look.

He smiled as he handed the book back to me, but he radiated a hardness to him that I hadn't noticed before, sort of a "don't fuck with me or I'll have to kill you and eat your innards" kind of vibe. Not that I could throw stones about the whole killing people thing. But I had always drawn the line at innard eating. "What are you doing here?" I asked him. More importantly, "How the hell did you find me?"

He frowned, lines creasing his forehead. "You told me you work here, remember? 'Just a bookstore clerk'?"

"I didn't tell you which bookstore I worked at."

"Of course you did." He said it with such confidence, such assurance, that I began to wonder. I *had* been feeling pretty reckless that night, and I'd felt an instant connection to him, like he saw past my fake names and my disguises right down to the real me. Normally, I wouldn't have done something so cavalier. But that night? I wasn't exactly in my right mind.

Mr. Ivanov cleared his throat loudly. I looked at John. "He's pretty anal about me not having friends here while I'm working. You'd better buy something or leave."

"I don't want to get you in trouble." He had a bemused smirk out of his face when he walked away. I heard the bell above the door ring. Fantastic. He strolls back into my life, only to disappear *again*. Figures.

I went back to shelving books, but no more than a minute later Mr. Ivanov called my name. I went up to the counter to see John standing there, with dozens of colorful paperbacks stacked in front of the register. Mr. Ivanov was staring at the books. The shocked expression on his face mirrored mine, I was certain. "He wants you to ring him up," Mr. Ivanov said.

"Uh...sure." I took my spot behind the counter and began punching the books into the register. Mr. Ivanov didn't believe in newfangled devices like electronic scanners, so I had to enter all of the prices manually. Once

Mr. Ivanov saw that John was, indeed, allowing his purchases to be tallied in good faith, he went back to doing inventory on the other side of the store, leaving John and I there alone. I expected him to say something, but he didn't, and the silence made me uneasy. "All these books are gonna be expensive," I told him.

"That's all right. I don't mind. I have the money."

I held up the book I was entering. "Seriously? I'm guessing you don't have any overwhelming desire to read *The Viking and His Virgin Bride*."

He shrugged. "The romance section was the closest."

I entered another book into the register, then another. If he was using his book-buying binge as an excuse to talk to me, he was doing a piss-poor job of it. "So, why did you disappear the night of the party?"

He sighed. "Dale, I..."

"No. Don't give me some bullshit excuse. If you weren't into me, that's fine. But you didn't have to bolt like I was Typhoid Mary or something. And you didn't have to come into the store today to feel better about yourself."

"It wasn't that. Let's just say that something came up suddenly."

"So suddenly that you couldn't even say goodbye?"

He didn't respond. I finished ringing up his books in silence. By the time I was done, his total was over three hundred dollars. He handed me a credit card. I stole a look at the name before I swiped it: John Goodwin.

I gave him the bags. "You should at least donate them," I told him.

He furrowed his brow. "What?"

"Donate the books. To a shelter or something. They always need stuff at those places, and these books would make the people there really happy."

He dropped his bags on the ground. "Shit, Dale. Just...shit." He ran his fingers through his hair. "You're not gonna make this easy, are you?" He leaned over the counter and lowered his voice. "Let's just stop pretending now."

"What are you talking about?"

"If you haven't figured out who I am yet, you will soon. And I'm sorry about that. I never expected...well, I didn't expect *this,* you know? But I'm not a good person to know. The more time you spend around me, the more danger you're in. So you need to leave New York. Go somewhere far away, somewhere no one can ever find you again. Because I'm not gonna be able to help you much longer."

Before I could respond, John turned and left, a bag of books in each hand. I stood there in stunned silence for a second, until I recovered enough to realize that I should go after him and demand to know what the hell he meant. I told Mr. Ivanov I would be right back, and then I bolted through the back into the alleyway that Ivanov's shared with the stationery store next door. I hoped I would intercept him on his way to the subway, but when I got outside I saw he was still standing right next to Ivanov's—at the mouth of the same alley I was in—talking on a cell phone. I dove behind the dumpster and listened.

"No, Gabriel, I can't do that." A pause. "I haven't been able to verify her identity. I don't even know whether she's a demon yet." Another pause. "No, I haven't been able to touch her yet. I know back in your day, you could go around touching any woman, any time. But here in the twenty-first century, we call that sexual assault, and I could get arrested." He stopped talking again. I could hear his heavy sigh even from where I was hiding. "Yes, Gabriel, I understand. I'll do what I have to do. I've been part of the Thrones for a long time, and they don't call me the Bloodhound for nothing."

He didn't speak again after that, so I peeked my head out from behind the dumpster. He hung up the phone and put it in his pocket. Then, instead of leaving like I expected him to, he lit a cigarette. He smoked the way you'd expect John Wayne or the Marlboro Man to smoke, holding it low and tight

between his forefinger and thumb. He leaned against the wall and exhaled. "Fuck," he said to himself. He ran his free hand through his hair. "Fuck."

He stamped out the cigarette, having barely smoked half of it, and left the alley. I stepped out from behind the dumpster and stared at the space he'd left behind, the smell of smoke and garbage invading my nostrils. It was only then that the full impact of the phone conversation really hit me. "Demon?" I said to the empty space. "What the hell?"

CHAPTER

D EMON. DEMON.
What the fuck?

Some nutjob was obsessed with me, and he was trying to figure out if I was a demon. Let's just ignore the fact that I'd almost had sex with said nutjob on a public pier.

I leaned back against the futon and covered my head with a fuzzy throw blanket, shielding my eyes from the setting sun streaming in through the windows. Ugh. This was absurd. John hadn't seemed like a nutjob. A little intense, sure, but not a nut. I'd been around enough of them to know.

I needed to look at the facts.

One...I wasn't even sure whether the phone call I'd overheard was about me. "She" could refer to anyone. It was just egotistical to assume he'd meant me. And John had mentioned he hadn't had a chance to touch her, whoever she was. John and I had certainly touched the night of the party.

But something *had* happened when we touched, an overwhelming, electrical sensation that was both painful and fantastic at the same time. The closest thing I'd ever felt to it was the shock of static electricity, but

that didn't even come close to what I'd experienced with John. It was more like what I imagined licking a high voltage battery would be. At first, it would hurt and burn your tongue, and you'd feel that strange numbness and tingling all the way down to your toes. Most people would have backed away, but I had kept going—because I realized I *liked* the way it burned.

Yeah. That was just...weird. It probably was just static electricity. That was the most logical explanation. I think it had stormed the next night. It was in the air or something.

Two..."demon" didn't necessarily have to be literal. Why would I even think it was? Maybe it was the name of a gang or something. John was the member of a street gang, and they were trying to track down a woman who was part of a rival gang, the Demons. That would certainly make a lot of sense with John's whole self-loathing, "I'm not a good person to know" thing. Thank God I'd gotten over those romance novel archetypes a long time ago.

John didn't look like a gang member. Weren't gang members supposed to have tattoos? Maybe his tattoos were made of invisible ink. That was a thing, right? Or maybe some gang members just didn't have tattoos at all. Unfortunately, everything I knew about gangs came from *Law & Order* marathons.

Three...I still didn't remember telling John where I worked. This was probably the easiest, and most logical, thing to explain away: I was feeling whimsical that night, and I must have forgotten. But it bugged me. Whimsical or not, it just didn't seem like the kind of thing I would do. I'd been on the run for ten years. My entire *life* depending on my ability to keep secrets. And telling a stranger where I worked would have been stupid even if I'd been a normal girl.

But of course, I must have done exactly that. How else would he have tracked me down at the bookstore? Occam's razor and all. When all else is

equal, the simplest solution is the most likely one. So it must have just... slipped out.

Ugh.

I grabbed my laptop from under the futon and turned it on. Once it came up, I went to Google and searched for "John Goodwin."

Approximately eight million search results. The first one belonged to a political consultant in Washington who looked nothing like the John I knew. The second link brought me to a law firm. Since I didn't feel like going through the other 7,999,998 search results, I tried again.

"John Goodwin, Gabriel" still gave me over six million results, the first one a YouTube video for some kid's school concert. Next.

"John Goodwin, Gabriel, Thrones," brought me to an HBO fan page. Not even close.

I had one more word left to try. I added "demon" to the search string, expecting to find some fantasy role-playing game or a motorcycle club. Instead, the first link that popped up read *"DEMONS are REAL...and they are Among Us."* I couldn't tell what the site was about from the description, so I went ahead and clicked on it.

The page looked like it hadn't been updated since about 1999, all neon text on a dark background. The page had apparently been written by some religious zealot, all about God and His Holy Wrath. I didn't see anything about John, Gabriel, or the Thrones on the page. The first thing I saw was a list of "Demon-infested Places," which made me laugh. As if demons were cockroaches or, better yet, a plague of locusts. The addresses were scattered all over the world, with a surprising concentration near Washington, D.C. (Or not so surprising, really; it would make a lot of sense if the government were populated by demons.) The only one nearby was a place called Devil's Spawn located in Midtown. Creative. I figured it was probably a biker bar or something.

I was about to click off the site when something caught my eye.

"Mentally unstable Peoples, and Drug Addicts, and those who are dying often have Strange reactions to DEMONS. Some report a Burning sensation when DEMONS are near, due to the FIRES OF HELL seeping into our Dimension."

My heart raced. The homeless man the other day had reacted strangely to me. He had said something about my light burning him. It wasn't the first time it had happened to me, either. I'd run into other homeless people during my time in New York who had reacted the exact same way. I'd chalked it up to them being crazy.

"DEMONS often boast great Strength and Stamina. They do not sicken or Injure easily, and they heal Quickly."

During my Rages, I had taken on people much bigger and, presumably, stronger than me. Even if I didn't remember, I'd seen the aftermath—every time I came out of a Rage, I'd wake up with a dead body beside me, and I'd walk away without a scratch on me.

"BE WARNED—DEMONS are very Violent and very Dangerous. They are the scourge of Hell upon this Earth!!!!"

For ten years I'd been running. But it didn't change what I was: a killer. Once upon a time, I'd been able to console myself with the fact that the people I'd killed deserved it. But what did that even mean? I'd acted as judge, jury, and executioner, all without even thinking about it. And now that I'd killed Andrew Seymour, I couldn't even say that anymore. I had probably killed an innocent man.

If anyone was the scourge of hell, it was me.

I felt a tap on my shoulder, and I nearly jumped out of my skin. "Jeez, Dale, relax!" Nik barely concealed her laughter. "I didn't mean to startle you. You were really in the zone there, weren't you? What are you reading

about?" I didn't answer her, not until she said my name again. "Are you all right?" she asked.

I closed my laptop. "I have to go to the library."

THERE ARE DOZENS OF LOCATIONS of the New York Public Library all over the city, but the one everyone always thinks of is the main branch on Forty-Second Street and Fifth Avenue, with its marble facade and its lion sentinels. I'd applied for a library card and gone a few times when I first got to New York, thinking that a building filled to the rafters with books would be paradise for me. Instead, something about it disconcerted me.

Maybe it was because it was so quiet. When you went up to the Rose Room, the main reading area, all you can hear is the *swish* of people turning the pages of their books, and the *clack, clack, clack* of people typing on their laptops furiously. When you walk across the room, even the tap of your shoes against the floor feels out of place, the weight of a thousand eyes staring at you in the glare of their tiny tabletop lamps. Sure, it was beautiful, with the vaulted windows, the chandeliers, and the cloud mural on the ceiling that looked more like it belonged in the Sistine Chapel than in a Midtown Manhattan library. But it felt oppressive, as if the room itself was telling me I didn't belong. I hadn't come back after that.

But I needed to go back to the Rose Room now, because the research desk was there—and really, I had no idea where to begin or what, exactly, I was looking for. I lingered in front of the desk until all the other patrons were gone. The librarian—a young guy in an oversized tweed jacket—barely glanced at me when I finally approached. "Can I help you with something?"

"Ummm...yeah." I swallowed. "I'm looking for information on demons. Not like, religious books, but information on...well, on whether or not they actually exist. In the real world, you know?"

The librarian stared at me for several seconds, a hard look on his face. "You'll need to go to Special Collections. Fourth floor."

I took one of the library maps out of the carousel and studied it. "I don't see a fourth floor on here."

He grabbed the map and circled a staircase with a red pen. "It's not a full floor. The elevator doesn't go up there. Take these stairs. It'll be the second room on your left."

The librarian's directions led to a door hidden behind a half wall. The paint on the door was peeling, and the wood had begun to splinter. The knob was loose when I turned it, and the metal steps groaned beneath my feet. When I got up to the fourth floor, half the lights were off. I half suspected the librarian was fucking with me, and the second room on the left would really be a broom closet.

Instead, I found a room lined with rows of books on plain metal shelves. There were no windows, and the only light came from a bare light bulb dangling from the low ceiling. It smelled like mold and old books. I sneezed. Twice. A rectangular table sat in the middle of the room, with only one chair. I guess they weren't expecting too many patrons up here.

"Why are you here?" said a voice from behind me. I turned.

A woman stood between two of the stacks, silhouetted by artificial light and dust motes. She was about thirty-five, and she wore a high-collared dress with a long skirt, and her hair was piled on her head in an elaborate up-do. Her waist was cinched so much in the middle that she must have been wearing a corset of some kind, and those old-fashioned, wire-framed glasses that actually looked like they were made of wire balanced precariously on her nose. She looked like she belonged in an Edith Wharton

novel, if Edith Wharton had written about creepy librarians. It takes all kinds in New York. She wasn't nearly as strange as the man I'd seen dancing in Times Square a few weeks earlier, wearing nothing but a tutu and a bra.

"I wanted to find out about demons. The guy downstairs directed me here."

She crossed her arms. "What kinds of demons? Many religious traditions have a belief in demonic-type beings. There's the Islamic jinn, the Hindu..."

"I don't care about that," I told her. "I found a weird website, and I wanted to find out whether demons are real."

"That's really a matter open to interpretation. Some people believe Santa Claus and unicorns are real."

"I don't believe in Santa Claus or unicorns, and I'm not a zealot. It's just that I've heard some stuff lately, and I wanted to do some research."

"Hmmm." The woman disappeared into the stacks. A few seconds later, she returned with a large, hardcover book and dropped it on the table, kicking up dust. "Start with this."

She walked away, her heels clicking on the floor, and I looked at the book. It was the size of a dictionary, and the binding was falling apart. I flipped through the pages. The first several chapters seemed to be about various religious traditions, and I was about to inform the woman that she had given me the wrong thing—despite my very clear directions to the contrary. But then the fourth chapter was titled, "Legends of Demons in Real Life." I began reading. The beginning of the chapter talked about stories and urban legends—apparently, people used to think that sleep paralysis was actually succubi stealing your soul—but then one section caught my eye:

In some Judeo-Christian theological circles, the rumor of angels and demons living among us on Earth persists to this day. Some scholars even speculate that Biblical lore was appropriated by these entities, changed and skewed for their own purposes (Atherton 155, Smith 78). One text, known as The Chronicles of the Fall and alleged to be a lost book of the Bible (Forsythe 14), even documents the angels' and demons' fall to Earth and the subsequent schism in their community.

It's easy to dismiss these tales as fiction, or simply antiquated religious dogma that didn't make it into the canon. But what's fascinating is that stories about people with inhuman strength, abilities, and longevity persist even in this age of skepticism. Stories about a man who lifted a train with his bare hands (Felton A7). Stories about a child who could move things without his hands (Richardson D12). Stories about a woman who can control the minds of the people around her (Channing A6). Stories about people checking into hospitals—and then mysteriously healing themselves (Turco B3, Howard C7, among many, many others). (See Appendix B for more examples of these types of inhuman tales.) But it makes sense that these angels and demons could have been living among humans for our entire history—because they look exactly like us. Humans, when confronted with an unknowable situation, tend to think of the simplest or easiest explanation. In earlier times, it might have been ghosts or witches or fairies—or, yes, angels and demons. But today, it might be a photographic error, an incorrectly recalled story, a fluke...

The section caught my attention, because it was exactly what I had been doing with John. How *had* he known where I worked? And what was that weird, electric feeling when he touched me?

I wanted to try to find The Chronicles of the Fall that the book had talked about, but there was no computer up in the Special Collections wing, only a row of old, wooden card catalogs. I went over to them and

tried to remember from my elementary school library visits how to search for a book without an author when you didn't have the assistance of a search engine. It took me about twenty minutes to find the correct card, and that was only after looking up the title in the bibliography for more information. Pathetic, I know, but considering the card catalog was covered in dust about a quarter of an inch thick, I wasn't the only person who didn't use it very often.

I found the book on the shelves and brought it back to the table. Unlike the first one, this book was in pristine condition. On the other hand, it just seemed *old*, the leather faded with age, the pages yellow and brittle, with that musty smell that old books often emit. I opened the book to the first page.

Early in the age of man, the angels lived in Heaven as the servants of God. But the archangel Zaphkiel was unhappy with his lot. Zaphkiel said to God, "Why dost thou favor man so? They are silly, simple creatures. They do not honor thee, and they have consumed the tree of life; yet they run free upon the Earth."

When God did not reply, the archangel Zaphkiel grew angry and resentful. He gathered followers who wished to roam the Earth, free as man and beasts.

When God learned of the archangel's treachery, He knew Zaphkiel and his followers must be punished. They were cast out of Heaven unto the Earth, with no remembrance of the paradise they had left behind.

They were cold, but they knew not how to build fires.

They were hungry, but they knew not how to hunt.

They were naked, but they knew not how to make clothing.

They wept and cursed, but still they could not remember anything before their fall to Earth.

After seven days and seven nights, they were found by a tribe of men. The tribe took pity on them and taught them the skills they needed to survive the long winter.

The angels survived, and they rejoiced.

For nine hundred and ninety-nine years, the angels and man lived together upon the Earth peacefully. But then a woman begat a child...

"I know you."

The librarian's voice startled me, and I jumped. She stood uncomfortably close to my chair. Her pupils were dilated, and she held something behind her back. "No, I don't think so."

"Yes. Yes, I do. Don't lie to me. I see you. I *see* you!"

My first instinct had been to protect my identity. But now it was becoming clear that this woman was either high on something pretty impressive—or completely, bat-shit insane. "Are you okay? Are you sick? Do I need to call a doctor?"

"Don't patronize me!" She whipped her hand around from behind her back, revealing a very small—and very sharp—letter opener.

I stood up and backed away from her. "All right. I don't remember where I know you from, but it's obvious you don't like me very much. So I'm just going to take my bag here, and I'm going to leave the library." I reached across the table slowly to grab my purse.

She stabbed my hand, pinning it to the table.

CHAPTER

"**W**HAT THE FUCK?" I PULLED the letter opener out of my hand. The woman tried to grab it from me, but I was stronger. I shoved her against a bookshelf, holding the letter opener to her throat. I could feel a Rage coming on, its red teeth sinking into me. *No, I don't want to do this.*

I took a breath. Another.

She's unarmed.

You have her pinned to a bookshelf.

She can't hurt you anymore.

I stepped back and tossed the letter opener to the ground. "I'm going to get my bag, and I'm going to leave."

I walked backwards until I felt my legs bump against the table. I tried to reach behind my back and grab the bag without taking my eyes off of her, but I couldn't find it. I looked away for just a second.

She screamed. I turned my head to see her lunging at me, the letter opener in her hand. I shoved her away from me. "Stop!"

The librarian froze.

It was strange. All that energy, all that inertia, all that anger, and she had just *stopped* right there in the middle of the floor, just a few feet from my jugular. But I wasn't going to complain. "I'm going to get my bag, and I'm going to leave. You're going to stay here. You're not going to follow me, and we're going to pretend this incident never happened."

I picked up my bag. This time, she didn't move. I took a step forward, but she still remained where she was. I bent down and grabbed the letter opener from the floor. "I'm keeping this," I said. She said nothing. I tucked it into the pocket of my bag, praying library staff wouldn't decide to search me on the way out.

I walked out of the room slowly, not wanting to spook her again.

When I got to the staircase, I opened the door and ran down all four flights of steps, emerging onto Forty-Second Street. I kept going until I got to the subway station and hopped on the first train that came by, not even bothering to look which line it was or what direction it was going in.

The other passengers stared at me as I sat down, and then I remembered that I had been stabbed in the hand and was probably bleeding quite heavily. I clutched my hand, trying to hide it as much as I could.

The next stop was Penn Station. I got off the subway and headed for a bathroom. It was evening rush hour, so the bathroom was crowded. Still, no one said anything when I went to one of the sinks and began washing blood off my hand. That was the best thing about New York, as far as I was concerned: most of the time, people knew how to mind their own business, especially when they were commuters from Long Island or New Jersey rushing to get their trains home, and you were a frazzled-looking twentysomething with blood on your hands and a *stay-the-fuck-away-from-me* vibe.

The blood stained the water red as it drained. I was afraid to look at my hand—although I was relieved it didn't sting when I washed it. I grabbed a hand full of paper towels, preparing to stem the flow.

And...nothing.

My hand was fine. Not so much as a scar remained to tell me I'd been stabbed—though I'd just washed the blood down the drain myself.

I ran through the possibilities. Maybe the librarian stabbed herself? Maybe it was paint? I couldn't stop staring at my hand.

An older woman tapped my shoulder. "Are you all right, honey?"

I flexed my fingers. Not even the slightest twinge. "Yeah, I guess I'm fine."

THAT NIGHT I FOUND MYSELF in Hell's Kitchen, in front of a bar called the Devil's Spawn. Hell's Kitchen had become as gentrified as the rest of Manhattan. The rents had skyrocketed, and the streets were lined with trees and benches. Somehow—in spite of the fact that I was just a few blocks from Central Park and the Broadway theaters—I had, apparently, arrived in the one part of the city that had remained untouched since the *Taxi Driver* era. It was quiet and dark, and the buildings looked run down. I half expected to see drug dealers and cigarette-smoking prostitutes hanging out on the corner, but all I saw was a lone homeless man sleeping on an overstuffed garbage bag. Music pounded inside the bar, vibrating the side of the building.

After I had been standing outside for a few minutes, trying to decide what to do, one of the patrons stumbled out of the bar. He was tall and middle-aged, with a heavy gut and a beard that would make Z.Z. Top proud, and he smelled like cigarettes and booze. He looked at me. "You... sssshouldn't...be...here. Vvvvvery dangerous."

"Thanks for the warning."

The man staggered toward me and grabbed me on the shoulders. In spite of his size and his proximity, I didn't feel threatened by him; the way he leaned his weight against me was more like I was holding him up than he was attacking me. "There's some...vvvvvery dangerous people in there."

"That's okay. I can handle myself."

"You sssshould...go home." He made an awkward attempt to pull me away from the building just as the door opened, illuminating us with the light from inside. He froze. "I didn't know," he whispered.

"Didn't know what?"

"I didn't know who you were, my lady! I'm so sorry! Please don't hurt me!" The man stumbled backward, tripping on a garbage can. I went over to try to help him up, but when I reached for him he recoiled. I backed off. It took him a few tries, but he finally managed to stand on his own two feet. "I've got a wife and two kids. You can have all my money. Or my dog, you want my dog? His name's Spot and he's very..."

I held up my hands to stop him. "I'm not gonna hurt you. I don't need your money...or your dog." What I couldn't figure out is *why* this man thought I was going to hurt him. He hadn't done anything to me. Not to mention that he was at least twice my size; even with the added strength I seemed to gain during a Rage, it would have been difficult.

The man knelt down in front of me, grabbed my hand, and kissed my knuckles. "Truly, you are merciful and...magnificent. Thank you."

He ran before I could say anything else, moving with a speed I wouldn't have thought possible from him. "Just when you thought a weird day couldn't get any weirder," I mumbled. But I was here now, and I'd run out of reasons to linger. Either I had to go inside, or go home.

I pushed open the door.

Unlike most Manhattan bars, the clientele of the Devil's Spawn looked pretty diverse. From grungy-looking biker types to leather-adorned dominatrices to Brooks Brothers-clad yuppies, there seemed to be a place for everyone. Except the more I looked around, the more out of place I felt. There was something about this place that made me feel like bugs were crawling under my skin, although maybe it was just that the place was filled with smoke. Thirty seconds after I got inside the door, I felt like I was choking. Apparently, they were telling New York City's smoking ban to go fuck itself.

The lights gave everything a yellowish cast. There were a couple of pool tables on one side of the room, where a woman in a too-short skirt with boobs hanging out of her top was playing against a guy who looked like he should have been modeling underwear on the side of a bus. The other pool table wasn't being used; too many people were sitting on it, watching the eye candy at the other table. Over in another corner were some old-school arcade games. A jukebox played loudly in the background. It took me several seconds to recognize the familiar beat of "Anarchy in the UK."

At the end of the bar, a man and woman were making out—except then I realized they weren't *just* making out. He reached up her leather skirt, too deeply to be merely brushing her thigh. Then he bit into her neck. She screamed; I couldn't tell if it was in pleasure or pain.

I felt something bump into me, and I turned to see two men—one tall guy in a "Fuck the Police" T-shirt, and one shorter, squatter guy with major armpit stains—fighting one another. They were already battered and bloody, and the crowd was cheering them on. The tall guy grabbed an empty beer bottle, smashed it along the side of the bar, and lunged. Pit Stains grabbed his wrists and head butted him, dazing the tall guy momentarily. I thought this would have been enough. The tall guy had obviously had it, and Pit Stains could claim victory while the other fought for consciousness. But

Pit Stains had other ideas. While the tall guy stumbled, Pit Stains grabbed his head and pulled it close, as if he was going to give the guy a kiss on the cheek. A second later, Pit Stains pulled away with something clutched in his teeth. The tall guy passed out altogether, his face now covered in blood. Pit Stains raised his arms above his head, and the crowd cheered. I looked harder and realized that Pit Stains had the tall guy's ear dangling from his mouth. Not one person looked like they were calling the police or the paramedics.

I took a deep breath and stepped around the still-unconscious (and now earless) tall guy and pushed my way up to the bar. There were two bartenders working the bar, one male and one female. The male bartender approached me; he resembled Mr. T circa 1986, complete with mohawk and bling. "What'll ya have?"

"Just a Coke, please."

"Just a Coke?" He leaned toward me. "It's safe in here, you know. We keep the tourists out."

"That's...fantastic." Though I wasn't sure how a bar this close to Times Square managed to keep *all* the tourists out, or how they would distinguish tourist from resident in this crowd. Nor was I sure how a place where I'd just seen someone receive an involuntary ear-ectomy could be classified as "safe."

"Just a Coke?" he asked again.

"I don't need any ice in it." It was obvious this wasn't the right answer; maybe this was one of those places that sold 190-proof grain alcohol or illegal drugs. But I'd wasn't about to break my vow not to drink alcohol anymore, not here. This was *not* the kind of place where I wanted my reflexes to be compromised.

The bartender returned a few minutes later with a glass of ice-free Coke and a check for seven-fifty. Damn. Now I remembered why I didn't usually

go out in Manhattan. I handed him a twenty-dollar bill. "I'm actually looking for someone, and I heard he might have been through here. His name's John Goodwin."

"Don't know him." He left before I could say anything else.

A few minutes later, he returned with my change and put it all on the counter. I pushed it back toward him. "Are you sure? He's in his thirties, about six feet tall, blond hair, brown eyes..."

The bartender took the bills and pocketed them. "Nope."

He walked away. I downed my Coke in record time, giving myself hiccups in the process. When the bartender came back, I held my glass away so he couldn't grab it. "Are you *absolutely* sure? He might have also been known as the Bloodhound."

"The Bloodhound?" the bartender repeated, loudly enough for the rest of the bar to hear.

The conversations around me stopped and people began to stare until the silence trickled through the whole bar. Even Pit Stains—still covered in the blood of his trophy—stopped. I cleared my throat. "So you do know him."

The bartender slammed his hands against the counter. "You listen to me. I don't know who you are, or where you come from, but we don't want him or any of his kind here. You tell the Bloodhound I run a clean business, and I don't bother nobody. So tell him to just leave me the hell alone. Now get out of here!"

"I was just..."

"Go!" He pointed to the door.

So much for that. I picked up my purse and went to the door, wishing I hadn't given the asshole such a big tip. But considering the whole bar was looking at me as if they wanted to tear me limb from limb, I figured it was better not to voice that sentiment.

When I was about half a block from the bar, I heard a voice calling, "Hey! Hey, you!" Since no one I knew ever came to this area, I figured the person wasn't calling me. But then she said, "You said you were looking for John Goodwin."

I turned, and I recognized her as the female bartender I'd seen working. She was tall and thin and had the kind of light brown skin that suggested mixed ancestry. She wore a yellow T-shirt that was purposefully frayed through the back, a short skirt, fishnets, and no bra. It was the kind of outfit that would have gotten most women, in most cities, arrested for indecent exposure, but this was New York—and very few women could pull off the braless, backless look as well as she did, anyway. But what was really intriguing was the tattoo on her back: a female warrior in full armor, her sword crossing the bartender's shoulder and ending at a point against her neck, as if it was just waiting to slice across her throat. Why anyone would get a tattoo that looked like it was trying to kill them was beyond me, but who was I to criticize anyone's aesthetic choices. "You know how to find John?" I asked.

"Maybe I do. What do you need him for?"

I thought quickly. "He and I went out a while back. We were just having a good time, and I guess we weren't as careful as we should have been, and...now I'm pregnant." I blinked my eyes several times, filling them with tears. "I'm not going to ask him for anything, not if he doesn't want to be a father, but I just...I just..."

"Save it," she said abruptly. "The John I know barely looks at women, let alone touches them. Try again."

Huh. The John I knew had looked, and he had *definitely* touched. "Maybe we're not talking about the same guy. Common name, you know?"

She shook her head. "Only one man is called the Bloodhound. So why do you really want him?"

I sighed. "I met him a few weeks ago. Something happened between us, and he kind of disappeared. Now I have some questions...about what I am."

"Which is what, exactly?" She squinted at me. "You didn't set off the alarms in the bar, so you're not human. Not completely, at least."

I wanted to protest, to deny her allegations, but I was beginning to think she might be correct. I shifted my weight between my feet. "I don't really know."

She stared at me, and I just looked back at her. Then she started to laugh. "Goddamn, you really *don't* know, do you?" I didn't respond, and she rolled her eyes. "There's a meeting at three a.m. on the first Saturday of every month. He'll be there."

The first Saturday of July was coming up that weekend. "Where is it? How do I get there?"

"It's suicide, you know." When I didn't say anything, she continued. "Take the Six train downtown and hop off at City Hall."

"Where is it from there?"

"Don't worry. You won't be able to miss it."

I nodded and began to walk away. Then it occurred to me that the information had come way too easily. I stopped. "Why are you telling me this?"

She shrugged. "Maybe I'm a good Samaritan."

"There's no such thing." I took a breath. "I just need to know...are you trying to help him or hurt him?"

She grinned. "I don't know. I haven't really decided yet." She turned and began walking away. "If you come back into the bar, ask for Ruth. They'll kill you otherwise."

CHAPTER

THURSDAY NIGHTS WERE MOVIE NIGHTS for Nik, Chaz, and me. Chaz was something of a movie buff, and for years he'd been dragging Nik over to his apartment every Thursday to watch whatever cinematic oddity he'd discovered on Netflix that week. Nik's tastes ran more toward contemporary blockbusters than obscure cult films, so I realized very early on that she looked at these Thursdays as something of a chore. On the other hand, it was obvious how close she and Chaz were—she told me he'd been her resident adviser during her freshman year at NYU, and they'd been fast friends ever since—so maybe she thought it was worth it to make sure she had a chance to hang out with her best friend at least once a week, even though he'd graduated from school now.

I'd started taking part in their ritual shortly after the warehouse party. I'd overheard Nik and Chaz bickering after he told her that their movie selection for the week would be *Harold and Maude*, starring Ruth Gordon. She groaned. "Chaz, I'm just not up to seeing a movie about some senior citizen Satanist."

"Ruth Gordon's not a Satanist in *Harold and Maude*. That's *Rosemary's Baby*. She's an eighty-year-old woman who gets involved with a twenty-year-old guy who repeatedly fakes his own suicide. Tom Skerritt makes a cameo as a motorcycle cop. Did you know the screenwriter's the same guy who directed *Nine to Five* and *Best Little Whorehouse in Texas*? Oh, and he directed one other movie I like...what's it called...oh, *Foul Play!* That's one's really cool. It's about—" Chaz and Nik were both staring at me like I'd grown a second head. "What? I like movies."

"Since when are you a walking Internet Movie Database? We took you for a bookworm," Chaz said.

"Just because you're a bookworm doesn't mean you can't be a movie nerd, too. I used to rent old movies at the video store up the street from me, back when I was in high school." This was true: my aunt hadn't allowed me to go out often, and I hadn't been able to afford much else. But was that Dale's truth? Should she really be a lover of classic movies and offbeat cult films like I was? Would she have spent so many of her evenings during high school in the local video rental place? Would she even call it a video rental place given that DVDs had long taken over as the dominant media form by the time Dale, five years my junior, was in high school? Maybe it didn't matter. Dale was me and I was Dale, and the lines were becoming blurry between us.

But neither Nik nor Chaz seemed to notice my worry. Chaz grinned at me and said, "You'll do." Nik rolled her eyes, as if she realized she'd been beaten.

After that, every Thursday night we dutifully took the subway and the PATH train up to Chaz's apartment in Hoboken (no easy feat from Brooklyn, but worth it since his apartment was twice as big and half as occupied as ours). We'd eat pizza, because we were all chronically broke and pizza was filling and cheap.

I don't remember what we were watching the Thursday after I went to the Devil's Spawn. Truth is, I probably wouldn't have remembered much of anything from that night if Chaz hadn't paused the movie sometime in the middle and said, "Earth to Dale. Come in, Dale."

I blinked. "Huh. What's up? I was watching the movie."

"No, you were *pretending* to watch. There's a difference. Usually by this time, you've offered commentary on the film or random trivia that no one in their right mind should know—except *moi*, of course, since you haven't stumped me yet. But you haven't said a word all night, and you've barely touched your food."

It was true. My slice of pizza still sat next to me. I'd taken maybe two bites. It tasted like cardboard. "I'm all right. I guess I'm just a little distracted."

Nik scooted closer to me on the couch and put her hand on my arm. "Dale, not to push, but...I have noticed that you've seemed a little distracted lately. Is there anything we can help with?"

This was why I didn't usually make friends. Eventually, they'd want to do stuff and know stuff, and I'd just have to lie to them again. I spent my whole life lying, but I didn't really like doing it. At this point, it had become one of those necessary evils, like flossing. I couldn't exactly tell Nik and Chaz: *So I met this guy at a party and he said some weird things, so then I did some digging and some other weird stuff happened and I think I might be a...*

Yeah. I couldn't say it. I couldn't even think it, really.

But Nik and Chaz were my friends, as stupid and masochistic as it might have been of me, and they were concerned. When you spend your whole life lying, you learn to lie as little as possible. It may sound counterintuitive, but it's true. The more you lie, the more likely you are to get caught in a lie—usually by contradicting one of the lies you've told earlier. So I told them as much of the truth as I could. "Remember that guy I met at the warehouse party last month?" They nodded. "Well, we've been...talking,

I guess, and it seems like there's something there. But, uh…I've learned some things about myself recently that make having a relationship difficult for me. Like, stuff about my family I didn't know." There. That was good. Just enough of the truth to sound truthful, but not enough to reveal anything strange.

Chaz swallowed a bite of pizza. "Dale, you don't have an evil twin running around out there, do you?" When I rolled my eyes, he wiped his forehead in mock-relief. "Thank God. My grandma always told me that I should *never* associate with twins, because one of them is always evil. Unless…*you're* the evil twin! The plot thickens!"

I rolled my eyes again. Nik gave me a concerned look. "Is it anything you want to talk about? Your family thing, I mean." I shook my head. "All right. So basically, your life is crazy right now, and you're wondering if you should get someone else involved in your mess."

Uh, sure. That sounded like what I said. "Pretty much."

"So you guys have been talking?"

If that was what you would call him randomly showing up in my bookstore, followed by me stalking him all over the city. "Yeah."

"Do you like him?"

That was a tougher question than it probably should have been. I liked the guy who had walked around Red Hook with me. I wasn't so sure about the guy who came into the bookstore. That guy was angry and aggressive—and still pretty sexy, much to my chagrin. And of course, there was the small matter of him thinking I was a demon. Yeah. That might be an impediment. I didn't suppose John and his pal Gabriel were from the Happy Demon Welcome Wagon. That would be too easy. "It's complicated," I said.

When Nik looked at me curiously, I shifted uncomfortably in my seat. "I mean…he's gorgeous, and there's crazy chemistry. I can't stop thinking

about him. But with all my family stuff going on, things are just really messed up right now. Plus...I just think we might be too different. You know, like he's from a different world from me, or something." There. That about summed up my feelings for John without saying anything at all.

"That's really tough. I'm sorry you're going through it."

Chaz paused the movie and threw his arms up into the air dramatically. "Oh, my God! Why can't you two just say what you mean? Dale, 'it's complicated' is just another way of saying, 'He's completely fucked up, but I'm trying to justify having sex with him anyway.' And what Nik wants to say is, 'He's probably a serial killer, but on the other hand, at least you'd finally get out of the apartment once in a while.' Now, are we done here? Because Harold is about to commit hari-kari, and it's the funniest part of the movie. You need to watch."

Chaz un-paused the movie. Nik frowned, and I could tell Chaz's comments had stung more than he intended them to. I was about to say something, but Nik spoke up first. "That's not what I was thinking at all! Stop being such a jackass and let me talk to Dale for a minute."

"But the movie..."

"Will wait." She turned back to me. "What I was going to say is that I think you should go for it."

I raised my eyebrows. "Just like that, huh? What about the whole serial killer thing?"

"What is the likelihood that he's actually a serial killer?"

"Well, uh..." Technically, *I* was a serial killer. But that was beside the point.

Nik stood up and went to the window, staring out toward the Manhattan skyline. "Have you ever been in love, Dale?"

"No." That, at least, I could be completely honest about.

"I have." She wrapped her arms around herself, like she would fall out of her skin otherwise. "His name was Yousef. We had English class

together during our senior year of high school. He was the most logical, rational person I'd ever met, total science nerd, completely left-brained. Sometimes during class I would say these off-the-wall things just to get a rise out of him. We used to get into these debates that would last the entire period!" She chuckled. "My parents freaked when they found out. The whole religion thing, they said, which was total bullshit. My parents hadn't even been to synagogue in years, and Yousef was an agnostic. He didn't have faith in anything that couldn't be tested using the scientific method, he said. So after graduation, we moved into an apartment together. He was going to UConn, working two part-time jobs to cover rent and books and tuition. I was working as a waitress at this little hole-in-the-wall place near campus, and I took whatever hours I could get. We hardly ever saw each other. But on those rare days when we were both off, when we could just watch television or have dinner together, it was wonderful. I felt more at home with him than I ever had with my parents, and I kept telling myself that it was worth it."

She was silent for a long time. "What happened?" I asked finally.

She exhaled. "He died. About six months after we moved in together, he was coming home from one of his jobs and crashed his car into a tree. They didn't find any drugs or alcohol in his system. The police thought he probably just dozed off at the wheel. He was just working and studying all the time. He never slept. Afterward, my parents felt guilty, so they offered to pay for my tuition to NYU. But between the tattoos and the dreadlocks, I think they've been regretting it ever since."

Her attempt at humor didn't do anything to hide the tears rolling down her cheeks. Chaz came over and put his arms around her. She sank into his embrace. "I'm sorry, Nik," I said. "I didn't mean to bring up painful memories."

She wiped her eyes, but she didn't pull out of Chaz's grasp. "That's not why I told you. I told you because sometimes you meet someone, and you just…can't get that person out of your head. It was like that for me. I used to stay up late at night, writing down things I could say to aggravate Yousef in class. I knew my parents wouldn't like it, and I knew we were young, but I didn't care.

Sometimes I think maybe, if Yousef and I hadn't fallen in love, he'd be alive today." Her voice broke. "But then I realize how stupid that is. Because I don't know what would have happened. Yousef might have died anyway, and then I would have never known what it felt like to have cereal on a Sunday morning with the person you love most in the world."

Hell. Here she was baring her soul, and my situation with John was so much more fucked up than she could imagine—and nothing like her sweet love story. "It's not like that between John and me."

"You don't know that. That's what you have to find out. And you *should* find out. But that's scary for you. I think maybe you isolate yourself because you're afraid if people know the real you, they won't like you."

Damn. She had no idea how accurate she was. "I don't know…" But I didn't sound convincing, even to myself.

She smiled at me, and there seemed to be a little bit of actual happiness behind it this time. "When are you going to see him again?"

I shrugged. "I've been invited to this party where I think he's going to be on Saturday night, but I don't know how to get there. I was told to take the Six train to City Hall, but the Six doesn't even stop there."

"Well, that's not exactly true." It was the first time Chaz had spoken in several minutes. "I remember hearing about this on one of those 'Lost New York City' tours. The old City Hall stop is at the end of the Six line. If you stay on the Six train at the end of the line downtown, you'll pass it as the

train turns around to go uptown. But it's not actually a stop anymore. It's been closed for like, seventy years."

"Hmmm." If John was into some kind of strange supernatural thing, like I thought he was, why would I assume he'd hang out at a bar or a restaurant like a normal person? Of course he'd be meeting with his buddies at some abandoned subway station.

Chaz gave Nik's shoulders a final squeeze. Then he un-paused the movie again. "I still think he's a serial killer," he said.

I snorted. "You may very well be right about that."

CHAPTER

AROUND 2:30 A.M. THAT SATURDAY, I got on the Six train heading downtown.

I wasn't quite sure what would happen. I half expected one of the MTA employees would shuffle through the train and kick me off, maybe even have me arrested for vagrancy if I was really unlucky. The other half of me thought that the train would keep on going and going into some train yard somewhere in Queens or the Bronx. How could I be sure this train wasn't due to go out of service for the night? How the hell was I supposed to know what happened to trains when they reached the end of the line?

Yeah, I probably should have verified Chaz's story about the turnaround before I got on the train.

When the train got to the end of the line, a tinny voice came over the intercom. "This is Brooklyn Bridge, the last stop on this downtown Six train. I repeat, this is the *last* stop on this downtown Six train." The other passengers filed off. Not a one of them spared a second glance at me, and no MTA employees combed the car with nets and/or Tasers.

The doors shut.

The train began to creep forward, inching into the dark subway tunnel. Slowly, slowly, slowly. It felt like I was in the darkness forever. I held my breath, wondering if I was heading into the abyss, never to be seen again.

The car jerked as the train headed into a sharp curve. Then I saw it.

I had expected an abandoned subway station to be dark, dreary, maybe even a little scary. This was anything but. Chandeliers hung from the ceilings, casting a warm glow on the station. Ornate green, white, and beige tiles decorated the walls and when I craned my neck, I could see skylights in the high cathedral-style ceiling. A staircase with the words "CITY HALL" above it led off the platform, although I couldn't see where. What I could see was that there was a light coming from somewhere at the top of that staircase.

The end of the train rounded the curve. I saw a flash of movement out of the corner of my eye, and I strained to see what had happened. Someone in another car had jumped off the train, landing on the City Hall Station platform. The person, apparently undaunted by the danger (and the fact that what he had just done was completely and utterly illegal) brushed off his pants and walked toward a staircase, illuminated by old-fashioned dangling lights.

I sat back in my seat, trying to process what I'd just seen. About a minute later, the train was back at the Brooklyn Bridge Station, heading uptown this time. I didn't want to switch trains here, fearing that someone might question why I was boarding the train at the end of the line. So I waited until the train got up to Canal Street, and then I got off and headed back over to the downtown platform.

A few minutes later another train came, and I got on again. When we arrived at Brooklyn Bridge, my car once again emptied out. As the train pulled out of the station, I ducked down, not wanting anyone on the City Hall platform—which, from what I understood, was supposed

to be abandoned—to see me. Still, I peered out the window as we rounded the curve.

This time, three people jumped off the train at the City Hall Station, once again heading toward that mysterious lit staircase. I realized then how they were doing it. New York City subway trains allow you to walk from car to car so that you can move to another part of the train if it was too crowded or hot or whatever. Mostly people just used the pass-throughs to get away from people who were smelly or talking to themselves. I'd used them once to get away from a man who was licking his lips and looking at me as if I were a prime rib. But I had also waited until the train was stopped before I moved, because I was too cowardly to walk between the cars of a train hurling forty miles an hour through the tunnels.

You weren't supposed to ride the gap in between cars, just move from one car to another as quickly as possible. That didn't mean people didn't do it sometimes.

The jumpers must have been riding the gap, waiting for the right moment to hop off the train onto the City Hall platform. It wouldn't have been difficult. City Hall had been a station at one time, so the platform was reasonably close to the train edge, and the train had to go slow through the station because of the sharp curve. Easy peasy. Yeah, right.

If the thought of walking between train cars made me nervous, jumping off of them scared the beejebus out of me.

I wanted to test my theory one more time—or maybe I was just looking for an excuse not to jump. I exited at Canal Street and waited until the downtown train came around again. This time, I got up and acted like I was getting off at Brooklyn Bridge, standing up and holding on to the pole as the train screeched to a stop. I noticed a woman moving toward the back of the car, as if she was going to get out with everyone else. Her eyes darted around the train suspiciously, and I did my best to appear like I

wasn't looking at her. When the platform doors opened at Brooklyn Bridge and the other passengers shuffled out, she grabbed the back door of the car leading to the gap between this car and the next.

As the last passenger got off, I ducked down again so that no one outside the train could see me. The doors closed, and we lurched forward. A few minutes later, we rounded the curve at the City Hall Station. Four people jumped off the train this time, including the woman I'd seen slip between the cars.

Well, that was that then. I guess I knew what I had to do.

I switched trains again. I boarded the very last car this time, figuring that anyone else who might be jumping off of that train would likely be looking forward toward the staircase, not backward to the interloper crashing their late-night rendezvous. When the train stopped at Brooklyn Bridge, I waited. The jumper I'd seen had moved to the gap while the train was still in the station, but I figured it was better to wait until no one could see me. Plus, then I could make sure another of the train jumpers wouldn't intercept me in the gap.

It had nothing to do with the fact that I would have rather stuck needles into my eyes than jump off that train.

When the train got back into the tunnel, I peeked out the window in between the two cars. No one was there. I opened the door and stepped out into the gap. The train jerked, and I grabbed on to a thin metal handle attached to my car—too thin, I realized, to support the weight of a grown adult riding outside a moving train. *Please let it hold.* The train righted itself, and I released the breath I'd been holding.

I finally willed myself to look out toward the side of the train. There was a gate, about the height of my mid-torso, linking the two train cars together accordion-style, designed to give the train maximum mobility while still preventing anyone from doing...exactly what I was planning to

do. I'd climbed fences higher than that gate as a kid, and the accordion folds of the metal would make good footholds. "I can do this. I can do this."

The light from City Hall Station came into view. The train honked.

I climbed on top of the gate.

The train started into the curve. My foot slipped. I screamed and grabbed the edge of the car for support.

The train honked again, twice this time.

I tried to pull myself back up, but my foot was stuck in the gate. I yanked it, once, twice. Still stuck.

We emerged from the tunnel just as the train rounded the sharpest part of the curve. I tugged again.

My foot jerked free suddenly, and I lost my balance again. I fell, one hand clinging to the gate and the other dangling precariously close to the bottom of the train. If I slipped, I'd likely be crushed between the train and the side of the track.

I put my feet against the gate and sprang forward.

I tumbled onto the City Hall platform, landing with a *thump* on my front. The fall took my breath away, and I just lay there for a minute, trying to figure out whether I was dead or alive. When I stopping shaking enough to move, I stood up and started walking toward the staircase.

City Hall Station was even more magnificent now that I was seeing it up close, with its arched ceilings and ornate skylights. I wondered why they had ever shut it down, why it had stood abandoned since World War II. It seemed a shame to keep this place shut away. Then again, if it hadn't been, it probably would have been covered in decades' worth of grime and graffiti and fossilized gum like every other subway station. As it was, it stood as a perfect time capsule, unknown to everyone except me.

I heard voices coming from the other side of the staircase. I mentally corrected myself: unknown to everyone except me, John, and his possé of subway jumpers.

I couldn't see anything from the bottom of the stairs, but there was a light flickering from somewhere on the top, off to the right. I crept up.

The voices became clearer. I recognized one of the speakers as John.

I peered around the corner.

I stared at what must have once been the entryway of the station. There was a boarded-up ticket window in the back, a depressing contrast to the beautiful rounded arches leading up to a stained-glass skylight. A group of six people stood in a circle, each wearing dark-colored bodysuits with an insignia on the left arm. The suits fit close to their bodies and seemed to give off a metallic sheen when the firelight hit them. I'd seen suits like this before, on a science show I'd watched once: the latest in body armor fabric technology, practically indestructible, yet thin and flexible enough to give you the maneuverability that traditional body armor lacked. The show had treated the fabric as if it was still a prototype. I guess these guys hadn't gotten the memo.

Another dozen or so people surrounded the circle, wearing street clothes. I could tell, somehow, that the street clothes-clad people were subordinate to the others. Maybe it was their submissive body language: heads down, shoulders slouched. But it was equally obvious they were part of the same group—the Thrones, I was guessing—because they all also wore the insignia on their body somewhere: a shirt, a belt buckle, a hairband. One man even had it tattooed on his leg. It was the tattoo, with its intricate, colorful artwork, that allowed me to see what it actually was: an angel, his body and wings completely covered in flames, his face contorted in agony, holding a sword above his head.

Lovely.

At first, I thought each of the six body armor-clad Thrones was holding a torch. But then I realized that the balls of flame I saw were actually hovering in the air, floating on their own accord. One of them held up a hand, and the balls of flame came together, coalescing above the center of the circle, where a man wearing cargo pants and a checkered button-down kneeled. I couldn't see his face, but I knew him immediately: John.

I also knew the posture of supplication was an act when he spoke. "I told you. I won't do it."

One of the bodysuit-wearing women sneered at him. "And who gave you the authority to make that decision, mongrel?"

I could practically hear his teeth clench. "Nobody told me she was Amara's daughter when I started this hunt. If you had, I wouldn't have taken the job in the first place."

There were murmurs around the circle. Another woman spoke. "But what about her crimes? The young man in Raleigh you told us about a few months ago, and the others."

Holy shit, they're talking about me, I realized. And they knew about the things I'd done. Fuck.

It occurred to me then that I didn't have an escape plan. I hadn't planned the whole jumping off the train thing in the first place, and now I was in an abandoned subway station with dozens of unknown people who knew about the things I'd done, and who apparently planned to do nefarious shit to me, and my only potential ally was surrounded.

How the hell was I going to get out of here? Jumping back on to the train didn't exactly seem like a feasible option, and the stairs to the street had likely been blocked off since the Truman administration—even if I didn't have to get through every single Throne to get there.

I was so screwed.

John didn't flinch. "She hasn't done anything worse than what we've done on behalf of the Thrones. On the other hand, if she were to disappear, it could trigger a full-scale war. I won't be a part of that."

A man with a mustache sniffed at him. "If Amara wants war, then so be it. You know they don't have the training or organization that we do."

"There are still more of them than there are of us. If anyone has the resources and the capability to pull them together, it's Amara. They may not have the martial training we do, but what they do have is an almost fanatical devotion to her." He hesitated. "I'm trying to think of the good of the Thrones. *All* the Thrones."

The body armor wearers erupted in angry shouting. Some of the plainclothes people, though, looked up for the first time. They looked… curious. John remained where he was, kneeling silently.

A man in body armor who hadn't yet spoken stepped forward from the circle. Something about him made me think of a highwayman of yore, stalking his victims through a blustery winter night. He stood at least a head taller than everyone else, probably around six foot six or six foot seven, and had the darkest skin I'd ever seen on a human being. I would have known he was in charge even if the others hadn't fallen silent as soon as he moved. There was just something about him, a presence, like he was the sun and the rest of them were revolving around him. Everyone except John, that is. I wondered if the man saw the defiance in John's pose, or if I was reading something into the situation that wasn't really there. "You are muddying the waters, young halfling, and I suspect you do so intentionally. You were given orders to find the girl, correct?"

John hesitated. "Yes, Gabriel."

"And you knew what you were supposed to do once you found her?"

John looked at the floor. "I did."

Gabriel nodded. "Indeed. Which means my options are limited now. I am sorry, John. I grew fond of you in the wake of your father's death, despite your tainted origins, and you've been a valuable asset to us through the years. But I cannot let this pass unheeded."

"I understand." John stood up, and Gabriel pulled out a gun, one of those old flintlock pistols with the rounded handles and wooden barrels I had only ever seen on TV.

I don't know what came over me then. "No!" I ran into the center of the circle and pushed John to the ground just as Gabriel pulled the trigger.

Gabriel lowered his gun and stared at me, his mouth ajar. The others stood as still as statues. I didn't know what to do next. Luckily, John was not as slow to react as I was. He grabbed my arm and pulled me to my feet. "Run."

We ran. "After them!" Gabriel yelled.

I heard footsteps coming behind us. A small, metallic disc whizzed by our head and attached to the wall. "Shit," John said. He grabbed my arm again and pulled me into a small room that must have once been a utility closet. "Cover your ears," he said.

I did. Less than five seconds later, bright, strobe lights began to flash through the vents in the door. But that wasn't the worst of it. The lights were accompanied by a high-pitched screeching noise. Even with my ears covered, my head spun, and I felt queasy. I crouched down, my head between my knees, tears rolling down my face. When my hands fell from my ears, he took my wrists and put them back up again, bracing them against my knees.

It felt like forever before the noise stopped; in retrospect, it must have only been a minute or two. John lowered my hands gently. "Just breathe through it," he said.

"What was that?"

"Sonic soundwave emitter, combined with a strobe light. It's meant to disorient and confuse. Most people freeze up when it starts, and then they're easy pickings."

"You okay to move yet?" he asked.

"I'm not sure."

"Try to stand up, at least. We need to be ready to run again."

There wasn't much room to maneuver in the closet, and John had positioned himself so that he was between me and the door, leaving just a couple of inches between us. When I stood, I accidentally brushed my hand against his shirt. It came away wet and sticky. "You're bleeding."

"Don't worry about it." He was breathing heavily, but he didn't give me a chance to ask him about it. "What the hell are you doing here? Are you crazy?"

"'Hi, Dale. Thank you for saving my life tonight. I really appreciate it.'" There was no trace of bitterness in my voice. Not even a little.

He grabbed my arms. I'd forgotten how much that zing between us stung at first, and the fact that his nails were digging into my skin so hard they would leave marks didn't help. "I told you to leave the city. I came here tonight to throw them off your trail. I knew what the consequences would be. I decided."

He decided? Gotta love macho asshole bullshit. "And what about when the next one came after me?"

I could hear the smile in his voice. "They'd never find you. If there's one thing you know how to do, it's disappear."

"You found me."

"I'm the best tracker they've got, and it still took me almost ten years. With me out of the equation, you'd be safe."

I wasn't sure how to respond to that. Kind of hard to say whether I'd be safe with John out of the equation when I didn't know what it added up to in the first place. Was that double variables or something? I'd always sucked at math. "I'm not going to apologize for preventing you from getting shot in the head."

"For the record, I had no intention of letting myself be killed."

"Did you forget the part where you had a gun pointed to your head? How the hell was I supposed to know you had some crazy kung-fu ninja plan to get out of it?"

He sighed. "I don't know how you got here, or why you would do something so half-witted...but thank you."

Well. Not exactly an apology, but it was something. I didn't say anything else, and about a minute or so later John spoke again. "I think we should be safe to go now."

He opened the door a crack and peered out. "It's clear." He left the closet and motioned for me to follow.

We ran toward the street exit. A few seconds later, I heard an electronic humming noise behind us, followed by a loud boom. "Dale, duck!" He pushed me to the ground as a black ball whizzed by, slamming into the wall above us. It dissolved into a quivering mass of legs and thoraxes.

My heart raced. I could barely get the word out. "Spiders."

"Mechanical spiders. Don't let them touch your skin."

But by that time, I was too panicked to listen, frozen in place by fear. The spiders scattered off in all directions, and I could only stare at them. They were no bigger than my pinkie fingernail, but that didn't matter when they started climbing up my shoes. "Get 'em off! Get 'em off!"

John bent down and began plucking the spiders off of my shoes, but that didn't stop some of them from making their way up my sock onto

my skin. Once they touched my bare skin, it began to burn and sizzle. I screamed.

"It'll be over faster if you help me," John said.

Pushing my fear to the back of my mind, I bent down and began plucking the mechanical arachnids off of my legs. In their wake, they left behind bloody red pockmarks. "It'll heal," John told me.

"Busy, Bloodhound?" asked a cold voice. I stopped what I was doing just long enough to look up. Four of the plainclothes Thrones surrounded us, two male, two female. Only one of them actually had a weapon pointed at us, though. The man I'd seen earlier with the tattoo balanced some kind of a rifle on his shoulder. It was very sci-fi looking, with a shiny, chrome barrel about an inch and a half in diameter and a blue light coming from the sight, aimed directly at the target—me. At that size, it looked like it was designed to take down elephants instead of people, and his shoulder dipped under the weapon's weight. He flipped a switch, and it emitted a high-pitched hum—the same hum that accompanied the appearance of those damn spiders.

Fuck.

John put his hand on my shoulder. "Just keep working on those spiders. I'll take care of this." He stood up slowly. His breathing was shaky, and he was sweating. "I'll come with you, Michael. But just let the girl go."

"Why should I?" The man, Michael, had a faint British accent. Usually, accents just made a guy sexier, but on him it had a distinctly disturbing quality. I half expected him to offer John some fava beans and a nice Chianti. "Who is she? A romantic thrall, perhaps? Or maybe—" He stopped mid-sentence, eyes widening. He spoke quietly: "She's the one, isn't she? Amara's daughter."

"Do you really think her legs would look like this if she were some all-powerful demon spawn?"

I glanced down at my legs. John and I had managed to remove all the spiders, but much of the skin between my ankles and knees had been burned away, leaving them looking like raw meat. It still hurt, but I ignored the pain, and the tightening feeling around my shins told me they were already healing.

"Then why did you save her life?" Michael asked. "Has the Bloodhound gone soft?"

"She's just a student down here to take pictures. Have Rebekah wipe her. No reason to draw undue attention."

The other three Thrones looked at Michael, who was apparently the leader of the group. "Where's her camera?"

"On her phone, fledgling. How many times have I told you that you need to be familiar with human technology in order to blend in with the human world?"

Michael considered this. I just hoped he wouldn't ask me to produce said phone, because I was probably the one person left on the planet who didn't have one. But one of the other Thrones, a woman, cleared her throat. "Michael, look at her legs."

They all looked down at my legs. The burns were almost healed, leaving behind smooth, unmarred skin. Michael glared at John. "You…"

Before Michael could finish his sentence, John whipped a small crossbow, maybe about eight inches long, out of his pocket and fired a bolt tipped in gold at Michael. Michael froze, his mouth agape. "I'm sorry, Michael, it had to be done."

John grabbed my hand, and we ran again, the other Thrones on our heels. We rounded a corner, and before they could see us, made another sharp turn down the steps toward the train platform. "What are you doing? How the hell are we gonna get out from there?" I asked.

A train honked in the distance as we ran down the steps. "The same way you came in," he said.

My eyes widened. "No fucking way! I could barely get off the train. We're going to the street exit."

I started toward the stairs, but John grabbed my arm again. "Gabriel has called in reinforcements by now. They'll be waiting at the street exit. This is the best way."

The train honked again, growing louder, and the headlights appeared down the tunnel. The other Thrones rushed down the staircase. "Dale, hold them!" he shouted. I stared at him in confusion. "Like you did before, when they were going to shoot me! Tell them to stop!"

"Stop!" I screamed at them.

One of them froze, but the two women kept charging us. "Damn," John said. He fired another gold-tipped bolt from his crossbow at one of them. It punctured her shoulder. She froze mid-step, one leg hovering over the steps. She tumbled and fell to the platform, still completely paralyzed.

The other woman held up her hand and whistled. Skittering noises echoed around us, and then the light beam from the train reflected off of many small pairs of eyes.

Rats. Hundreds of them. They charged us.

"Shit!" John reached back into his pocket, pulled out a pistol, and fired at the woman. It didn't fire a bullet, but some kind of dart with a needle in the front. She screamed, collapsing to her knees. She recuperated quickly enough to jump up and run away, the rats following.

The train emerged from the tunnel. I looked at John. "I can't do this."

"Then you'll die," he said flatly. Then he linked his hand with mine. "You tried to save my life. Now I'm trying to save yours. We jump, on my count. One...two..." he squeezed my hand, "...three."

We jumped.

CHAPTER

8

I SLAMMED INTO THE ACCORDION GATE. It knocked the wind out of me, and I couldn't get a foothold on the side of the train. The train rounded back into the tunnel, curving sharply. My left hand slipped, leaving me flailing toward the wall. I swung myself forward and grabbed the gate again, my feet still dangling.

"You have to get over, Dale!" John shouted. He was already standing on the other side. How the hell had he jumped all the way over the gate?

The train jerked, and I held on tighter. "I don't think I can."

"I won't let you fall. Trust me."

Tears ran down my face, but I nodded. He leaned toward me. "Lift your feet and find the step. It's at the bottom of the gate." I had visions of my feet being crushed into a bloody pulp between the train and the edge of the track, and I froze. "It's all right, Dale. The gate is right in front of your feet."

I edged my right foot forward, locating the triangular bend at the bottom of the gate with my toes. John nodded. "Good, now the other one." I inched my other foot forward. "A little more to your left, just a little... there, you have it. Now just climb."

With my feet secure, the climb wasn't any more difficult than it had been on the way out—less so, with John giving me directions on where and how I needed to move. When I reached the top, he held out his arms to help me over. I stumbled into him as I stepped onto the train car, and he steadied me with his hands. My skin buzzed from the contact, and I was surrounded by his butterscotch scent. He was breathing as heavily as I was. "Thank you," I said.

He looked me in the eyes, and for one moment frozen in time I thought he was going to kiss me again. Then he shook his head, and the spell broke. "We need to get inside the car," he said.

"Right." We opened the door and entered the car. John sat down on the closest seat, resting his head against the wall, while I stood up and paced back and forth between the poles. I had too much adrenaline surging through my body to stay still. The train stopped at the Brooklyn Bridge Station, and the doors opened. A few people boarded the train; luckily no one got onto our car. We were a macabre sight, exhausted and panting and covered in blood that may or may not have been our own. "There are too many people here," I said. "We should get off at the next station."

"They'll look there. Better...stay on...long as we can."

I glanced over at John, and I gasped. Besides the blood on his clothes, his skin was starting to turn a sickly gray color. His eyes were closed, and sweat beaded over his forehead. "Holy shit, John, what's wrong?"

"Mmmmm fine. Just gimme...a little time."

I bent down and unbuttoned his shirt. In the center of his stomach was a large welt, the size of a golf ball, that had turned a dark gray color. Darker streaks radiated from it, as if he was rotting from the inside out. But that wasn't what really alarmed me. No, what got me was the fact that his stomach was moving on its own accord, as if the creature from *Alien* was about to burst out of his skin. For all I knew, it was. "What the hell is this?"

John cracked his eyes open and looked at his stomach. "Silver," he groaned before he lost consciousness.

I RAN THROUGH THE AUTOMATIC doors of the emergency waiting room entrance, carrying John in my arms. "This man needs help! He's dying!"

The woman at the desk took one look at John's pallid skin and bloody clothing and picked up the phone. Seconds later, an orderly took John from my arms, almost buckling under John's solid bulk. A second orderly came up, and together they loaded him onto a gurney.

A doctor in green scrubs raced out behind them, a stethoscope in her hands. "What happened?" she asked.

"I don't know exactly. I think he was shot." I kept clinging to his hand. The electric charge between us was so faint it was almost gone.

She put the stethoscope to his chest. "Pulse is thready. How long has he been unconscious?"

"Maybe fifteen minutes. Check his stomach. I think there's something with his stomach."

She removed a pair of scissors from her scrub pocket and cut open his shirt. "Significant discoloration of skin, no visible injury...oh God..." John's stomach had started moving again. The doctor gaped at him momentarily before collecting herself. "Get him in back! Have a crash cart ready!" she ordered. The orderlies pushed the gurney through the emergency room doors. I tried to follow, but one of the nurses stopped me. "You can't come in here, miss. The doctor will let you know when there's any news."

I nodded, staring at the doors that were still swinging from the momentum of John's gurney.

From my left, I heard someone clearing their throat. The woman who had first phoned for help still stood there. "Sammy almost fell down when he tried to grab that guy off of you! How were you able to carry him in here like that?" she asked.

Shit. "Adrenaline, I guess."

"That must have been a hell of a lot of adrenaline. That's some Wonder Woman shit right there! How did you…"

"Where's the bathroom?" I asked. She pointed down the hallway. I thanked her and took off as quickly as I dared without looking like I was running from her.

There was a cart with folded scrubs outside one of the rooms. When I was sure no one was looking, I grabbed a purple set from the top. I felt bad about stealing, but the idea of sitting around for hours covered in John's blood—and my own—was worse.

I changed out of my blood-soaked T-shirt and shorts and into the scrubs. I threw my soiled clothes into the trashcan and washed my hands.

The lights went off.

I heard the whirring noise of a backup generator, and a few seconds later the emergency lights came on. A voice came through the overhead speaker: "Ladies and gentleman, please do not be alarmed. We are working to ensure power is…"

The speaker cut out, and the emergency lights went off. The hum of the backup generator died. From outside the bathroom door, I heard people screaming.

They'd followed us.

I ran out of the bathroom and stumbled through masses of people to get back to the waiting room. I found it in chaos. The only illumination were the lights from outside—which all had full power—and people were panicking. Several were crying. Others were yelling at the woman

at the desk, who was holding a flashlight and trying to calm everyone down. "It's all right," she called. "Everything is going to be fine." She didn't sound confident.

I approached her, cutting off the people flocking around the desk. "Give me your flashlight," I ordered her.

She handed it to me without a word. The people standing behind me yelled in protest, but I ignored them. I flicked on the light and pushed through the double doors of the emergency room. I had to find John, and we needed to get out of here now.

If I thought the waiting area was in chaos, I hadn't been prepared for the actual emergency room. It was dark, and people wearing scrubs ran from bed to bed with lanterns and flashlights in their hands, shouting at one another. Patient beds ran up and down the walls, each separated by thin curtains. Some of the patients were crying. No one noticed me.

The beds were all hidden by curtains, so I started to peek behind them, apologizing softly when I shined my light into the eyes of a bewildered patient.

A loud crack broke through the room as someone kicked the doors open. I caught a quick glimpse of some of the Thrones I'd seen earlier. A man wearing fitted body armor carried a black box, about eighteen cubic inches, with a plunger on the top of it. It reminded me of the dynamite detonator boxes you'd see in old Westerns. In spite of the darkness, all of them were wearing sunglasses. I ducked behind the curtain as their leader began to speak, keeping an eye on them through the slit. "Ladies and gentlemen, we apologize for the inconvenience. I'd say this isn't going to hurt, but it probably will." He pushed down the plunger.

I jumped onto the bed and covered the man there with my body, doing my best to protect my own head and neck with my arms. But instead of the shrapnel I expected, a bright light flashed through the room. I closed

my eyes tighter and tried to cover the eyes of the patient beneath me without hurting him. Seconds later, I heard the sound of multiple bodies simultaneously hitting the ground. "Spread out. Look for them. They'll be around here somewhere," I heard the leader say.

I opened my eyes. Underneath the curtain, I could see the fallen body of an orderly. In the darkness, I couldn't tell if he was dead or just unconscious. I could move, which was a plus, but I felt like a punk rock band was beating its drums inside my temples. I edged off the bed slowly, trying not to throw up.

I hadn't looked at the patient in the bed before I jumped on top of him, but now I did, clutching my flashlight with unsteady hands. I couldn't tell how old he was, and his face and body were so mutilated and torn that his best friend likely wouldn't have been able to recognize him. The smell of blood and rust permeated the air around him. If there was one thing I knew, it was death, and if this man wasn't dead already, he would be soon—and he had been that way long before the Thrones had marched into the emergency room.

I was about to leave when I heard the *clomp, clomp, clomp* of several pairs of feet thudding along the tile a few beds behind me. They hadn't peeked behind my curtain, hadn't spotted me yet, so I slumped to the ground as quietly as I could and played dead.

Clomp, clomp, clomp. They opened the curtain of a bed across the aisle.

A pause. *Clomp, clomp, clomp.* They opened the curtain of the bed behind me.

Clomp, clomp, clomp. The curtain sheltering me opened. I held my breath and tried not to move. A few seconds later, the curtain closed and they moved on.

I waited until their footsteps had faded before I allowed myself to breathe again. I stood up and peered out the curtain, when I heard a scratchy noise, too close to be coming from outside. I switched on my flashlight.

The mutilated man was looking at me. Dear God, he's conscious.

Several of his teeth were missing, and half of his lip had been torn apart and was dangling down near his chin. A gash, more than an inch wide, cut his face nearly in half diagonally, bisecting his nose into two distinct pieces. What little skin wasn't bloody was covered with embedded grime, as if the poor guy had been dragged across asphalt. For a horrible second, I wondered if this was John, if his condition had deteriorated so much that he'd been left this rotting husk. But no, this man was dark haired. Not like John. More like Andrew Seymour had been. "Light," he rasped.

"Is my flashlight too bright?"

I switched off my flashlight, but he grabbed my hand with surprising strength. "Your light," he said. His eyes filled with tears, and he took a shuddering breath. Then he closed his eyes, and his grip on my hand relaxed.

There were no alarm bells, no doctors and nurses rushing in calling a Code Blue. Nothing like you see in the movies. Just a man who died in the dark with a stranger. I knew I should do something, find his family or call a priest or something. But I could hear the clomping footsteps getting closer again, and I just didn't have time. "I'm sorry," I told him, pushing the thoughts of the last time I apologized to a dead man out of my head. This man deserved to die in peace, without my ghosts interfering.

I left the dead man behind and slipped between curtains, spending as little time exposed as I could. I searched so many beds, saw so many sick and injured people, and I began to wonder whether I would find John at all. Had he been taken in for surgery? Was he already dead? The thought hit me hard, and I willed myself not to panic.

I finally found him lying on a gurney in the back of the emergency room, his eyes closed, shirtless, with an IV dripping into his arm. His stomach was still gray and discolored, but at least it didn't look like it was about to burst open.

I shook him. "John?" The zing I normally experienced when I touched him was still muted. "John, wake up. We have to get out of here!"

His eyes snapped open. "Where are we?"

"The hospital. The Thrones are here. They cut the power, and now they're searching for us."

"Damn." He reached down and pushed against his abdomen. He winced. "You shouldn't have brought me here, Dale." He sat up and ripped the IV line from his arm, tape and all. "Which way is out?" he asked. I pointed back toward the main door. "All right. Let's go."

He got off the gurney—and as soon as he did, his legs gave out from under him. I grabbed him so he wouldn't fall. "Are you all right? Were the doctors able to figure out what's wrong with you?"

"Don't worry about it. Help me to the door."

I wrapped my arm around him, holding my flashlight with my other hand, and we made our way to the doors. Once we pushed through them, the man in the body armor with the detonator box stood there, flanked by two other plainclothes Thrones. He smiled at John. "So the mongrel bastard isn't dead, after all."

John shrugged. "Ezra, I envy you, really. I'm just a bastard by birth. But you? When people call you a bastard, you've earned it."

Ezra scowled. "If you turn the girl over, I'll agree to give you a five-minute head start before I contact the others. It should be enough to get you out of town and away from Gabriel. Call it loyalty for everything you've done for the Thrones over the years. You deserve a fighting chance."

John pulled away from me, bracing himself unsteadily against his own legs, panting. "Come closer," he whispered shakily. Ezra leaned in. "You're forgetting…one thing."

Ezra's eyes narrowed. "What?"

Before Ezra could react, John whipped out his crossbow and fired it into Ezra's exposed hand. "I don't need a fighting chance."

Ezra collapsed, his eyes still open, his mouth gaping in surprise. The other two Thrones, a man and a woman, rushed us. "Dale, tell them to stop!" John yelled. "Like back at the subway."

"Stop!" I yelled. Nothing happened. They kept charging us. "Shit!"

The male Throne grabbed me, but he only managed to get one of my arms. I took the other hand and swung up at him, crushing the heel of my hand into his nose. It made a crunching noise, and he released me, blood dripping down his face. But then he was back on me, angry this time. He threw me toward the wall, and I collided with a small set of movable drawers.

I was too dazed to move for a second, and the Throne advanced on me. I pulled open the drawers and dug through the instruments blindly, until I found what felt like a scalpel. I waited until the male Throne was nearly on top of me, and then I stabbed him in the eye.

He screamed and collapsed. I pushed him off of me and jumped up. The female Throne had John on the floor, and he wasn't moving.

Ezra's detonator box was on the floor. I grabbed it. It was metal, and heavier than it looked. Good. I swung the box around and hit her on the head. She fell over, unconscious.

I shoved her aside and bent over John. "Oh my God, John! Did she hurt you?"

He pushed himself up, cringing with pain. "Don't worry about me. Worry about getting out of here."

I helped John to his feet. "What about…all of them?" I motioned toward the people who had collapsed when the Thrones used their light thingy.

"We can't help them. They're already dead. C'mon."

I put my arm around him, and we ran through the double doors. The scene in the waiting area was very much like the one inside the ER, bodies strewn all over the place. Ezra had apparently used his light thingy out here, too. I felt red bleeding into my vision. "We should have killed him." My voice was dark and deep, fueled by the Rage that was threatening.

"No time now. We need to go." John's voice was unsteady, and he was panting. It was enough to snap me out of it, to bring me back to the here and now.

We ran out the door, emerging onto First Avenue. "We need a car," John said. He scanned the street and then pointed to the opposite corner. "There."

A dark BMW was parked along the side of the street, its lights on, its driver slumped over the wheel. I darted across the street, still clinging to John, ignoring the car horns honking at us. When we got there, John pulled the door open. "Dale, tell him that he parked his car tonight, got drunk, and then forgot where he parked it. Tell him not to look for it any more tonight, that he should just wait until Monday."

I did. The driver just stared at me, still half-asleep. "Huh?"

"John, it's not working."

"Try again. Like you mean it this time."

I tried again, staring into the driver's unfocused eyes. I could feel the instant his resistance dropped, like a sudden change in air pressure that makes your ears pop. His eyes glazed over, and he staggered away from the car. I got into the driver's side and began adjusting the seat and mirrors as John stumbled over to the passenger's side. Once he sat down, he looked behind us. "We need to go. Now."

I looked in the rearview mirror. The two Thrones we had fought earlier had run out of the hospital and were getting into a car of their own. "Fuck."

I pulled out of the parking space and floored the gas. A taxicab almost hit me, blaring its horn as I sped through an intersection. "Dale…"

The Thrones' car was still on our tail. "Hang on!" I made a sharp right down a side street, blasting the horn at a homeless man who was walking across the street. He darted out of the way, and I rolled through another red light. At the next intersection, I turned right, nearly fishtailing the vehicle when I took the turn too fast.

I saw an exit sign for the highway and made a sharp left turn, cutting across several lanes of traffic. Tires screeching, more honking. I just pressed the gas down harder, whipping us around the sharp curve of the on-ramp and merging into an impossibly small hole in the traffic, whizzing across until I got to the left lane. When I glanced into my mirror again, I didn't see their car. I slowed down to a normal pace. "I think we lost them," I said.

John didn't respond. I risked a quick glance at him. His eyes were closed, and he was breathing heavily. "Are you all right?"

"Just keep going."

I switched on the overhead light. John's face was now a pale gray, and his lips were blue. Worse, his stomach was moving on its own again, as if dozens of tiny hands were pushing out against him, trying desperately to get out. As I looked at him, he leaned over and threw up on the floor. "John…what the hell is going on?"

He leaned back against his seat, not bothering to open his eyes. "I'm fine. Don't worry. Just keep going."

"You're obviously not fine. What's going on?"

He cracked his eyes open. His irises had turned silver. "I'm dying."

CHAPTER

An hour later, I found myself helping John inside a second-floor room of a motel off the highway that was just this side of charge-by-the-hour. But it was clean, and that was the most important thing for our purposes. In the hand I wasn't using to brace John's weight, I carried a bag from a local Wal-Mart filled with bandages, bath towels…and kitchen knives. "This is a bad idea," I said as I covered the bed with a towel.

He lay down on the bed without responding to my comment. He was shivering, and his skin was bluish gray. "The bullet I was shot with is called a fractal bullet. It's designed to fracture inside the body. Right now, I have pieces of shrapnel drifting toward my heart, and I won't be able to heal until they're all out. I'll help you as much as I can, but obviously I can't cut into myself."

"And the fact that everything I know about medicine comes from watching *M*A*S*H* reruns back in high school doesn't bother you?"

"That still puts you head and shoulders above most of the doctors I've met."

He retched. I managed to throw a trashcan in front of his face before he puked on the bed. I filled a cup of water for him from the bathroom and

gave it to him when he stopped vomiting. He was still shivering, and the towels were already covered in sweat. "It has to be now, Dale. I can't wait any longer."

"I don't know if I can do this."

"You can. We'll just…take it slow."

I ran to the bathroom and washed my hands thoroughly. By the time I got back, John's breathing had become choppy. Then, I removed a knife block and rubbing alcohol from the shopping bags. Once I separated the knife block from its protective plastic coating, I pulled out a paring knife and poured alcohol over it.

John pulled off his shirt, but he couldn't get it over his head. I took it off for him, tossing the sweat-soaked cotton to the floor. I wet some gauze pads with the rubbing alcohol and swiped his abdomen with them. "Don't… need…that." John's teeth were chattering so hard I could barely understand him. "Germs can't hurt me."

"I don't fucking care," I told him. "Tell me what I need to do."

He pointed to the center of the blackening welt, which had swelled to the size of a softball. "I was shot here. If you cut about two inches above and below, you should be able to pull the shrapnel out. You bought tweezers, didn't you?"

I nodded, and I pulled them out of the bag, wiped them down with more alcohol-soaked gauze, and put them on a washcloth I'd placed on the nightstand, along with more gauze, needles, thread, and butterfly bandages. I took a deep breath. "Here goes nothing."

I placed the tip of the knife about an inch above the scar and cut. Cutting skin is not like chopping vegetables or even cutting into a well-cooked steak. The closest I can come to describing it is that it's like cutting up raw chicken, if the chicken was bleeding on you and convulsing so

hard you thought it would knock you off the bed. "Fuck, John! You need to hold still!"

"C-c-c-can't."

I crouched above him, using my legs to pin his shoulders and torso in place. Then I tried again. John cried out, turning his head into the pillow to muffle his scream. A tear leaked out of his eye. Still, I only managed about an inch before stopping, and I hadn't made it all the way through the tissue. "I need to use one of the sharper knives."

"Too...big," he panted.

"At this rate, it's going to take me hours to get an incision big enough for me to work with."

Unspoken were the words *I don't think you can last that long.* The fragments were killing him.

I could see the fear in John's eyes. But finally, he nodded. I pulled one of the bigger, longer knives out of the block, wiped it down, and cut. Blood welled from the incision, but I kept going, pushing down with the knife to work my way through the muscle layer. John clenched his fists, digging into his palms with his fingernails. When I had made about a three-inch-long cut, I stopped. "I think that's long enough. Do you need to take a break?"

John took a ragged breath. "Just get it over with. Please."

I pulled the incision apart with my hands. God, there was so much blood! It oozed over my fingers, covering my knuckles. His insides were a mess of ichor and slime, and I had no idea whether that was a good thing or a bad thing because I had no idea what the inside of someone's abdomen was supposed to look like in the first place. Now I knew why the doctors on TV always asked for suction. "I don't see anything."

"Dig," he wheezed. "Use the side of the knife, if you have to."

"Jesus Christ." I lengthened the incision another inch and spread it open with my fingertips. After rooting inside him for a few minutes,

something caught my eye—a *glittering* something. It was a tiny fragment of silver wedged into what looked like his intestines. It was smaller than my pinkie nail, surrounded with pus and inflamed, red flesh. I grabbed the tweezers. "Take a deep breath."

"Why?"

"Because I think this is gonna hurt." Before he could say anything else, I grabbed the fragment and yanked it out. He cried out, and his body bucked so hard that even all my weight on top of him couldn't stop it. When he finally stopped, I tossed the fragment onto the nightstand. "How many more?"

"I don't know. Half a dozen maybe?"

I could feel the blood draining from my face. "John, they're so small. I don't know how I'll find them all."

He nodded weakly. "All right. There may be one thing I can do. Move the lamp so it shines directly into the wound." I did so. He closed his eyes and took a deep breath, then another, then another. It was like he was falling into a trance of some kind. "I can feel them," he said. "Touch me."

"I don't..."

He grabbed my wrist and pulled me toward the open cut, moving my hand down toward his belly button. "There. Can you see it?"

I leaned in closer to him, and there it was, a tiny piece of metal flecked with blood, shining in the lamplight. I reached for it with the tweezers and pulled it out. This time, John didn't lurch, but he squeezed my wrist as I pulled it out. He released me, his body relaxing, and I tossed it onto the nightstand. "How are you doing that?"

"A meditation technique I learned years ago. I've had to repair a lot of my own injuries over time."

I didn't know what that meant, and I didn't want to ask. "Do you need a break?"

"No, let's keep going." He took my hand and guided me to his left side, near his rib cage.

We followed the same technique for three more fragments. Beads of sweat dripped down John's face, and his breathing grew labored. The last fragment was wedged into an organ—his liver, I thought, but I wasn't sure. By that time, he was too weak to move, his body having given up the fight against the pain. I removed the bullet and dropped it onto the nightstand. His body remained limp, and his expression didn't change. "Please tell me that was the last one."

"Think...so."

I sighed in relief. The worst was over, but John's stomach was still gaping open in front of me. I pulled the needles and cotton thread I'd purchased out of the bag, but John grasped my wrist. "No. Just pull it together with the butterfly bandages and tape it up."

"You're crazy. It's too big for that."

"No. It'll heal. Just give me...a minute."

"John, there's no way something like this is going to close without stitches. It's too big and too wide."

"Just leave it. It'll be fine." He opened his eyes and looked at me. "If it doesn't work, we'll stitch it. But...I just can't take any more right now, you know?"

"All right." I put down the needles and thread and instead used the butterfly bandages to close up the wound the best I could. I covered it with gauze and held my hand there, trying to stop the blood that was already seeping through the woven cloth.

John closed his eyes and took several slow, deep breaths. Several minutes later, I felt the skin beneath the gauze growing hot. When it was too hot to touch anymore, I pulled my hand—and the gauze—back.

The incision had already healed into nothing more than a soft pink line. The scar from the original bullet wound had faded to an off-white color.

John opened his eyes. I met his gaze. "Are you a demon?" I asked.

He smiled. "You mean you don't know? I'm not a demon. *You* are."

He passed out.

CHAPTER

10

JOHN REMAINED UNCONSCIOUS FOR THE next several hours, waking only to puke into the garbage can next to the bed. I paced the room, trying to deal with what I had learned.

I was a demon.

I was a demon, and I apparently had some kind of Obi-Wan Kenobi mind powers that I had never noticed before.

I was a demon, and I had just spent the last several hours jumping off of a subway train, stabbing someone in the eye with a scalpel, and digging around in John's stomach.

I checked on John. His skin was still warm, especially around the wound site, and the cool washcloth I'd applied to his forehead was now tepid. I rinsed it in cold water again and reapplied it to his forehead. My skin tingled, stronger than before, at the contact, and John stirred. "John? Are you awake?" I whispered.

John's eyes sprang open. He leaned over the side of the bed. After puking into the trashcan again, he fell back onto the pillow and closed his eyes. Within seconds, his breathing had resumed a steady rhythm. I

sighed and got up to clean the plastic bin. Again. At least he hadn't puked on the bedsheets.

Three hours after John passed out, I was no closer to answers. My feet were tired, and I was worried that I might wear a hole into the cheap carpet. I'd already washed all the knives, and I'd left the bullet fragments on the nightstand, not knowing if John would need them or not. The towels... well, there wasn't a whole hell of a lot I could do about them. There was less blood on them than you would imagine, but no amount of bleach was ever going to make them usable again, even by the standards of this shithole. Besides, ten years of running from my own crimes left me with an instinctual aversion to leaving blood-soaked towels behind. I had put them on the floor for now; I figured we'd shove them into a bag and toss them somewhere far, far away after we left.

I sat on the bed next to John and put my hand on his forehead. He was still hot, but not as much as he had been a few hours earlier. I lay down on the pillow next to him and closed my eyes, inhaling his butterscotch smell. I didn't think I would fall asleep, since my head was still spinning, but as I felt his warmth next to me and listened to his steady breathing, I slowly drifted off.

When I opened my eyes again, John was staring at me. "Hi," I croaked.

"Hi, yourself." He gave me a weak smile. He was still too pale.

"What time is it?"

He rolled over and looked at the bedside clock. "About midnight. We should start moving again soon."

God. A whole day had passed. I sat up, rubbing the sleep out of my eyes. "How long have you been awake?"

"Not long. I didn't want to wake you."

"How are you feeling?"

He took a deep breath. "Still shaky, but better than before, thanks to you."

"I want to check your incision."

He lay back on the bed and bared his shirtless chest to me. The cut I had made in his skin had faded into a pale white line, as if it had been made years ago instead of a few hours. The bullet entry wound was still raised and puckered, but it still looked like a much older scar than it was. Still, his skin retained a grayish tinge. "So…are you okay now?"

"Not exactly." He sat up gingerly.

I'd been in a hurry while I was looking for whatever passed as medical supplies at the twenty-four-hour Wal-Mart, but somehow I'd had the foresight to throw some clean T-shirts and sweat pants into the cart for both of us. I left John's on the nightstand. He pulled the shirt over his head, the blue color of it emphasizing the unhealthy pallor of his skin. His hands were shaking, and I thought he was going to throw up again. "What's going on, John? Did I miss some of the bullet? Do I need to go back in?"

"No, nothing like that." He took several deep breaths. There were lines of pain etched into his face. "There was silver inside the bullets. It's in my bloodstream now. It's toxic to me—to *us*."

I frowned. "But you said you weren't a demon." *And I am.* That was the part I was still having trouble getting my head around.

"I'm not. I'm an angel."

My thoughts spun around me too fast to say anything at first. John must have sensed my confusion, because he remained silent, waiting for me to speak again. "So we're enemies?"

John didn't speak for a long time. "Yes. Not *us*, specifically, but historically, angels and demons are enemies."

"So those people at the subway station…were they angels, or were they demons?"

"They were angels. Part of a militant group known as the Thrones. Not all angels are Thrones, but they run everything in the angelic world. No angel would risk going against them."

"And they were upset with you because you didn't bring me in?"

He didn't speak for a long time. "No. They were upset with me because I didn't kill you. I was hired to assassinate you."

Panic overtook me. My breathing accelerated to the point where I was near hyperventilation. John got off the bed and crouched next to me. "Easy, Dale. Take it easy. I'm not going to hurt you."

By the time I was able to speak again, there were tears in my eyes. "I don't understand," I said. "How is any of this possible? Why are they even after me? Do they just try to assassinate all the demons in the world?"

"No, much as they would like to. Even if that were possible, it wouldn't be a practical use of their resources."

"So why? Is it because..." but I stopped myself before I said anything else. I didn't know how John had found me, didn't know what he knew about my past—and if he didn't know, I wasn't going to tell him.

He cringed as another spasm of pain overcame him. He grabbed the trashcan and pulled it closer to him, but he regained control of himself before he needed to use it. "Here's what you need to know for right now. First, you're a half demon. Your father was human, but your mother was a full-blooded demon."

I froze at the mention of my mother, a woman I didn't remember, whose picture I'd never seen. When I was a child, my father told me keeping pictures of her around made him too sad. "My mother is dead." I told him.

"No, she's not. That's the second thing you need to know." He got up from his crouch and then sat next to me on the bed, putting us on a more even level. "Your mother, Amara, is the most powerful and influential demon in the world. She also disappeared almost three decades ago. Gabriel—

the leader of the Thrones—thought that your death would be enough of a catalyst to bring her out of hiding."

"That's impossible. My father told me she died when I was six months old. He could never even *talk* about her!"

He ran his hands through his hair. "If we were back in New York, I could show you my research, my notes..." He sighed. "Look, you already know you're different. I suspect you've known for a long time now, long before you were willing to admit it to yourself. You also know you have power. The reason I'm *alive* right now is because of your power."

"I can control people's minds." The words felt wrong in my mouth, even though I'd seen it myself less than twenty-four hours earlier.

"Yes, and you can make people do what you want them to do. Just like Amara. You've probably been doing it subconsciously for years." He paused. "Did your father ever tell you how she died?"

"Cancer."

John gave me a skeptical look. "Pure-blooded angels and demons are immortal. Their half-blooded children are, as well. We can be killed, but we don't die of natural causes. Do you really think that one of the most powerful demons in the world was killed by *cancer*?"

My voice was barely more than a whisper. "I don't believe it."

"What matters is that Gabriel does."

I sniffled, trying to hold back tears. John cringed again. This time, he grabbed the garbage can and vomited in it. I ran to the bathroom and got him a cup of water. When I got back, he chugged it down without a word. "It's getting worse, isn't it? Whatever's making you sick?" He nodded. His teeth were chattering so hard that he probably couldn't speak. "So what do we do?"

"I have a friend in Vermont who should be able to help."

He stood up, but his shaky legs couldn't support his weight. He braced himself against me. "What if you d—what if you get sick before we get to Vermont?"

The solemn look in John's eyes told me he knew what I had really been about to ask. I waited for him to reassure me. *I'll be fine. Don't worry so much.* But he closed his eyes, the shivers going through his body becoming more violent. "Just keep running," he said. "Just keep running and don't stop."

CHAPTER

JOHN AND I DIDN'T TALK much on the drive. He wrapped himself up in some blanket we took from the motel and closed his eyes as soon as I started the engine. "Head east until you get to Hartford," he said. "Then take I-ninety-one north."

"I-ninety-one north to *where*?"

But a soft snore from next to me let me know that he was already asleep.

For the first couple of hours, he alternated between sleeping and throwing up in the garbage bags we'd "borrowed" from the motel's stash. Since I couldn't stand the smell, even concealed as it was beneath layers of plastic, we had to stop every time he threw up. We must've hit every gas station and convenience store between the motel and Hartford. Every time we found one that was open, John would hand me some wrinkled bills and ask me to buy him either a sports drink or water, which he'd chug before the next exit.

As the sun rose, John spent less time throwing up and more time unconscious. I didn't know if that was a good thing or a bad thing.

I knew when we were getting closer to our destination, because John opened his eyes and started giving me directions to turn down windy back roads. We ended up pulling into the parking lot of an old-fashioned amusement park, complete with wooden roller coasters, a lighted Ferris wheel, and a carved wooden sign that read "Funland" over the entrance gate. "Is this the right place?" I asked.

"Yes." He clenched his jaw, just a little, but I'd been in the car with him long enough to recognize the signs that another wave of pain was passing through his body. "Just park as close to the entrance as you can."

It was a Monday morning, so the park wasn't crowded, and we were able to park fairly close to the gate. John wrapped his arm around me as we walked up to the ticket booth, and we looked like any other couple out for a day of fun at Funland. If we were walking slowly because John was leaning most of his body weight on me, and if his normally tan skin was the color of a midwinter snowdrift, nobody noticed but me.

When we got to the ticket window, John released me and took a step forward. "We're here to see Isaac," he said. The girl at the window—who couldn't have been more than seventeen—handed us orange bands to put on our wrists. John wrapped his arm around me again and we stepped forward to the turnstiles. The security guard took one look at our armbands and waved us through without checking our bags the way he had been for the other guests.

The park smelled like funnel cake and popcorn and was themed to look like a Renaissance festival, with fiberglass castles and thatched-roof shops with signs that said things like "Ye Olde Tavern" and "Funland Marketplace and Shoppe." The female employees roaming the park wore corsets and long skirts, and the males wore tunics and tights.

John led me to a long, thin building in the middle of the park, plain and austere enough that it didn't quite look like it belonged. A sign on the door said "STAFF ONLY." He knocked twice, paused, then knocked four times.

Several seconds later, a man wearing a red polo shirt with the word "Funland" over his lapel opened the door. He was maybe an inch or two shorter than me and had a small, wiry build bordering on too thin, the kind of build you often see on adolescent boys. Despite his size, he carried himself with the easy confidence of someone who knows exactly who he is and what he's doing, and I guessed him to be in his mid-twenties. His dark skin and eyes suggested Middle Eastern or Indian ancestry. He leaned against the doorframe and folded his arms across his chest without a word.

"Hey, Isaac. Long time." John released me and collapsed to his knees.

Isaac and I both grabbed for him at the same time, pulling him over the threshold of the building. Once we closed the door behind us, Isaac turned to me. "Help carry him," Isaac ordered. Before I could answer, Isaac grabbed his ankles, leaving me to grab his shoulders.

On our right were several cots lined up along the wall, the kind you'd see in the nurse's office of an elementary school. On the left were several desks with old computers on top of them. A young woman, dressed in the same red polo as Isaac, groaned when she saw us come in. "Another drunk? At this time of morning? I told Marcie three seasons ago that we should get rid of all the grog stands. But no, she said, it goes so well with our theming. Let's just ignore the fact that 55 percent of our ticket sales go to children under twelve."

Isaac said nothing, and we walked toward an elevator in the back of the office. I heard the woman's voice behind us again. "Aren't you going to put him in a cot?"

Isaac's hesitation was so slight that I wouldn't have noticed it if I hadn't been looking for it. "No. I don't want to risk any of the parents seeing him.

We've got that school group from Montpelier here today. I'm taking him to the bowels."

The woman rolled her eyes. "It's your funeral." She went back to her work.

Isaac pushed the button for the elevator. We took John inside and braced him against the wall, leaning his weight against my body, as Isaac swiped his employee identification card and typed a code into the keypad. The elevator descended for what seemed like a long time, and I struggled to keep John's awkward weight from falling.

The doors opened into a long, dusty hallway with cement floors and cinderblock walls. Rows of florescent lights flickered on along each wall, and the whole place smelled like garbage, even though I didn't see any. Isaac scooped down and picked John up in a fireman's carry, similar to the one I had used on our way to the hospital the previous night. He didn't even strain as he scooped John over his shoulders. I gaped at him. "If you could do that, why didn't you just do that in the first place?"

"To make you feel useful."

We stopped in front of a door labeled "Storage Area B." Isaac swiped his employee badge and punched in his code again. When we got inside, we were greeted by yet another door, metallic and heavy, just a few feet in. To its right was a palm scanner. Isaac placed his hand on it. Less than a second later, the door clicked open. Isaac walked through the entryway with John still over his shoulders. I followed.

A screeching alarm went off.

Isaac calmly set John on the floor and pulled out his phone. After he read something on the screen, he stopped and glared at me. Before I could ask what I'd done to upset him, he crouched down next to John and shook him. When John didn't respond, Isaac slapped him across the face. Hard.

John groaned. "What?"

"Did you know that she's a demon?"

Even in his weakened state, John managed to roll his eyes. "Who do you think you're talking to?"

"And you brought her *here*?"

"The Thrones are trying to kill her. I'm trying to save her. Put her into the system, Isaac."

Isaac looked at his phone again. "She's coming up as Amara's kin."

"I know. She's Amara's daughter." John met Isaac's eyes. "Put her into the system, fledgling."

The command in John's shaky voice was obvious, as was the fact that he had just pulled rank on Isaac, however that worked. Isaac sighed and turned to me, the alarm still screeching in the background. "Give me your hand."

When I hesitated, he grabbed my wrist roughly and pulled my hand toward him, palm up. He retrieved a small lancet—similar to one you'd see at a blood drive—out of his pocket. He pressed it against my fingertip and pushed the button. I felt a small prick. He squeezed a bead of blood out of my fingertip and pressed it against another palm scanner that flashed with red lights. An electric tingling flowed through my hand. The sensation was vaguely familiar, but I couldn't place it. A tube attached to my fingertip and whisked the blood away. The flashing red lights turned green, and the alarm went silent. Isaac opened the door into a large apartment.

I looked down at John, but he was already out again. Isaac hoisted him up in his arms and carried him into a bedroom, placing him on a queen-sized bed covered with a puffy duvet. Although John wasn't conscious, he was shivering. Isaac wrapped the duvet around him before he turned to me, that eerie calmness still emanating from him. "What's wrong with him?"

"I'm not sure. He was shot yesterday with some weird fragmenting bullet. I think he called it a fractal bullet. I cut him open and pulled all the

pieces out. He got a little bit better, but then he got worse again. He said something about there being silver inside the bullet."

"Oh, hell." He immediately unwrapped John from the duvet burrito and then ripped the brand-new shirt I had purchased off his chest. "Three doors down on the right is my bedroom. I need you to go and grab an IV bag, catheter, and stand from my closet. Then go into the second drawer of the dresser and get one of the syringes with the yellow cap and one of the syringes with the purple caps. And then in the bottom drawer, there are empty syringes and disposable needles. Get me one of those, too, along with the biggest gauge needle you can find."

I ran down the hall to Isaac's bedroom. Even in my rush, the room made me freeze. It was filled with medical equipment: blood pressure cuffs, rubber gloves, bedpans, and prescription bottles covering the dresser. The bed wasn't even a regular bed, but an adjustable hospital-style bed with metal rails on the side. Before I had too much time to contemplate that, I heard Isaac yell, "Bring the defibrillator too!"

It took me three trips to get all the gear Isaac requested. By the time I completed my final trip, Isaac had attached the large-gauge needle to the empty syringe. He pressed his fingers against John's stomach, along the side of the raised scar where the bullet had entered his body. He plunged the syringe into John's stomach and pulled the plunger up. It filled with blood, which was normal. The distinctly silver sheen the blood gave off probably was not. "What's wrong with him?" I asked.

"He's been poisoned." Isaac injected the medication in the yellow and purple-capped syringes into the IV bag and squeezed it gently, mixing the solution together. "Silver is poisonous to angels and demons when taken internally. That's where the whole 'silver bullet' thing came from. But if the silver doesn't hit the heart and the bullet is removed from the body, the victim can heal. So the Thrones came up with something better: fractal

bullets. When the bullet hits the body, it will fragment, and those pieces will drift toward the heart unless they're removed. But they also liquefied the silver and put it *inside* the bullet. Even if the pieces are removed, the silver still hits the bloodstream. It's one of the few weapons that's almost guaranteed to kill an angel or a demon."

I stared at John's limp form on the bed. "Is he going to die?"

"He should be dead already." Isaac wrapped a tourniquet around John's wrist, cleaned it off with an alcohol pad, and felt for the vein. He inserted the needle into John's hand, taped it down, and attached the tubing. "I don't know if he'll survive. His body will flush the poison out of his system, or it won't. There's nothing else we can do."

"John was drinking a lot of water and Gatorade on the way here. Will that help?"

"Maybe."

How reassuring.

Isaac left the bedroom. I followed, and he closed the door behind us. We crossed into a living room area. I hadn't checked out the apartment when we came in because I was too worried about John, but now I had a chance to look around. The whole place was white—white plush carpet, white furniture, even the cinderblock walls were painted white—and very modern looking. It was very clean, with a hint of Windex and Lemon Pledge in the air. A square chandelier with tube-shaped lights hung from the ceiling, and a large sectional couch, big enough to be a bed, sat along the wall. To the left, a small, galley-style kitchen was separated from the rest of the room by some kind of curved shelving unit, which was adorned with black-and-white pictures, the only hint of personalization in the apartment. I examined the photographs closer. Each of them focused on a specific body part: a hand, an elbow, a close-up of an eye so focused that I could count every lash.

Isaac took out his phone again and touched the screen. Several seconds later, the lights got brighter, simulating the daylight that was completely absent from this subterranean sterility. I sat down on the sectional. It was more comfortable than it looked, the cushions hugging my tired body. "This is really nice. Do you live here? Right under the park?" I asked.

"Yes."

I smiled. "You're living my childhood dream, you know. When I was a kid, my dad took me to Disney World. After the vacation ended, I told him I wanted to move there and live in Cinderella's Castle. He told me that nobody actually *lived* in the park, that it closed at night and everyone went home."

"When you own the park, you can do whatever you want."

"You bought a *theme park*?" I had never actually thought of someone *owning* a park before. In my mind, they were all controlled by faceless, monolithic corporations.

He shrugged. "I needed a place to live."

Ooooh-kay. I could tell by the tone of his voice that he didn't want to talk about it anymore, so I changed the subject. "So are you a doctor or something? I saw all the stuff in your…"

"No."

And this time, it wasn't a "let's change the subject," but a complete shutdown of the conversation. Isaac touched the screen of his smartphone again, and some music came on—something soft and classical, with piano. He pulled a book out of a glass case behind us, sat down on the other side of the sectional, and began to read without giving me another glance.

I took the hint. I leaned against the back of the sectional and closed my eyes, allowing the music to soothe me. Minutes later, I was asleep.

WHEN I WOKE UP, MY shoes had been taken off and I had been covered with a blanket. I heard two male voices in the background. In my sleepy state, I couldn't recognize them at first.

"How could she not know any of this?"

"She's never been exposed to this world. Amara disappeared when she was just a baby. Dale believed her mother was dead all these years."

"I don't like it. She's a security risk. Not to mention your history with…"

"I know!" the other voice interrupted. "Do you think I haven't considered all this? But it's necessary. She needs to be able to take care of herself." The other voice did not respond. I heard a sigh. "I'm asking you as a friend."

"Sometimes you ask too much."

By this time, I had identified the voices. I opened my eyes. John and Isaac were standing in front of the sectional, just a few feet away from me. John still had an IV attached to his hand, hung off of a rolling stand next to him. But he looked stronger and healthier than he had since the subway, and his skin had lost that sickly grayish pallor. I sat up. John looked at me and smiled. "Nice sleep?"

I ran over and wrapped my arms around his shoulders, careful to avoid the IV tubing. He hugged me back, enveloping me in his warm butterscotch scent. As he touched my skin, I realized the electric zing between us was back in full force. "You're okay now? I was so worried."

I felt his smile against my cheek. "No need to worry about me, Little Demon. I'm fine now."

"'Little Demon'? Don't try to distract me by being cute."

"You don't like it?"

"Don't change the subject. Isaac said you might not recover. He said the silver in your bloodstream was poisoning you."

"Well, Isaac's a pessimist and a grump. It takes more than a few drams of silver to keep me down."

We'd held on a little too long, and it was getting awkward now. I pulled away and stepped back, trying to recover my equilibrium. "Yeah. So silver, huh? Good to know. But I thought that was just werewolves."

John and Isaac exchanged a look. John spoke first. "Dale…werewolves aren't real. Neither are vampires, fairies, leprechauns, or the Tooth Fairy."

"No, of course not. Obviously. I mean, angels and demons are real, but vampires and fairies? Absurd! Positively absurd! Whatever would make me think such a thing?"

He sat down next to me, shifting the IV stand out of the way. "There's truth at the core of most stories. There are angels and demons who can shape-shift into different forms, and silver is toxic to us. Myths, legends, even *religions* are humans' way of understanding and categorizing the world around them, but they didn't always understand everything, or convey it correctly. Furthermore, time and mistranslation has often skewed even their misunderstood truth, like a game of telephone. Most of the supernatural stories you have heard can be traced back to our kind."

I nodded, but my confusion must have still been evident on my face. John continued. "It's like *Titanic*."

I glanced at Isaac, who shrugged. "The ship?" I asked.

"Not the ship, the movie," John said, as if it should be obvious. "A good chunk of that movie was true. There really was a ship called the *Titanic* that hit an iceberg on its maiden voyage and sank. But a first-class passenger named Rose and a third-class passenger named Jack didn't really meet and fall in love on the ship."

"Yeah, but everyone knows which parts of that story are true and which parts are fictional," I said.

"They do *now*. The last *Titanic* survivor only died a few years ago. Many of their children and grandchildren are still alive. But what about in a hundred years, when the memory has faded even more and all most people ever encounter are secondhand historical texts? What about in a thousand years, when scholars look at the video cassettes of the movie the same way we might look at a piece of pottery from the Ming Dynasty? Add in some supernatural intrigue, and that's pretty much how our history works, in a nutshell."

I nodded and leaned against the back of the couch again, trying to process his words. "You watched *Titanic*?" I asked.

I didn't think it was possible, but John's cheeks turned a little red. "I have to move and interact in the human world. I watch movies to make sure I can keep up with humanity's evolving nuances."

"But *Titanic* was a historical movie."

"It was incredibly popular and influential."

"What exactly did it tell you, besides that every ten-year-old girl in the country was crushing on Leonardo DiCaprio? Also, for the record, we *already* look at video cassettes as if they're pieces of pottery from the Ming Dynasty."

John turned to Isaac, giving him a "See what I put up with?" look. "She's right. No one uses video cassettes anymore." I chuckled, but Isaac's maintained a straight face.

John rolled his eyes and turned to Isaac. "Anyway…as I was saying, the reason I brought her to you, as opposed to someone else, is because she shares Amara's power."

"Mind control?" Isaac asked. When John nodded, he swore under his breath. "How powerful?"

"Powerful. She's been using it unconsciously for a while, I suspect, and I've seen her take hardened Thrones warriors and freeze them in their tracks. But she has no idea how to implement it consciously or how to control it. She's like a nuclear bomb waiting to go off. I can help her with her physical training, but you're much more adept with mental gifts than I am. That's why I came to you." John's tone became pleading. "You know I wouldn't put you in this position if I had anywhere else to go. But you're one of the few people I know who the Thrones don't control."

Isaac massaged his brow. "You owe me for this." He looked at me. "Are you ready?"

They had just spent the last several minutes talking about me like I wasn't there, and Isaac still looked like he had a stick up his butt. I looked between the two of them. "All right, but which one of you is going to be Kate Winslet? Because I'm sure as hell not wearing a corset."

CHAPTER

12

ISAAC TOOK US TO THE kitchen of his underground apartment, where there was another door armed with a palm scanner. John had removed the IV tubing so he could move around more easily, but I wondered if it was premature. He was still a little pale, and there were bags under his eyes. He looked over at me and smiled. I realized he had attributed the concern on my face to the wrong thing when he spoke. "Don't worry—Isaac added you to the system. The alarm won't go off again. The system is just scanning you."

Isaac placed his hand on the surface of the reader and waited until the light turned green. As we passed through the entryway, my skin prickled. I rubbed my arm. "It almost feels like…when John touches me." Minus the growing sexual tension that I'd been trying very hard to ignore, but whatever.

We headed down a long hallway, with Isaac in front. "The detector is infused with John's blood," he said.

"What? Why?"

"John has a powerful ability to detect supernaturals. Hasn't he told you anything?"

John grunted. "I was a little busy with the whole 'trying not to die' thing." He looked over at me and then brushed my arm with his finger. That electrical zing that I'd noticed the first time we met danced over my arm. "It's strongest when I have skin-to-skin contact," he said. "I can't control the response then. But I can project it outward, too." He removed his hand from my skin and hovered it over me, and lingered there. I felt the zing again, fainter this time, just enough to raise the hairs on my arm.

"I still don't understand what that has to do with taking your blood for an alarm system."

It was Isaac who answered. "I assume you've heard of AziziCorp." I nodded. It was impossible *not* to have heard of them. Everyone had an Azizi smartphone or an Azizi computer or an Azizi tablet. Even as disconnected as I was, I still had an Azizi mp3 player tucked into my backpack—which was sitting with the rest of my stuff in Nik's apartment in New York City.

Isaac continued. "John's ability is a coveted one. Children and people near death can sometimes sense us, but most of us have no way to identify each other. My father, Abraham, is the founder of AziziCorp, and he's half-angel. He uses the company as a front to develop technologies specifically engineered for angels. Years ago, he discovered that when you infuse John's blood into the right type of computer circuitry, he could create a supernatural detection device."

John brushed his fingers against my T-shirt. Shivers ran down my spine, and they had nothing to do with John's supernatural radar. "They don't take much, Little Demon, and not very often. I can always make more."

"You can stop calling me 'Little Demon' any time. Also, an alarm system that's powered by blood? That's pretty macabre."

"Duly noted." John grinned.

Isaac ignored us. We got to the end of the hallway. Isaac pressed his hand against another scanner. There was a click, and Isaac turned the handle of the door.

Isaac's subterranean complex was impressive, and this room was the most impressive I'd been in yet. The soft glow of the recessed lights gave the impression of a dewy morning glow, in spite of the fact that I hadn't seen the sunlight since John and I arrived the day before, and the room smelled like lavender and chamomile. On the wall opposite of us was a huge fountain, the flowing water illuminated with blue, green, and purple LED lights. Large cushions covered the floor. Isaac motioned for me to sit down, which I did. He sat across from me, his legs akimbo. John remained standing, leaning against one of the empty walls.

Isaac spoke first. "So what's your range?"

"My *what*?"

"How many people can you manipulate at the same time, and how far does your reach go?"

"I don't know."

Isaac frowned. "All right. We'll start with something simpler. How is your ability represented in your mind? Tactile, visual, auditory maybe…"

I looked at John helplessly. He got the hint. "I tried to tell you, she doesn't know any of this. When she uses her power, she's been operating completely on instinct. She didn't even know she was doing it until the other day. Right now, she's got nothing but raw power."

"Hmmm." Isaac removed his phone from his pocket and swiped his index finger across the screen. Seconds later, the lights faded into a muted twilight glow. He swiped again, and mellow, chiming music came on in the background, the kind you would expect to hear if you were getting a seaweed-and-peppermint facial in Chelsea. Isaac looked at me. "I need you to close your eyes. Concentrate on your breathing."

"Shouldn't you at least buy me dinner first?" Isaac said nothing. John folded his arms across his chest and shook his head. "All right, all right, fine."

I closed my eyes and focused on the in-and-out rhythm of my breath. "Okay, good," Isaac said in a soft voice. "Inhale, hold it for two, and then exhale. Keep following that pattern, and clear your head of all other thoughts."

Isaac went silent. I let the music fade into the background and concentrated on my breath. In and out, in and out, in and out. But I couldn't sustain it very long, and my mind started to roam. Free-form thoughts danced through my head. The community swimming pool my father used to take me to on the hottest summer days. The smell of popcorn in the independent movie theater in Alphabet City. The way the sky lights up during a nighttime thunderstorm.

The body of Andrew Seymour, covered in blood.

My eyes snapped open. "I can't do this." I got up, tripping on the stupid cushion in this process. "No offense, but this is all a little too New Age-y for me." I headed for the door.

Isaac gave an exasperated groan and whipped out his phone again, kicking the lights back on. John intercepted me at the door. "It's all right, Dale."

My hand shook even as I grabbed onto the doorknob. "I was fine before, and I'll be fine now. I don't need this."

"We almost didn't make it out of New York because you can't control your abilities." Blunt words, but true ones. "I want you to be as strong as possible. I want to know that if anything happens, you can protect yourself."

My eyes filled with tears, and I lowered my voice to a whisper. "I don't think I can do this."

"You can. I'll be right here with you."

After a few seconds, I nodded and wiped the wetness from my eyes. I sat back down on my pillow across from Isaac. John sat next to me. Isaac glanced up from his phone. "Are you done yet?"

I exploded. "Why is he here?" I asked John. "I need to work on using my powers, okay fine, I get it. But what exactly is he adding to this process?"

I expected Isaac to get mad. But instead, he just calmly put his phone away. A few seconds later, an orange tabby kitten crept into the room and mewed. I had no idea where he had come from or how he had gotten in, given Isaac's rigorous security. But the kitten was disheveled and too thin. I crawled toward him slowly so I wouldn't scare him. "It's okay, little guy. I'm not going to hurt you."

The kitten mewed. Then, suddenly, it began to grow, morphing before my eyes into a full-sized lion. He opened his mouth and roared, hot fish-breath on my skin, incisors the size of cucumbers getting perilously close to my neck. I back-crawled away very, very slowly.

The lion vanished. I looked over at Isaac and John. Isaac burst into laughter. "What the fuck was that?" I asked.

"*That* was what I add to this process. John's ability doesn't work mentally. Mine does. I can cause people to see and feel things that aren't really there."

I peeled myself away from the wall and took an unsteady breath. My hands were still shaking, and I didn't think I would be able to stand up right then. John folded his arms across his chest and glared at Isaac. "Was that really necessary? What the hell did you show her?"

"It was just a cat."

I jumped up. "It wasn't a cat. It was a fucking *lion*." I stopped and caught John's eye, realizing the implications of what he had asked. "You mean you didn't see it?"

Before John could speak, Isaac answered. "No, he didn't see it because he has shields around his mind, blocks that even I can't get through. Your

mind, on the other hand, is completely unshielded. You don't know how to use your abilities, and anyone else with mental powers could use *their* abilities against *you*."

I looked over from Isaac to John, who had a sober expression on his face. Great. No help there. "All right, I get it," I said. "What do I need to do?"

Isaac motioned to the cushion I had been sitting on earlier. I took a seat again. This time, John sat down next to me, close enough to be almost-touching, and Isaac sat across from the two of us. Isaac took out his phone again. The lights dimmed, and the music came on. "Close your eyes," he said. "If your mind wanders, don't panic or get upset. Just come back to this moment, back to your breathing."

This time, with John's steady presence next to me, it was easier to banish thoughts of Andrew Seymour. When my mind started to wander, I just refocused on the warmth radiating from his body, the butterscotch richness that always permeated his scent, the sound of his breathing, in sync with mine.

After a few minutes, Isaac spoke again. "All right, Dale. Picture yourself reaching out with your mind, your energy reaching out from your brain into the room. What does it look like? What does it feel like?"

I did so, but I had no idea whether something was actually happening or it was all in my imagination. "It's like...wispy arms. Or tentacles maybe."

"Good. Now what I'd like you to do is try to reach toward me with those tentacles until you find my mind. Touch it if you can. Open your eyes if you need to. Tell me what it feels like."

I shifted the tentacles, reaching out toward Isaac slowly toward him until I felt...something. "It's like there's an eggshell around it," I said.

"Could the tentacles break that shell?"

I poked at the shell with my mind—my *tentacles*. "Yes. Easily."

"How about now?"

I felt again. This time, the shell was harder, more substantial. "It's like a wall of steel. I don't know if I can get through it this time."

"Go ahead and try. I don't expect you to get it right the first time, but it'll be good practice."

Since Isaac's shield felt like steel to me, I imagined my tentacle turning into a blowtorch. In less than five seconds, the bright blue flame pierced into his mind. I didn't order him to *do* anything, didn't make him quack like a duck or spend the rest of the day hopping on one foot, but I *had* him, and in that moment I could have made him do anything I wanted him to do. I opened my eyes to find Isaac staring at me, trying to hide the terror in his eyes. "I'm sorry," I said.

"No, you did exactly what I wanted you to do. You were just…faster than I expected." He stood up and paced the room. "I think you should try John next."

I was about to agree, but John growled next to me. "Isaac…"

"You want to know, don't you? You want to know how strong she is, what she's capable of. That's one of the reasons you brought her to me. This is the best way to test her, and you know it."

"That's not the point."

"So what is the point, John? Are you more concerned that she won't break through your barrier, or that she will?"

John and Isaac glared at each other, having some sort of silent man-to-man communication, and I didn't understand the byplay that was going on between them at all. I tried to diffuse the tension. "I'm actually getting a little tired…"

"No, Dale, he's right." John took a deep breath. "I know what you're trying to do, but he's right. You should go ahead and try."

I nodded. And then I closed my eyes.

John's mind was even easier to find than Isaac's had been, maybe because the feel of it, the feel of *him*, was already so familiar to me. But it was covered by a shell that was even harder than Isaac's had been. In my mind, I saw it as diamond, flawless and impenetrable. "I don't know..."

"Just go ahead and try," Isaac said.

It would have made me feel better if *John* had said it. He hadn't objected, but every muscle of his body was tense. I closed my eyes again and visualized my tentacle chipping away slowly at John's shield with a chisel, working my way through slowly. Just as I thought I was making some progress, the tentacle snapped back at me. I opened my eyes, my head pounding. Snot dripped down my face. I reached up to wipe it away and realized it wasn't snot at all, but blood.

Isaac handed me a box of tissues. He looked almost sympathetic. "I guess I should have warned you about the blowback."

John stood up and motioned for me to follow. I did, but I felt dizzy and my knees buckled beneath me. John caught me before I could crash to the floor. "I think we've had enough for today," he said.

I DIDN'T SEE JOHN FOR the rest of the day. I spent most of it asleep on Isaac's cozy sectional holding an ice pack to my eyes, trying to get rid of the massive headache I developed from the "blowback" of trying to break through John's shields. Isaac did wake me once, to apologize and put some food in front of me, which I ate ravenously before falling asleep again.

John woke me that night—although I only knew it was night because Isaac's automated lights had been turned down to their darkest setting, leaving only a tiny bit of light to illuminate the path between the living

room and bathroom. Plus, I had that disoriented, groggy feeling you get when you're awoken in the middle of the night. "What time is it?" I asked.

"Around four." Before I could object to the ungodly hour, he threw a thin pair of sweatpants and a T-shirt at me. "Get changed and meet me back out here in a few minutes."

I staggered off of the sectional into the bathroom and changed. When I came back, he was sitting in the spot I'd just vacated, the television remote control in his hands. "I wanted to show you something," he said.

"And *something* couldn't have waited another, say, four hours or so?"

John ignored the comment and hit a button on the remote. A video began to play, black-and-white surveillance footage. The date on the bottom right of the screen was over nine years earlier. I recognized it immediately. "Do you recognize this place?"

"It's the homeless shelter in Huntington, West Virginia." And the footage was date stamped the night of my second Rage.

John pressed the "Play" button, turning on the grainy footage.

It was about eight months after the prom. I'd been on the run since then. I'd cut my hair into a short bob, dyed it black, and started calling myself "Moonshadow," because I was eighteen and angsty and the gothy thing worked for me at the time. I found myself sharing a room with four other people in Huntington, West Virginia—still too close to Pittsburgh for my comfort, but I was hoping to save up enough money with my two waitressing gigs to go farther west, to California maybe, or New Mexico. I'd always heard it was beautiful in New Mexico.

But the owner sold the building to some big corporation that was building a strip mall, and we were kicked out. After bouncing from couch to couch for a while, I ended up in the homeless shelter. I was in and out of there for about a month, because I couldn't find another place I could afford and I didn't know what else to do.

The shelter had been crowded that night. It was one of the coldest days in West Virginia history, and everyone who could get off the streets was. The place reeked of people who hadn't washed properly in months, and the bleach the staff used every morning to wash us away. There was this tiny old woman, maybe about eighty years old, and she wasn't all there. She took her wallet out of her oversized purse and began to count her money, dozens of fifty- and hundred-dollar bills. Two other women approached her—Tonya Tompkins and Alexis Sanchez, though I didn't know their names at the time. When the old woman refused to give them her money, they began to rough her up. One of them pulled out a knife.

I remembered getting up. I remembered my body shaking, a red haze overtaking my vision. And that was all.

On the screen, I grabbed the knife and stabbed one of the women in the throat. She fell to the ground, blood gushing from a severed artery. The second woman jumped on me, her fingers bent into a claw shape and thrusting for my eyes. I grabbed her wrist and twisted until her hold loosened. Then I slammed her against the wall. She slumped to the floor, eyes closed, body limp. She would die a few days later from massive brain injuries. After she released her hold on me, I shook my head as if coming out of a trance. Everyone else in the room had frozen. I glanced from the bodies, to the blood on my hands, to the horrified stares of the others in the room. And then I ran.

The whole thing had taken less than forty-five seconds.

John paused the video and turned to me. I was shaking, my body not sure whether to run or freeze in place like a cornered animal. "They would have hurt that woman," I said.

"Except we both know that wasn't the only time you've killed. Not even close."

I had heard John and the Thrones at the subway station talking about my crimes. But when John and I had left New York together, I had hoped… honestly, I didn't know what I had hoped. "What do you want from me?"

"What I want," he gestured toward the video, "is to know where the *hell* that woman was when we were fighting on the subway platform and at the hospital."

I felt like I had swallowed cotton. "I don't know what you're talking about. You already know that was me in the video."

John sat down next to me, his legs nearly brushing mine. "What I know is that ten years ago, the Thrones put me on assignment to find a young half-demon who had just murdered her classmate because she was jealous that he went to the prom with her friend and not her." John looked at me like he expected me to interject, but I didn't. "I knew that this young woman was the daughter of Amara, arguably the most powerful demon in the world, and that she had inherited her mother's abilities. For a decade I chased her, following the pile of bodies in her wake. When I finally found her in New York, I expected a cold-blooded, sociopathic killer."

I stood up and turned away from him. "I did kill all those people. You know it, and I know it. What I don't know is why you didn't just kill me like you were supposed to."

CHAPTER

13

J OHN CROUCHED BEFORE ME. "Do you really think so little of me?" He rubbed his thumb against my wrist, massaging the pulse point there. "When I finally caught up with you in New York, I watched you. I watched you smile at asshole customers and feed all the homeless people on your block. I watched you read all the new releases in the store when no one was looking and laugh so hard that tears ran down your face. I watched you before I spoke to you at that party. You were so alone that night. I wasn't even going to approach you, but I just couldn't stand how *apart* you were. And then you ignored me and jumped into an argument with a man twice your size to protect someone you'd just met that night." He smiled at me. "You saved my life, Dale. Whatever happens, however this plays out, I am not going to hurt you or let you be hurt, not if I can help it."

Emotion welled up inside me. I bit my cheek, holding it back. "Why did you show me that video?"

John stood, immediately flipping back into hardass mode. "On the subway platform when the Thrones were coming after us, and again at the hospital when Ezra and his people had us cornered, you froze up, and it

almost got us killed. It's not unexpected. It's how most people react when confronted with violence. But you're not most people, and the homeless shelter was neither the first nor the last time you've been confronted with violence. So here's what I want to know: what happened between then and now to make you freeze up like that?"

I didn't speak. I couldn't. I just stared at him with what I'm sure was a terrified look on my face. John ran his fingers through his hair. "Look, Dale, at this point, I don't care what you've done in your past. All that matters are the present and the future." I still didn't answer. "All right, fine. Just tell me this: is it something you think you can replicate?"

My voice was nearly a whisper. "No."

John sighed. "All right, then. Let's do this the hard way."

IT WAS STILL DARK WHEN we left Isaac's underground lair and headed up into the amusement park. John wore a pair of jeans and a gray T-shirt, and he had a set of keys dangling from his wrist from one of those bands that looks like a telephone cord. In his other hand, he held a flashlight. The park was completely deserted, the flashing lights off, the rides silent. "Aren't you worried that someone will catch us?" I asked.

"The janitorial staff is all gone by midnight, and none of the opening crew get here until eight. Besides, if anyone does catch us, we'll just tell them we have Isaac's permission. Which we do."

"It's so strange that he *lives* at the park. I know his place is all pimped out and everything, but you'd think he'd be sick of coming through the garbage tunnels."

John shrugged without looking at me. "Walt Disney had an apartment at Disneyland."

"Yeah, but he didn't *live* there."

John hesitated, his walking pace slowing just a fraction. "Sometimes people don't have anywhere else to go." He stopped in front of a building and unlocked the door. "We're here."

The sign above the door read "Kiddie Korner," complete with the final "r" turned backward. John flipped the lights on and led me inside. The inside was just a large room, about the size of a football field. It had been set up as a play area for smaller children, with tables and chairs for the adults. The Renaissance theme continued here, too—in the center of the room stood an indoor climbing gym that was set up to look like a castle, and the walls were painted with trees with the words "Enchanted Forest" above them. Scattered around the rest of the room were large stepping blocks, child-sized huts, and a plastic rocking horse. The floors were covered with foam rubber pads. To the parents, it must have been attractive because it was indoors and air conditioned. To me, it smelled like vomit and dirty diapers and didn't justify being dragged out of bed at four a.m. "What are we doing here?"

"Training." He walked out to the middle of the room, next to the castle. John was over six feet tall, but the thing was still more than twice his height. "Since you don't seem to know whether you can replicate your reactions at the homeless shelter, we're going to have to start from scratch. The techniques I'm going to teach you are based on Krav Maga, a form of martial arts used by the Israeli military. It focuses on real-world combat situations, on results rather than technique. You're unstructured and undisciplined at this point, so I think that will work best for you. So let me ask you this: what do you think is the first rule to defending yourself?"

"Stick 'em with the pointy end?"

"Funny. I watch HBO, too. No, the first rule is that you avoid confrontation whenever possible. It's not fight or flight; it's avoid or evade. How many exits are there to this building?"

I looked around. Besides the door we came in, there was an alarmed emergency exit on the opposite side. "Two."

"Incorrect. There are four." He pointed at the main exit and the emergency door. "One and two, of course. Three," he pointed to a door labeled "Employees Only" and said, "if you go through that door, you'll find there's another exit behind the building. It's where park employees dump the trash. And finally, four." He pointed up to a vent in the ceiling. "You should be small enough to get through there. If you crawl through the duct, it connects to the food court eventually."

"And how the hell do you propose I get up there?"

Without a word, John jumped onto the castle, climbing its sides until he reached the pointy part of the turret. He couldn't stand up all the way, because he was too close to the ceiling, so he wrapped his legs around the turret, reached up, and tapped the vent. He smirked at me, as self-satisfied as a cat with a tuna can. "Pretty much like that."

"You're just showing off."

"No." He released his legs and jumped to the ground, landing as gracefully as a gymnast. "*That* was showing off."

I rolled my eyes. Men. "So you want me to climb to the top of that thing?"

Just like that, John was all business again. "No. I want you to know that you *can* climb to the top of it, if that's your only exit route. But given the choice, it's certainly not ideal. Those metal ducts will cut the hell out of your knees and hands."

"You talk like you've been up there."

"Not that one. But others, yes. Which brings us to the second rule, and it's a big one. A physical confrontation should be your option of last resort.

Run, get away from the situation, hide if you can't do anything else. Don't engage if you don't have to. Once you get into a fight, you run the risk that you will lose."

"I've done pretty well for myself so far," I grumbled.

John circled me, looking up and down, examining my body. The whole thing would have felt sexual, if he wasn't so clinical about it. "You're fast, and you have good instincts, I'll give you that. But you're going up against Thrones who have trained for *years* to neutralize demons. I know, because I trained many of them. You're also female. Even among angels and demons, males are on average bigger, stronger, and faster than females."

"That's sexist," I said.

"That's biology. With a human male, you'll always have the advantage. With a male Throne, that'll be taken away. The female Thrones have learned to compensate in other ways. Your biggest advantage is your mind control ability, which only works erratically at best."

"So basically, I'm fucked."

"No, not at all. You *did* hold your own against the Thrones in the subway station, and then again in the hospital, and that's important. You also have me on your side. I know how they fight, and I can teach you how to work against that. I want to get you to the point where we minimize the freeze time, and you react on instinct. So that brings me to the third rule, and it's that once you're engaged in a confrontation, there are no rules. There's only one thing you have to do."

"What's that?" I asked.

His golden brown eyes met mine. "Survive."

OVER THE NEXT FEW DAYS, we fell into a surprisingly easy routine. I'd sleep through the morning and early afternoon. In the late afternoon, after his shift at the park was over, Isaac would take me into the room with the fountain—what he called the "Oasis Room"—and we'd work on my brain. I found it easier and easier to find the boundaries of Isaac's mind no matter where he was in the room, or even if he was standing outside. He put up different levels of shields—everything from fragile eggshell to titanium solid—and I would punch through them with my mind and order him to do something, like hop on one foot or sing the alphabet.

"You're putting a lot of trust in me, you know," I said to him on the afternoon of the third day. "You're letting me punch through your shields *on purpose*, and once I do, I could make you do anything."

"Could you?" He placed his hands behind his back and faced me. "Okay. Try me."

I reached out and touched his mind, which was, not surprisingly, covered by solid shields. I punched through easily—and hit another layer of shields. Again, I took them out, encountering another layer, and another, and another, until I finally gave up in frustration. "What you have to understand," Isaac said, "is that there's a lot of willpower associated with a mentally-based ability. When I'm in the presence of an enemy, I reinforce my layers of shielding with redundancies, and I know I can have them down faster than you can go through them. That level of shielding, though, takes considerable effort to maintain, so I relax them some when I feel I'm safe. And, of course, when we're practicing. I'll teach you how to do that, too. When it comes to shielding, you are a mere Padawan and I am a Jedi Master."

"Did you just make a *Star Wars* joke?"

"I never joke about *Star Wars*."

Every night, John would wake me up. We'd go into the park and basically play a modified version of hide and seek. If I made it back to Isaac's apartment in the tunnels before John could catch me, I'd win. If I won, he promised, we'd stop for the evening, and I might actually get to obey my circadian rhythms and sleep during the night, for once. If not, we'd go back to the center of the park and do it again, over and over again, until nearly sunrise.

Of course, John always won.

On the third night, I decided to do something a little different. There was a gigantic carousel smack dab in the middle of the park, surrounded by high fencing that stretched out another fifteen feet or so from the edge. Every time we had tried this exercise, I had gone around it, which added a not inconsiderable distance to my run. John was faster than I was, and his endurance was better than mine. The added distance just gave John more time to catch up with me, even with the head start he always gave.

That night, when John and I split up, I decided to cut down the middle and go *across* the carousel, rather than around it. It was an ordeal. The metal fence around it was taller than I was, tapering to sharp points on the top, and the slats didn't provide much in the way of footholds. I struggled to climb over, the sound of John chasing me getting closer and closer all the time. Finally, I made it over, and I ran across the carousel to the other side of the fence. This time around I knew what to do, and I made it more easily. Still, the sharp points tore a hole in my shirt. I ignored it and jumped to the ground.

About five seconds after I jumped the fence, I heard it rattle behind me as John arrived at the carousel. Damn. How was he so close? He's given me a head start—he always gave me a head start—and still he was right on my heels again. "I'm impressed, Little Demon," he called. "You used the

geography around you to your advantage. But it's not enough. Not when I'm your opponent."

I couldn't help it. I turned around and looked at him. John had backed up until he was about fifty feet away from the fence. Then, he sprinted back toward the carousel. When he got near the fence line, he *leapt* into the air, sailing easily over the pointy spikes and landing in a crouch position. For a second, all I could do was stare. "Holy shit."

He rose and gave me a cocky grin.

I ran.

CHAPTER

I WAS STILL SOME DISTANCE FROM the tunnel entrance, but I threw everything I had into the sprint. What the hell? I didn't even know what John had just done was physically possible. There had to be something in the laws of physics that said, "Thou cannot leap over tall fences in a single bound unless thou art Superman." Was that it? Did John have the power to levitate himself? What he had done was inhuman, but I kept forgetting that John wasn't really human.

Then again, neither was I.

I heard metal rattling behind me again, and I realized John was climbing the fence on the other side. He probably didn't have enough space inside the fence to get the necessary running start. This could give me the advantage I needed. I cut through the bathrooms, emerging on the other side, and ran past the games area to the office and the tunnel door. I could still hear John closing in on me. I reached Isaac's door and placed my hand on the palm scanner. After what seemed like forever, the light flashed and the door clicked open. I ran into Isaac's living room toward the overstuffed sectional, our agreed-upon home base. John caught the door before it

slammed shut and followed me in. He was so close I could almost feel his breath on my neck.

A lot of things seemed to happen at once.

I reached the sectional, my legs brushing the sides. Safe.

John was so close he didn't have time to stop his momentum. He crashed into me and we both fell back on the couch, him on top of me.

He hovered over me, as sweaty and out of breath as I was. I locked eyes with him. "I won," I said.

"Yes, you did."

"You got arrogant. If you hadn't jumped the fence, you probably could have caught up with me."

"You're right."

"So what do I get?"

"What do you want?"

I didn't answer. I couldn't, because his body was so close to mine and his eyes were filled with heat. He reached over and stroked my skin through the hole in my shirt, over my collarbone and down toward the slope of my breast. I shivered as electric currents overwhelmed my body, and I couldn't tell what part of it was John's ability, and what part was my own desire. He stared into my eyes, his pupils dilating. "What do you want, Dale?"

I didn't think about it. I leaned toward him.

He jumped away, moving to the other side of the room with almost the same speed as he'd used to chase me down. I sat up, feeling cold without his body to keep me warm. "John…"

He wouldn't look at me. "You won fair and square, so no more training tonight. Tomorrow night we'll head back to the Kiddie Korner. I've taught you how to hide and how to run away. Tomorrow we'll start working on how to fight."

He reached into his pocket and pulled out something—a piece of Werther's candy, its distinctive gold foil immediately recognizable. He still wouldn't look at me. The lack was killing me. "John," I said.

He finally turned, his posture closed, his face guarded. "What is it?"

There was just so much. And in the end, I said none of it. I pointed to the candy wrapper, which he was crumpling in his hands. "That's why you always smell like butterscotch."

He looked at the wrapper, then back at me, then back at the wrapper again. He sighed. "Goodnight, Dale," he said, and then he retreated into his bedroom.

I DIDN'T SEE JOHN AT all the next day. His bedroom door was open, so I peeked inside. His bed was made with military precision, the blankets folded up on the bottom, the sheets so tight you could bounce a quarter off of them. There was no sign John had even slept here the night before. When Isaac came back from the park to take me to our session in the Oasis Room, I asked him where John was. He shrugged.

"Do you know when he'll be back?"

"Nope."

"But he will be training with me tonight, right?"

"Don't know."

"Are you capable of actually forming a sentence?"

Isaac remained expressionless. "Probably," he said.

I rolled my eyes and followed Isaac to the Oasis Room for our session.

Several hours later, I found *The Princess Bride* playing on television. I was able to make it through Westley and Buttercup's harrowing escape from the Fire Swamp before I dozed off. Some time later I awoke with

a gasp, jumping up from my comfortable perch on the sectional. The television was still on, playing some infomercial for a hands-free vegetable slicer. John was looming over me, his arms folded across his chest. "Why aren't you ready to go?"

I stretched and wiped the sleep out of my eyes. "Well, good evening to you, too."

"We train at the same time *every night*, Dale. I'm not sure why you thought tonight would be different."

I stood up, facing him. Even at my full height John still dwarfed me by a good nine inches of solid muscle. Still, I tried not to let it intimidate me. "Between our midnight romps through the amusement park, and Isaac's meditation woo-woo shit, and *being on the run from people who are trying to kill me*, I feel like I haven't gotten a minute to breathe in almost a week now. I'm exhausted, and I'm overloaded. So if I take some time to myself—while you're MIA, by the way—to watch one of my favorite movies and doze off on the couch, you're just going to have to suck it up and deal with it!"

To my surprise, John chuckled. "I guess you'll be ready to fight tonight, then. Go get dressed."

After I dressed and splashed some water on my face, we returned to the Kiddie Korner. John said the location was perfect for sparring, because it was padded—thank you, litigious parents—and because it had obstacles like a place you might end up fighting in real life likely would. I almost mentioned how *unlikely* it was that I'd end up fighting in a place that smelled like microwave pizza and day-old puke, but John still seemed to be in a prickly mood and I figured discretion was the better part of valor, in this case.

"Angels and demons are very hard to kill," John said as he moved a plastic teeter-totter to the other side of the room. "That's why the Thrones'

offensive techniques focus primarily on disabling your opponent, rather than killing them. The idea is that once you disable your opponent, you can use a more surefire weapon to kill them."

"Like the fractal bullets?" I thought of the night I pulled the tiny pieces of metal out of his body and shivered.

"Yes, exactly. But the materials and technology for those weapons are often very expensive. You don't want to lose your bullets or waste them just to hit a leg or an arm. At worst, your victim might lose a limb, but they probably won't die."

"Comforting," I said grimly.

"It should be. That's their weakness. While they're fighting to harm, you'll be fighting to kill."

I remained silent, though my hands were shaking. He studied me like one might study an insect, its wings pinned to a cardboard mat. "Your mother is known to be one of the best fighters in the demon world."

"I'm not my mother," I snapped—maybe too harshly. But how else could I respond to comparisons to a woman who was no more real to me than Santa Claus?

"No, I know you're not Amara." He took a breath and ran his fingers through his hair. "But...I know your history, Dale. I've been following you for ten years, and I've watched that video from the homeless shelter over and over again. I know what you're capable of. So why is it making you so uncomfortable in the training arena?"

It was on the tip of my tongue to tell him about the Rages. But I just couldn't do it. "I—I don't know."

"I don't want you to be taken by surprise again like you were at the hospital. If you hadn't grabbed that scalpel..." his voice trailed off. "It's just...if I can get you to react faster, without fear, then you'll be safer from the Thrones." I didn't say anything, and he came over and put a hand on

my shoulder. "They will be vulnerable to you. I promise." His fingers grazed over my skin.

I pulled back, the sensation too much for me. "I understand. Let's get started."

"All right," he said. Then he lunged at me.

He moved fast. Before I had time to react, he grabbed me. My mind caught up to what was happening, and I struggled against him.

And he pinned me to the ground in two seconds flat.

He released me, and I stood. "I wasn't ready," I told him.

He lunged at me again.

This time, when he grabbed me, I managed to shift my weight forward and use his own momentum against him, rolling him over my body. The maneuver caused me to lose my own balance, and I landed on top of him. "Better." He grabbed me and threw me back onto the mat, capturing my throat with his hand. "But not good enough."

I kneed him in the balls, not hard enough to hurt him but enough to get his attention. He released me and jumped up. I stood and shoved him. "What the fuck, John?"

He stood and brushed himself off. "The Thrones don't fight fair. They're predators, and they'll strike when you least expect it."

I turned away from him. "You said they would be vulnerable to me."

"'Vulnerable' doesn't mean 'sitting ducks.' Try harder." He got into his fighting stance again, one foot in front of the other, knees slightly bent, hands ready to jab. I put my hand up to stop him. He rolled his eyes and relaxed. "Fine. We'll take a break."

I sighed in relief and went over to the water fountain along the far wall, chugging it down until I felt like I was about to swim away. "I want to get you trained in weapons, too. I'd like you to at least know how to use a knife and a gun."

I turned back toward John's voice, but I didn't see him. "A gun?"

"Yes. We'll start you with a revolver. They don't carry as much ammunition as the semi-automatics and they're tougher to conceal, but they're easier to shoot for a novice. I'm most concerned about effectiveness here."

I still didn't see him. I started walking the room, searching for him. "But...a gun?"

"It's one of the most efficient ways we have of doing potentially grievous damage to a body."

"But I thought you said I would be trying to kill the Thrones. A bullet wound won't kill them."

His voice came from somewhere behind me. I followed the sound as he spoke. "We'll get some of the fractal bullets, maybe some incendiary ammunition. A shot to the chest with either of those should do more than enough damage. And a shot to the head...well, those will usually kill most people, regardless of the type of bullet."

"But...*you're* not armed."

His voice was much closer this time, no longer echoing off the wall. "I'm armed all the time, Dale. I've usually got at least two guns and multiple knives in my pockets."

I whirled around to find him right in front of me. He lifted the leg of his pants. Sure enough, there was a gun holstered around his thigh. I gaped. "How did I not know this?"

"I conceal them, Dale. The only reason to wear a weapon in plain sight is to intimidate people."

I didn't respond. Seconds later, I saw something move from the corner of my eye. I lunged.

John grabbed my arm, spun, and tossed me to the ground. He intended to charge before I could stand, but I ripped off a kip-up and found my feet, poised to strike.

"You'll be in a position of more power if you can get me on the ground," he said. "Use my weight against me, if you can."

He made a grab for my arm. I crouched and used his own momentum to roll him over my back, throwing him to the ground. He jumped back up before I could get to him and shoved me against the wall. I punched him with the heels of my hands. He flinched, but didn't release me. I tried to shove against him, but it was like a brick wall was pressing against my body. "Don't rely on your upper body strength," he said. "You might be a demon, but you're still female, so it's not going to be your greatest strength, not when you're up against a supernatural male. Think of what my weaknesses are, and then figure out your strengths."

I grunted—it was the only answer I could manage at that moment—and I hooked my foot around the back of his knee. It buckled, and he lost his balance. He tumbled over without releasing his grip, bringing me with him. As I was falling with him, I thought about something he said. I had my strengths…but I was ignoring my biggest one. As he turned me over onto the ground, I reached out to his mind with mine, testing his shields. When I found a flaw—a small, almost imperceptible one, but it was something—I met John's eyes. "Release me."

The blowback came. It felt like a drill was boring into my brain, and blood leaked out of my nose. John glared at me. "No."

"Release me!" It felt like my skull was going to split in half.

John's face tensed, and a single drop of blood trickled out of his ear. For a second, I thought I had him—but then he tightened his grip. "No."

I was pinned. I was pinned to the ground, and I couldn't make him let me go. For the first time in my life, I was helpless, completely at his

mercy. Tears started rolling down my face, and I started to hyperventilate. "John, please..."

He released me, finally, but I knew it had nothing to do with a compulsion and everything to do with the pure, undiluted terror rippling through my body. He jumped up and stepped away from my prone body, not once looking at me. "What the hell was that, Dale?"

I sat up. My fear was turning to anger, fast. "You told me to use my strengths! If I really have this mind control power, shouldn't I be using it?"

"Not on *me*."

I stood up and wiped the blood off my face, ignoring the throbbing in my temples. "Part of the reason I fucked up in the hospital was because I didn't know how to use my powers. If you don't want me to be caught off-guard like that again, I need to incorporate them into my training sessions."

"You *do*. With *Isaac*." He grabbed my arm roughly. "I do *not* want you in my head. Never. You will not try that again. Do you understand?" When I didn't answer, he gripped me tighter, his voice becoming more frantic. "Do you understand?"

"Fine. Yes."

John released me. My nose tickled from the blood still dripping down my face. I wiped it away. My head was still throbbing. My only consolation was that there was still blood on *his* face, too, a drying streak running down his neck. He rubbed his forehead. "We're done for tonight," he said. He walked through the door without speaking to me again.

ONCE AGAIN, JOHN WAS MIA the next day, but I didn't want to see him any more than he probably wanted to see me. I slept for most of the day until my headache finally disappeared, and by the time I got up it was time to get

ready for my training session with Isaac. After I showered and got dressed, Isaac was waiting for me in the living room. "John told me about what happened last night," he said. "Will you be all right for today?"

I shrugged, trying my best to appear nonchalant. "Why wouldn't I be?"

"Because John said you almost caused your brain to hemorrhage last night."

"Oh, is that all?" Well, that explained the headache and the bleeding. Had I hurt John last night? I hadn't been the only one bloodied. "Is John all right?"

"He's fine. He's concerned about you."

"Then why hasn't he come to *see* me? Or to apologize? He really had acted like a douche last night. I was just doing what he told me to do. I didn't know he would freak out about me using the powers *that he was training me to use.* Well, if you see him, you can tell him I'm fine. And I'm not concerned about him."

Isaac shrugged. "All right." He headed for the door, leaving me to decide whether to follow—or not. I always got the feeling Isaac didn't care much either way.

During our sessions, Isaac would guide me into some sort of meditative state, and I'd work on building the shields around my mind. At first I couldn't tell whether I had succeeded or failed, and I had to rely on Isaac's assessments to tell me how well I'd done. But after a few days of practicing both with Isaac and on my own, I started to get a better sense of when and how to put my shields up. I imagined a brick wall around my mind, linking the layers together, cascade-style, to reinforce them upon themselves. The previous day, Isaac had finally announced that he couldn't break through my shields. I considered that a victory.

That day, I crouched down to take off my shoes, but he held up his hand to stop me. "Not today," he said. Without another word, he opened the

door, leading me into the sour-smelling tunnel hallway. He led me down an unfamiliar corridor to a set of elevator doors. He pushed the call button. I heard a loud rattling noise, and the elevator doors shook. I raised my eyebrows. "Are you sure this thing is safe?"

"It hasn't broken yet."

Fantastic.

The elevator took us to the back side of the park, near the garbage dumpster and blocked from the public's view by a large wooden wall. Two teenagers smoked cigarettes behind the wall; I recognized them as park employees because they were wearing the Renaissance Fair-style clothing that all of the front-end employees wore. As soon as they caught Isaac's glare, they stubbed out their cigarettes and darted to the other side of the wall, back to the public section of the park. Isaac didn't say a word, but he had just the hint of a smile on his face. "You scared them off," I said.

"Likely."

I was already irritated with him for the non-answers he had given me about John, and I was already feeling pissy about John's strange behavior. So I snapped at him. "Is it some kind of a power trip for you, scaring unsuspecting teenagers?"

He didn't hesitate. "I don't need a power trip. I'm already the boss. They know they're not supposed to smoke on park property. That's why they ran. They were wrong." He hesitated. When he spoke again, his voice was softer. "Besides, I can't condone them doing something that might make them sick or kill them one day."

"It's their choice. Not like it's a secret how bad it is for you."

"They're young. They don't know what they're giving up yet." He looked over at me, his eyes level with mine. "You're young, too."

I snorted. "Yeah, I'm a baby. How old are you exactly? Twenty-three?"

"I'm forty-seven."

My jaw dropped. With his flawless skin and tiny, almost frail-looking body, I had guessed he was no older than twenty-five, and the only reason I hadn't guessed younger was because I figured a teenager—even one with family money—wouldn't own and run his own amusement park. Granted, he couldn't help his height, or size, but still. "You are fucking with me, right?"

He started walking with a determined stride, heading toward the café. I followed. "Angels and demons are often much older than they appear. John is over three hundred years old, for example."

I stopped dead in my tracks. "Now I *know* you're fucking with me."

Isaac hadn't noticed I stopped until he heard me speak. He turned around, the same neutral look on his face. "He told me he was born in 1680. I remember the Thrones celebrating his three hundredth birthday back when I was a kid, so that's probably accurate. As for the other part of your statement, given John's obvious attraction to you, fucking with you would be ill-advised. Besides..." he didn't bother to hide the smirk, "I'm much too old for you."

It took me a second to figure out what he meant. Then I blushed. "I didn't...I wasn't...it's just an expression! You didn't really think I was being literal, did you?"

He shrugged. "I live in a tunnel. I don't get out much. Although at least, unlike John, I don't have the habit of referring to World War I as 'The Great War,' and calling fashionably dressed men 'macaronis.' Sometimes even in the same conversation, which is odd."

I was flabbergasted. Here he was, talking like this was all perfectly normal while telling me that the guy I'd been crushing on was over three *centuries* my senior. The guy who'd touched my skin and looked at me as if I was the most desirable woman in the world was a full-grown adult while Benjamin Franklin was still in diapers. "This can't be happening."

Isaac stepped closer to me. "Immortals don't look their age. You'll have to get used to that."

I couldn't deal with the implications of that, not on top of everything else. "I don't want to talk about this anymore."

"Fine." There was uncharacteristic anger in his voice, though I couldn't figure out why.

We walked over to the café, which was full of people sitting at the outdoor tables, chowing down on corn dogs and French fries and funnel cakes—sometimes all at once. Isaac pointed to a man sitting by himself at a table, wearing Dad jeans and a fanny pack and likely waiting for some children who were gleefully enjoying the Merry Olde Roller Coaster for the zillionth time. "What kind of shielding does he have?"

I tried to tune out everything else, concentrating only on the man. I reached toward him with my mind. "It's like a soap bubble," I said. "There's something there, but it's weak and fragile. If I push through it, it'll break easily."

"That's how it is with most humans," he said. "It's not that humans are incapable of shielding their minds. But why would they bother? They don't know that we exist. What about…" he pointed to a teenage girl farther away from us, "her?"

Once again, I reached out with my mind. This time, I was met with firmer resistance. "She's shielded," I said.

"Not as common with humans, but not uncommon, either. Instinctual survival instinct, probably. Can you break it?"

I tested it with my mind, poking and prodding until I found a weakness. "It's like…" I struggled to find a good analogy, "you know how you can lock the bathroom door in your house, but it's easy enough to just pop the lock with a screwdriver or even kick the door open if you really wanted to? That's how it is."

Isaac nodded. "A fair assessment. You'll find that kind of shielding is common among angels and demons. Full shielding requires a lot of energy and effort, and most don't bother maintaining it most of the time. Bathroom lock shielding is good for detecting intrusion attempts, though. If a hostile attempts to breach your shields, you'll generally know it before they get in…unless they're strong enough to plow right through before the victim even knows what's happening."

"But what about John?" I massaged my temples instinctively. Even though my head had stopped hurting, I couldn't get that whole "brain hemorrhage" thing out of my mind.

"John has chosen to keep full shields up all the time."

"Why?"

He shifted his weight between his feet. "That's something you should ask John about."

"Yeah, but he doesn't tell me anything. I only know about his power because you brought it up. Hell, I didn't even know how old he was!" Isaac hesitated, wavering. I seized the opportunity. "I'm trusting my life to this man, and he knows *everything* about me. I should at least know something about him."

Isaac sat down at one of the tables, rubbing his temples with his fingers. I sat down across from him. He sighed. "John's parents were murdered by a demon when he was a kid. He saw the whole thing."

Jesus. "How old was he?"

Isaac shrugged. "Not sure. Young, though, maybe eight or so. The story is legend in the Thrones. John's father was the leader of the organization until he was killed. Gabriel took over afterward and took John in. John was basically raised by the Thrones." I remained silent, trying to process the new information, and I was startled when Isaac spoke again. "John has spent the last three centuries searching for the demon who killed his

parents. That's why he's such a cold person. I don't think he's really let anyone in since his parents died."

I thought about the previous night, about how John had touched me with naked lust in his eyes. He hadn't been cold then.

When I didn't push further, Isaac spoke again. "I want to try something a little different now. It's time for you to actually use those powers of yours." He pointed toward a lone teenage boy dressed in a tunic and tights, a park employee on a break. "I want you to go up to him and make him do something."

My throat felt suddenly dry. "Something like what?"

"Maybe just make him go back to work. He takes too many breaks."

"I'm not going to use my training sessions as a means to further allow you to terrorize your employees."

"Does he look terrorized to you?" I folded my arms across my chest stubbornly. Isaac rolled his eyes before he caught himself and disciplined his face back into its neutral expression. "It doesn't matter what you make him do. The point of the exercise is getting you to use your abilities consciously and offensively."

"I don't feel right about it."

Isaac shrugged. I was getting so tired of those damn apathetic shrugs. "You won't hurt him. Not unless you want to."

I wanted to scream at him. How the hell could he understand my concerns about the moral implications of making someone do something against their will when he apparently used the teeny tiny bit of authority he had to scare his teenage employees? But Isaac was right. Something had happened the night of the warehouse party, something I still couldn't explain. I didn't have to hurt the boy. I could make him do something silly, like hop on one foot or sing the national anthem. That wouldn't be so bad. Nothing permanently damaging there, right?

I took a deep breath and walked toward the boy's table. My stomach clenched. Forget butterflies—it was more like elephants were trampling through my intestines. He had his head buried in a book, so he didn't see me approach. A man after my own heart. If only he were ten years older— or three centuries, whatever.

I cleared my throat, and the teenager looked up at me. "Is anyone sitting here?" I asked. He shook his head and turned back to his book without a second glance.

An inauspicious beginning, certainly. But I wasn't going to let that stop me. "Nice weather we're having today. I'm glad it's not super hot. I bet you are, too, in that outfit." He made a noise, something between a grunt and a groan. I took that as an affirmation. "I remember going to an amusement park one time with my dad when I was a kid, and it was so hot that day that I felt sick after a few hours. Then we discovered it was way cooler on top of the Ferris wheel. We must have rode that thing a dozen times before we finally just gave up and went home." The teenager glanced at me, but otherwise didn't respond. "So how do you like working here? I was thinking about maybe applying for a part-time job, but I've heard the owner here is a real tyrant..."

Finally, the boy looked up at me. "Is there something you wanted, ma'am?"

His voice cracked on the last word. God, he must think I was some kind of pervert or something. "No. Nothing at all. I was just…making conversation, I guess. Sorry to bother you."

The kid went back to his book, and I sat back in the uncomfortable metal chair, trying to figure out how to salvage the situation. I reached out toward him mentally, and there he was, his mind as open and unprotected as a baby chick. He glanced back at me, no doubt feeling my eyes boring a hole into him. "Are you all right?"

"Jump on one foot," I told him.

"Excuse me?"

"Just...jump on one foot."

I could feel the command going toward him, and then bouncing off of his—totally unshielded!—mind and dropping like dead weight. The teenager looked at me again, his eyes widening. "Lady, I really think you need some help."

"Sing the national anthem!"

He stood up and backed away, not taking his eyes off of me. "I'm going to get security."

Shit. I put out my hands in a placating gesture, giving him an embarrassed chuckle. "Oh. Crap. I'm sorry. I just...I thought you were someone else. My bad."

The kid continued to back away, tripping on a chair that someone had pushed out from another table. Once he recovered his footing, he broke into a run and got out of there as quickly as he could.

I stayed where I was until I heard Isaac clear his throat behind me. "I've never seen anyone run from the food court that fast before. Unless they're vomiting."

"I don't need your sarcasm right now," I told him.

"It's not sarcasm. E-coli is nothing to joke about." He sat down across from me. "I assume running away was *not* what you asked him to do."

"What tipped you off, Sherlock?"

"I don't know. Your pleasant demeanor?" He sat down across from me. "So what happened?"

I wiped sweat off my face. "I felt his mind, felt that he had no shield, and then I just...couldn't do it."

"Performance anxiety?"

I wasn't sure whether he was mocking me or not, but his face was perfectly serious. I sighed. "Has it ever occurred to you how unethical this is? How immoral?"

Isaac pursed his lips. "How so?"

"These are people's *minds* you want me to mess with. You want me to take away their free will. How can I do that with a clear conscience?"

"What about that man at the party? The one who was bothering your friend? John told me about what happened then."

I shrugged. "I didn't know what I was doing then. Now I do."

Isaac cringed, his face pained, although I couldn't figure out what I had said to cause it. He took a deep breath. "These people who are coming after you don't fight fair. They won't stop until you're dead."

"But John will help..."

"You can't count on John. John has his own goals. You can't always depend on him to protect you."

"I thought he was your friend."

"He *is* my friend. But I'm not blind to who he is."

"And since I don't actually *know* who he is, I guess I'm just screwed."

I got up, my chair scraping along the pavement, and walked away. When I was a few feet from the table, I heard a noise behind me, a sharp intake of air through clenched teeth. I turned back around. Isaac rested his head against the table, his eyes shut. His olive-toned skin had gone ghostly pale, and he was sweating. I knelt down beside him. "Are you okay?"

"Head," he mumbled.

I was an idiot. I had been so consumed by my own self-pity that I failed to notice that Isaac apparently had a raging migraine coming on. "Do you want me to help you back to the tunnels? Or have someone get one of those medical emergency cart thingies?"

He shook his head, but even that slight motion seemed to cause him more pain. "Can't move yet."

"Okay. No problem. I'll be right back."

I ran up to one of the food vendor carts, cutting past everyone else in line. "I'm sorry, but my friend's got a migraine. I need a cup of ice and a plastic bag in case he throws up."

The vendor didn't have any plastic bags, so I got a popcorn tub instead. I returned to the table. "Where does it hurt the most?" I asked. Isaac pointed to his right temple. I pushed the cup of ice against it. He recoiled against the shock of the cold at first, but then he reached up and took hold of it himself. His hand was clammy, I noticed, and he hadn't even touched the ice yet. "My best friend used to get migraines back when we were in high school. She said that putting ice on her head was the only thing that helped. Well, that, and Mocha Frappucinos from Starbucks. I must have gained about fifteen pounds in the summer between junior and senior year, and to this day it's still the only way I can drink anything remotely coffee-like. I half suspected she just used her migraines as an excuse so her parents would buy her overpriced sugar foam whenever she wanted." I chuckled. It had been so long since I'd thought about that, so long I'd thought about anything other than the horrible night our friendship came to an end.

After a few minutes, the lines of strain seemed to ease on his face, and he lifted his head up and blinked slowly. "Are you all right?" I asked.

"Not really." His voice was raspy. "Would you please get me some water?"

I went back to the food vendor and got him a large cup of water. When I returned to the table, he drank it down in one gulp. "Need more?"

"Not now," he replied. He grimaced and placed the cup of ice back against his head. "Mocha Frappucinos?"

"There's gotta be a Starbucks around here somewhere, right? Honestly, I'm surprised you don't have a 'Ye Olde Starbucks' right here in the park."

He was silent for a long time after that, just rubbing his right temple with the cup of ice. Finally, he set the cup down and looked at me. "I have a brain tumor."

I gaped at him. "What? Are you serious?"

"I was diagnosed three years ago. It's malignant and inoperable."

"But how? You're an angel, right? I thought angels and demons lived forever. Isn't that what you just told me?"

He gave me a wry smile. "Genetics don't really play fair. Pure-blooded angels and demons are immortal, but once you get further away from the pure-blooded ancestors, it gets complicated." He winced again and put the cup of ice back to his temple. "Purebloods cannot reproduce with other purebloods, so they look for humans to breed with. Supernatural genes are, apparently, dominant, so those half-blooded children inherit their parents' supernatural qualities, including immortality. But what if the half-blooded child has a baby with a human? The quarter-blooded baby may inherit *all* the traits of their supernatural grandparent, or none. More often than not, it's a mix of both." He smiled at me, but it didn't reach his eyes. "I'm one-quarter angel. I got just enough supernatural to keep me from dying six months after my diagnosis, but not enough to stop the cancer or keep it from killing me indefinitely."

"That's why you have all that medical equipment in your room," I said, lamely.

He nodded. "I get headaches and seizures. I have a palliative care nurse come in to check on me several times a week, but I've asked her not to come while you're here. I've been on an upswing recently, and it's been nice to feel normal for a change."

"But…Jesus…isn't there anything they can do? Like chemotherapy or something?"

"Maybe if I were fully human. But supernatural physiology reacts strangely to drugs. Likely the 'cure' would be worse than the disease." Tears slipped down my face, and Isaac reached out and grabbed my hand. "Hey. Don't worry. My angel physiology is keeping me alive and mostly well much longer than expected."

"But I don't understand. Why are you just hanging out in an amusement park like this? Shouldn't you be in a hospital or something? Where is your family?"

He looked at the ground. "Not all angels are Thrones, but the Thrones control everything about angelic society. They only use humans to breed, because they can't do it themselves. But the mixed-blooded children's humanity is considered a weakness, and they are never afforded equal status within the Thrones' hierarchy. Anyone 'too human' is exiled."

The pieces started to click together. "They kicked you out when they found out you were sick."

He nodded. "My father couldn't afford to lose the Thrones' good graces, not when AziziCorp was finally making strides with supernatural tech, so he handed over my share of the inheritance and sent me away. He doesn't know where I am. No one in my family does."

"Guess I'm not the only one with a shit family."

"It wasn't their fault. It's just the way things are." He looked up at me. "John was one of the few people from my former life who bothered to track me down. No one else ever bothered to look. He's one of the only people I consider a friend."

And yet you told me not to trust him. But I didn't say it. Now was not the time or the place for that conversation. I pinched the bridge of my nose to stop more tears from coming. "How long do you have?"

"I don't know. But who does, really? 'Immortal' and 'unkillable' aren't the same thing. Remember that."

Small solace. But at least I had a *chance*. "I'm sorry," I told him.

He gave me a one-shouldered shrug. "Me, too."

JOHN DIDN'T COME THAT EVENING, which left me able to get ten straight hours of uninterrupted, *glorious* sleep. I didn't know if John was around or not, but his bedroom door was closed, so I assumed so. Not that it mattered. His geriatric ass could be in Timbuktu for all I cared.

When I got up around 11:00 the next morning, John's bedroom door was still closed. I was curious about whether he was inside, whether he was even *alive* in there, but I wasn't going to demean myself by putting my ear to the door to listen. So I showered and got dressed. Ate some yogurt and a banana. Watched some daytime talk shows.

You know. Quality time.

When Isaac came home from his shift, John emerged from his bedroom. He looked fresh and invigorated, with no trace of the damage I'd done the other night. I don't know what I expected. That he'd still have blood on his face? That he'd be clutching his face in his hands? I'd washed my face, and my headache was long gone, so I don't know why I'd expected anything different from him. Still, it was a little bit disconcerting to see him walk in as if nothing had ever happened. "I'm going to join you and Isaac today, Dale," he said.

"Uh…fine. No problem. Thank you for asking." Although he *hadn't* actually asked. Judging by the tight expression on John's face when I said it, my slip hadn't escaped his notice.

We headed into the Oasis Room, John in front, with Isaac and me following. Before we could cross the threshold of the door, Isaac took my arm. "I just…I wanted to thank you for helping me yesterday."

I released a breath I hadn't even realized I'd been holding. "Don't worry about it. I was afraid you'd feel awkward about it." I certainly did.

"No."

He hesitated. Isaac could be hard to read. He wasn't exactly the most expressive person on the best of days, and he seemed to believe that someone might charge him for the number of words he used. "Is there something else?" I asked.

"I just wanted to let you know that you didn't do anything wrong."

"Uh…thank you?"

He took a breath as if he was going to say something else, but then he walked into the Oasis Room without another word.

I followed. Once I passed the threshold, John closed the door behind me. I sat on the overstuffed pillows on the floor and started to take off my shoes. "You don't need to do that," John said. "Isaac and I want to talk to you first."

I looked over at Isaac. He wouldn't meet my eyes. "Is that so?"

John sat down across from me. He was close enough to brush my legs with his, but he didn't. Instead, he rested his arms on his knees and leaned toward me, his body open and relaxed. It was so different from John's normal stick up-his-butt tightness that I knew it was deliberate. "Isaac told me about what happened yesterday. That you couldn't use your abilities on the boy in the park."

I glanced over at Isaac. He still wouldn't meet my eyes. "Yeah. So?"

"So I'm concerned."

"Concerned about what, exactly? That I didn't want to fuck with the head of some teenage kid who's never done anything to me?"

"That, combined with your inability to use your powers on me the other night."

"That was different!" I exploded. "I didn't want to mess with the teenager because it's wrong to use powers like this to manipulate people just for the hell of it. I couldn't use my powers on you because you have these crazy-ass impenetrable shields around your mind. And then you got mad at me for even trying!"

"Regardless, it speaks to an inability to control your powers, and I don't know if Isaac is the best person to help you."

I finally caught Isaac's eyes. "I don't know if there's anything else I can do for you," he said.

I rubbed my face. "So what exactly do you suggest? Do you have any other friends lurking beneath amusement parks who you can ask?"

John didn't hesitate. "I think we should find your mother."

What the fuck? "You've got to be kidding me."

"She has the same abilities as you, Dale. She should be able to help you find your trigger and use your abilities whenever and wherever you want."

I stood up and stepped away from them. When I got over to the LED-lit fountain on the wall, I stuck my fingers into the flow of water, willing it to calm me. "I don't think that's necessary, John," I said. "I've made a lot of progress with Isaac already. I've learned how to control my shields, and how to sense and penetrate other people's minds. I can get into Isaac's mind with no problem, no matter which shield he throws at me."

"But you haven't been able to control him, have you?"

"I haven't tried." I didn't want to. To do so would seem like a violation—especially in light of what Isaac had told me the day before. Isaac's brain was already betraying him. I didn't want to add fuel to the fire.

"And you couldn't control the boy at the park yesterday."

"It was my *first* try! It's not like pulling an Obi-Wan Kenobi on someone is *easy*, and I've made a lot of progress over the last week. C'mon, back me up, Isaac!"

Isaac nodded. "It's true."

Gee, thanks. "If I keep working with Isaac on my mental stuff, and with you on my physical stuff, I'll get better. Just give me more time."

John stood up, folding his arms across his chest. "Isaac can only take you so far in your training. Amara is the only other person in the world who has your ability."

I turned away from him. "I don't care. I'll figure it out."

"It doesn't make sense for you to plateau here with Isaac when we can track down your mother and she can help you explore the full scope of your abilities."

I spun around and faced him. "She *abandoned* me, John! Up until a week ago, I thought she was dead, and now you march into my life and tell me that, not only is she *not* dead, she's the most powerful fucking demon in the world. She could have come back any time she wanted. But no, she left, and she stayed gone, even after my dad died. So fuck her! I want nothing to do with her."

"'Fuck her'? That's it? That's all you have to say?"

I ran my fingers through the fountain water again. "I'll figure out my powers."

"You might not have *time* to figure them out! The Thrones are already tracking you, and they won't stop until they find you. You need to stop thinking like an abandoned child, Dale!"

I gaped at him. "You asshole."

He stepped into my space, close enough that he had to look down into my eyes. "I might be an asshole, but I'm also right."

"Fuck you, John!" I shoved him away. "Why don't you take a little *fucking* responsibility, for once? I was doing fine before you came along."

"Seven murders in ten years is *fine*?"

"I had a job. I had friends. I was *fine*. And now I have *nothing*. The Thrones are only after me because of you! You painted a big fucking target on my back!"

He froze as if I had hit him. When he spoke again, his voice had softened. "You're right," he said. "The Thrones might have been after you initially because of who your mother is, but I'm the one who led them to your doorstep. I'm the reason you're in this mess. And for that, I'm sorry."

His sudden capitulation caught me so off guard that I didn't know what to say. "Thank you."

He kept his tone soft. "But…it doesn't change the fact that you *are* in this mess. By now, the Thrones have traced your current and former identity. They're interrogating your friends in New York…"

Wait, what? "What do you mean…interrogating?"

He hesitated. "It's standard procedure for the Thrones. If they can't find the person they're looking for, they'll question the people closest to them."

I could barely breathe. "You're telling me the people who used mechanical spiders to sear the flesh off of my legs and killed an emergency room full of people are now 'interrogating' my friends?"

"They'll probably be all right, as long as they cooperate."

I looked at Isaac for confirmation. Once again, he wouldn't meet my eyes. "Why the hell didn't you tell me?" I asked John.

"We were already gone, and they didn't know anything. I didn't think it was that important."

"What the hell? They're my *friends*, John!"

"No, they're not, Dale. You've only known them for a few months. They don't know the first thing about you, not even your name."

His words stung. More than I wanted to let on. "What the fuck does that matter, John? All they ever did was try to be nice to me. Now the Thrones might be filleting them, and you didn't think it was important to

mention to me." I marched over to the door and pressed my hand against the palm scanner until I heard the lock click. "You know who else doesn't know the first thing about me? You."

CHAPTER

IT WAS A DREARY, OVERCAST day, chilly for July even in Vermont. Still, the park had a decent crowd, and it didn't take me long to find a middle-aged man staring at his cell phone while his kids were on the carousel. "Can I borrow your phone?" I asked.

He eyed me up and down. If my Wal-Mart special yoga pants and oversized T-shirt weren't enough to make me look white trashy, my disheveled hair and tear-stained face probably weren't helping. "No. Sorry."

I snapped. I reached out for his mind and seized it, grasping it in my mental talons. "Give me your phone. Now."

I felt a release of pressure inside my mind. The man's eyes became unfocused, his pupils dilated. He handed me the phone without another word.

I switched the screen over to telephone mode. I hadn't carried a cell phone since high school, and one of the consequences was that I still remembered the telephone numbers for everyone I knew. It came in handy now. I dialed Nik's number. It rang once…twice…three times. "Please pick up," I whispered.

I almost started crying when her voice flooded the line. "Nik, it's Dale," I said.

"Dale, where the hell have you been? I've been so worried. I was going to call the cops! But I wasn't sure if I should. I remembered you said your asshole ex-boyfriend worked in law enforcement, and I was afraid…"

I interrupted her. "Don't worry about that right now. I need to warn you. There might be some people looking for me. They'll come to you, and they might come to Chaz. Whatever you do, just…tell them whatever you know. Don't worry about me."

There was a long silence on the other end of the line, and I started to panic. "Nik, are you still there?"

Her voice was quiet. "They've already been here."

I stopped breathing. "Are you all right? Tell me everything."

"I'm fine. They all dressed in black suits, and they talked weird, like really formal. I thought they were cops or feds or something, but they never showed me any identification or told me what agency they were from. I've told them I don't know where you are, but they just keep coming back. And on Monday they took Chaz and…"

"They took Chaz? Is he okay? They didn't hurt him, did they?"

"They kept him overnight, and they…" she hesitated. "He'll recover, physically, but he's just not *right*, Dale. I don't know what they did to him, but I think it might have really screwed him up in the head."

My eyes filled with tears. "God, I'm so sorry. I didn't know this would happen when I left, and I never meant to get either of you involved with this." There was silence on the other end of the line. I could imagine her face: hard, accusatory, hurt. "Look, Nik, if they come back again, just…tell them everything. Whatever you know, whatever you can think of, just tell them. Tell them about this phone call, too. I don't matter here, all right? Just keep yourself safe. Tell Chaz, too. Keep yourself safe." I hung up the

phone before she could say anything else. I gave the phone back to the man and walked away.

I wandered through the park. It was nice—parents with their sticky-faced children, young couples walking hand-in-hand, young teenagers running through the park on their own for the first time. I bought a soft pretzel and sat on one of the benches. I chewed the pretzel slowly, letting the salt crystals dissolve on my tongue.

Someone cleared their throat next to me. It was Isaac. "I don't want to talk to you," I said.

He sat down next to me anyway. "You left before we could finish our conversation."

"That wasn't a conversation. That was an ambush."

He had the good grace to cringe. "I'm sorry."

"Yeah." I took another bite of my pretzel.

We sat in silence for a couple of minutes, until he spoke again. "Do you want to ride the Ferris wheel?"

I stared at him. "I'm pissed at you."

"You can be just as pissed at me from on top of the Ferris wheel."

I couldn't argue with that.

As a Funland employee—I was beginning to think that no one knew he actually owned the place—Isaac was able to get onto the Ferris wheel without standing in line. As his ride partner, I had the same benefit. It was one of those huge wheels that towered over the park, with dozens of cars in different colors that took a good eight minutes to fully load and unload. We sat across from one another, and the car began its slow climb to the top.

Neither Isaac nor I said anything until we were well off the ground and the wind was blowing through the car. "You really don't think you can help me with my powers anymore?" I asked.

"I'm not sure it's my help that you need."

"What are you talking about? You've helped me so much. I never would have known how to project outward with my mind or how to shield myself without you. And I know if we work on the whole mind control thing some more, I'll get it." My voice sounded whiney, or maybe just a little desperate.

He shook his head. "Your problem isn't strength or focus. Your problem is your unwillingness to control people, your fear that it violates their rights."

"It does violate their rights. Why should I be able to force people to do things they wouldn't otherwise do?" I hesitated. "But wait…I *can* do it, if I'm angry or upset enough. Like just before you found me, I was able to use my power to get a man to give me his cell phone. I was just so pissed at John and so worried about Nik and Chaz, and I did it without even thinking. It was…really easy, actually."

Isaac paled. "Who did you call?"

"Nik. I just wanted to make sure she and Chaz were…"

Isaac grabbed my shoulders. "Have the Thrones found them?"

"Yes. They questioned both of them, and I think Chaz might have been tortured."

Isaac pulled out his phone and began texting. I'd never seen Isaac look even the slightest bit ruffled. He was shaking now. "Hell," he muttered.

"Look, I know John doesn't think Nik and Chaz are real friends, but they're important to me. I wanted to make sure they were all right. I know John's your friend, but I don't care if he's pissed off about it."

"Do you think that's why I'm upset?" He kept texting furiously even as he yelled. "Did it occur to you that the Thrones are likely monitoring Nik's phone?"

I froze. In my anger and panic, I had violated the number one rule of being on the run: never look back, because someone is always looking for you. "I didn't think about it."

Isaac sighed and leaned his head against the back of the car. "It's all right. You were mad, and you were feeling protective of your friend. It's probably fine. Even if the Thrones intercepted the call, it'll take them time to isolate…"

His voice trailed off as the sky above us darkened. I looked up, thinking we were in for a sudden thunderstorm. Instead, I saw a long, cylindrical object flying in the air. It was a shimmery gray color that almost disappeared into the sky, and its presence blocked out what little sunlight there was on this cloudy day. "What the hell is that? A blimp?" I asked.

"It's not a blimp; it's a zeppelin." Isaac pulled his phone out of his pocket and began texting frantically. "Fuck. We're out of time."

"I don't understand." But I was afraid I did.

"The Thrones are already here."

CHAPTER

A PANEL ON THE BOTTOM OF the zeppelin opened, and dozens of body armor clad figures jumped out. Instead of plunging to the ground, about half of them flew higher into the air. The rest descended slowly to the ground, as if they were taking an elevator rather than fighting gravity. They were wearing some kind of packs strapped to their backs, and even in the darkness I could see blue flames coming out of the bottom of them. It reminded me of *The Rocketeer*, if the rocket pack had been designed by Apple and marketed as the iRocket.

The Ferris wheel—which had still been creeping upward for loading and unloading as the zeppelin descended—stopped suddenly, and the lights that illuminated the spokes turned off. I thought it was just because the ride operator had figured out something was going on and stopped the ride, but then I looked around and realized *all* the rides had stopped, every light had turned off, all the music stopped, and every piece of machinery had ground to a halt. Several large spotlights switched on inside the zeppelin, scanning the ground. "They cut the power," I said.

"Yes." Isaac continued to swipe at the touch screen of his phone frantically. "I'm texting John. We can't take on that many Thrones. He might be your only means of escape."

I could hear the sounds of people screaming, though we were high enough in the air that it was faint. I looked down. The tourists were scrambling, running for the exit, hiding inside the makeshift buildings around the park, even crouching behind garbage cans and benches. They were sitting ducks, every last one of them.

One of the floating Thrones came to a stop in the air, hovering about halfway between the zeppelin and the ground. "Ladies and gentlemen!" she called out, her voice projecting through the entire park. "No need to be alarmed. We are searching for someone. A woman."

She gestured toward the zeppelin, and a picture appeared on the side. *My* picture. My senior-year high school portrait, to be specific. Ten years out of date it might have been, but I was still easy enough to recognize. "Oh, shit."

Someone screamed. A moment later, one of the Thrones flew upward, holding a woman in a fireman's carry. The woman was fighting him, kicking and thrashing, but he barely seemed to notice. He nodded to another of the Thrones, who flew over to him. They grabbed her by the arms and dangled her in front of the female Throne. The woman's legs waved back and forth, desperately trying to find ground where there was none, and she started to cry. "Is this her?" one of the male Thrones asked. I could see where they'd make the mistake. She was about my age and complexion, with brown hair instead of auburn.

The female Throne tapped an earpiece. Seconds later, she spoke. "Gabriel says no. Let her go."

They dropped her. Her screams echoed through the park as she plummeted to the ground.

Isaac reached through the Ferris wheel car to the outside door, jiggling the handle from the outside. "There's a trick to these," he said. "If I could just...there." The door popped open. The Thrones seemed to be busy searching the ground, and they didn't notice. Isaac stood on the edge of the car, the back of his feet hanging over the edge. "Each of the spokes of the wheel is like a ladder. You can use them to climb down."

"What about you?"

He half-shrugged, then smiled—big and toothy and bright. Dimples plunged into his cheeks. "You know, I've always wanted to be a hero. Funny, huh? A short computer geek with a brain tumor." His expression became serious again. "Get to the ground. Find John. Get out. Don't worry about me."

"What about..."

But Isaac had already climbed to the roof of the car, grabbing on to one of the rungs of the wheel spokes. But he wasn't climbing down like he had told me. No, he was working his way from rung to rung to climb *up*, toward the zeppelin and the crazy people with rocket packs who had just dropped someone from the sky. I wanted to call after him, but he was *fast*, and by that time he was already far enough above me that he wouldn't be able to hear me. He looked down and gave me a little wave, not a greeting so much as a "get your ass in gear."

I hoisted myself to the car roof and grabbed on to one of the rungs. The good news was that the car was at a forty-five-degree angle with the ground, which meant I was able to lie flat along the slats and shimmy down toward the center. The bad news was that, in doing so, I faced directly toward the ground. *Don't look down,* they say. Yeah, not so easy when the ground is right in front of you—and two hundred feet below. A wave of vertigo crashed into me. I closed my eyes and took several deep breaths, but just for a few seconds. I couldn't afford any more.

Isaac and I weren't the only ones who had abandoned their cars and were trying to make their escapes via the wheel spokes. All around me, other people were trying to make their way across and down, taking their chances with gravity in the hopes of escape. All I could hope was that the Thrones didn't notice me among the masses of fleeing people. My hair was shorter than it had been in the high school picture, and my curves had all settled into their rightful places, but my face was the same. For ten years, I'd used makeup and hair dye and clothing and fake glasses to disguise who I really was. Now, absent all of that, it was clear that I hadn't really changed all that much. I might as well have been running around the park naked.

I eased my way down to the next rung, gripping the sides until my knuckles turned white. As quickly as I could manage between the vertigo and my blinding panic, I made my way to the apex of the wheel. It was round, not much wider than the rungs on the way down had been. Worse, *all* of the spokes connected to it, which made finding a place to get my footing difficult. But I had to use it to branch off onto one of the other spokes, one that would take me to the ground. If the amusement park workers could do it, so could I.

I set my right foot on it first, followed by my left. I shifted my body so that I was in a more upright position, balancing precariously on the narrow, circular perch. Using the spokes above me for balance, I took a step down. Then another. Another. My chest was even with the wheel's apex now, the rest of my body below.

My foot slipped.

I grabbed the apex frantically, barely able to get a grip because my hands were shaking so badly. I took a slow breath, trying to will my heart to slow down and get my adrenaline to more manageable levels.

My left hand was throbbing, wedged between two joints on the wheel's apex, and my right foot was still dangling in the air. I glanced down, but

I was at such an angle that I couldn't see where the rung was or how far my foot was from it. Fantastic. I moved my foot slowly, carefully, until I felt something that I hoped was the rung. I flexed my muscles, testing the sturdiness and the width of it. When everything seemed all right, I eased my foot onto it.

Then came my hands. I moved my right hand first, shifting it onto the next lower rung. No problem. My left hand proved more difficult, stuck as it was. I wiggled it, but it held tight. I was afraid to pull it, fearing that I would lose my precarious balance. I needed to think.

The Thrones' spotlight moved over me, scanning the area. I held my breath. *Please don't see me, please don't see me.* It seemed to linger for a moment. Then, it moved on, scanning other parts of the park. I released my breath.

I didn't have time to wait. I braced my feet as well as I could and grabbed the rung I held with my right hand more tightly. Then, I yanked my hand out with a sickening crack. The world turned white for a second, and I bit my lips, trying not to scream from the pain. When I could think again, I looked at my hand. Already it was turning blue and purple, and I was pretty sure a couple of my knuckles were broken. My hand felt tight and stiff, my body already trying to mend itself together, but without the aid of anything to split it with, I knew it was pretty well fucked.

I heard another scream, followed by a thud. The Thrones had just dropped another innocent person from the sky. I needed to get out of here. Now.

I managed to get down a few more rungs, using just my legs and right hand. The climb was slower than it had been before. Tears ran down my face, the pain in my hand too much to take. When my nose got too snotty I stopped for a second and looked up. Isaac had made it to the top of the

wheel now, where he was balancing on the uppermost car. "What the hell are you doing?" I said to myself.

I didn't have to wait long. I heard a loud crash above me, and I looked up. A large dragon had landed on top of the Ferris wheel. It opened its mouth and roared, orange flames exploding from its mouth. I could feel the heat even from where I was, almost to the bottom of the wheel. Several of the Thrones froze in the air, while others kept moving as if they didn't even see it.

The Thrones' leader projected her voice through the park again. "Kill it!"

"What the fuck? There are dragons now?" But something nagged at the back of my mind. Neither John nor Isaac had ever mentioned anything about dragons. But I did remember how Isaac had once conjured up a lion so realistic I could smell its breath. I raised my shields to their highest levels, and the dragon disappeared. I lowered them, and it reappeared. "Oh, wow."

Isaac was using his ability to distract them. He was trying to give me time to escape.

I tried to move faster, not wanting to waste the opportunity he'd given me. The Thrones were still distracted by the dragon illusion, shooting and slashing away at its scaly body. Isaac was better than I had given him credit for. As the Thrones "injured" the dragon, holes and cuts appeared in its large body, complete with oozing blood. Even though I *knew* it wasn't real, it was pretty damn close, and it was giving the masses of people on the ground time to run away.

But then, one of them spotted Isaac on the roof of the car. The leader called out, "The illusionist is on the top of the wheel! Grab him!" Two Thrones stopped in midair and made a beeline for him.

"No!" I screamed. "Not him! It's me you want!"

The Thrones grabbed Isaac from the top of the wheel. The dragon disappeared abruptly, and they pulled Isaac into the air. "Not him! I'm right here!"

No one heard me. I kept rushing down. Too far, I was still too far.

Isaac's legs were kicking as the two Thrones dragged him to their leader. "I remember you," she said, her voice still projecting through the park. "I thought you'd be dead by now."

I couldn't hear Isaac's response, but I suspected it was something along the lines of *go fuck yourself*, judging by the harshness of her next words. "You've been hiding the girl. You know what she is, and you've been keeping her from us. You are a traitor to your people. Tell us where she is now, and maybe we'll spare you."

Once again, I couldn't hear Isaac's reply. "Just give me up, Isaac," I whispered. "Just tell them where I am. Save yourself."

But when the leader's voice echoed in the air again, it was even colder than it had been before. "Then you're of no use to us." She raised her arm, and the two Thrones holding Isaac dropped him.

Isaac didn't scream. He was silent as he fell through the air and landed on the ground with a dull thud.

Without thinking, I released my tenuous grip on the rungs and jumped to the ground. It must have been another fifty feet. I landed on my feet, sending shockwaves of pain through my ankles and legs. But somehow, I managed to keep upright, and I ran to where Isaac lay.

Isaac's neck was bent at an unnatural angle, and his eyes were open, staring into nothingness. But part of me wouldn't accept it. I crouched down, ignoring the pain in my legs, and placed two fingers on his neck, fumbling for a pulse. I felt nothing. "C'mon, Isaac, wake up!" I struggled to remember the CPR course I'd taken in high school. I began doing chest

compressions, trying to remember how long I was supposed to do it before I gave him a breath. "C'mon, Isaac, just wake up. Please, Isaac, please."

I heard footsteps in front of me, and a large set of boots appeared in my vision. I looked up and saw the Thrones' platoon leader in front of me. She was tall, blonde, and Nordic-looking. She folded her arms across her chest. "That didn't take very long," she said. She motioned to a couple of the other Thrones who closed in around Isaac and me. "This is her. Take her to Gabriel. He wants to question her before we do anything else."

The two Thrones—big, burly-looking men with scowls on their faces—each grabbed me by the shoulders. I flung my body weight forward, jerking the two men off-balance. One released me, but the other didn't, grabbing my other arm and pushing me into the ground. But he'd made a mistake. He'd left my legs free. I kneed him in the groin, hard enough that he'd be singing soprano for a week. The movement caused pain to shoot through my leg again, and I realized I must have injured it worse than I thought.

But the groin kick wasn't enough to get the Throne to release me. His hands gripped my upper arms, his muscles thick and veiny. I did the only thing I could think of: I rolled my head to the left and bit him.

Human teeth aren't designed to tear through living flesh, but with a little jaw strength and a lot of determination, it's amazing what they'll do. I wiggled my head until it tore the flesh from his arm, and then I spit it on the ground. The big guy screamed, loosening his grip and giving me the opening I needed. I head-butted him hard, relishing the crunch as his nose broke. The combination threw him off enough that I was able to roll over, pinning him beneath me. I slammed his head into the ground, knocking him unconscious before he could capture me again.

As I jumped up, I heard the Thrones' platoon leader say in a sardonic voice, "You're supposed to be the strongest men in the unit, and you can't handle one demon?" She tapped her earpiece. "Calling all troops to the

front of the Ferris wheel. We need assistance capturing the demon. Bring a body bag for the weak-blood. We'll have Azizi senior dissect his brain and see if he can replicate the illusion ability for our tech."

I turned to her, wiping away the blood from my mouth. A red haze filled my vision.

She smirked.

The Rage flooded my body, and the world went black.

CHAPTER

17

THE NEXT THING I REMEMBERED was John gripping my hand, tugging me along. We were running. Everything hurt. I tried to stop. "No, no, no, we have to keep going," John said. He carried a large rifle in his other hand, the one that wasn't clinging to mine.

We were in a parking lot. What parking lot? Were we still at the amusement park? "Isaac?" I croaked.

"Is dead. But you already know that."

"What? No. He can't be. We were on the Ferris wheel together, and the Thrones came…"

"And he sacrificed himself to save you. Don't muck that up by being stupid now."

I heard a loud boom behind us. A few seconds later, the mechanical spiders I had seen during the fight in the subway station skittered toward us. One of them found my leg. I shook it off. "John!" I screeched.

"Ignore them. You'll heal."

Another blast rang out behind us, and a bolt of electricity struck me in the shoulder. I screamed and fell to the ground. John swore. He crouched

next to me, propping me up on the side of a car. The right side of my shirt had been shredded by the blast. He tore it away, revealing a snowflake-like red mark running across my shoulder, down my arm, and across my chest. He took my wrist in his hand, checking my pulse. "Are you having trouble breathing?" I shook my head. "Any numbness or weakness?"

I flexed my arm and hand. "It feels tingly, like it went to sleep."

John nodded. "That's normal. Give it a minute. You'll be fine. But for now, stay down."

I followed, too woozy at that point to do much else. John jumped up and positioned the rifle over his shoulder. He fired about a dozen shots in rapid succession. I heard two thumps—people falling to the ground, a sound I'd heard too many times that day. John ducked back down next to me. I gaped at him. "You just shot those people like it was nothing."

He gave me a look. "I'm an assassin. What do you think that involves? Light scolding?"

I couldn't answer—and I didn't really want to, because he sounded pissed. He grabbed my arm and we took off running again, zig-zagging between cars. He stopped at a dark green, older model Ford Taurus. He broke the passenger's seat window, reached inside, and popped the door lock. Once the door was open, he brushed the shattered glass off of the seat. "Get in and open the door for me!"

I did as I was told. John hurried around to the other door and got inside, tossing the rifle into the back seat. He ducked below the steering column and pulled something out from his pocket. I thought it was another gun, but it was something else altogether: a Swiss Army knife. He used the screwdriver attachment to remove the panel underneath the steering column. Once he exposed the wiring, he switched attachments and stripped about half an inch of covering off of a green wire and a red wire. Then, he touched the two wires together. They sparked, and the engine turned over.

He revved the engine a few times before he shifted the car into reverse and pulled out of the parking spot. "Get down as low as you can," he said.

I did, jamming myself between the seat and the glove compartment. John spun the wheel around, shifted into drive, and floored it, flying through the parking lot. I heard a bang, and then glass shattering; the Thrones had shot out the back window. John's only response was to push down the gas petal and drive faster.

I was nauseated and in pain, so I closed my eyes and took deep breaths, relishing the feel of the fresh air on my face. I don't know how long I was like that—no more than ten minutes, probably—before John spoke again. "I think we've lost them. You can get back into the seat now."

I pushed myself up into the passenger's seat, using my uninjured (or at least, less injured) right hand. My left hand had, by this time, curled up into a claw-like position that I couldn't wrench it out of, and I didn't bother trying. Both my knees had swollen to the size of cantaloupes, and my left ankle looked like it had a softball protruding from the side of it. The snowflake-like markings on my shoulder had begun to fade, though, which was kind of a shame: of all the injuries I had received that day, it was the least ugly. My clothes were stiff with blood. *Whose* blood, I had no idea, and I wasn't sure I wanted to find out.

We were on a two-lane, winding road surrounded by trees. I smelled flowers in the air. John gripped the steering wheel tightly, and I thought I could hear his teeth grinding. "We'll have to ditch the car soon," he said finally. "It's too conspicuous with the broken windows. We'll stop at the next large parking lot we see, and I'll hot-wire another car. I'll need to switch the license plates on this one, too, and I'd like to abandon it off of the side of the road somewhere. Preferably in a ditch or something, somewhere no one will find it for a while. Are you up for driving for a bit?"

I glanced down at my swollen knees. "I don't think so."

John slammed his hand against the steering wheel. "Dammit, Dale. What the hell were you thinking? Isaac sacrificed himself to save your life, and you hovered over his body like an idiot!"

"I was trying to save him!"

"...And then instead of running and hiding like I told you to do, you attacked them! There were at least a hundred of them there. Are you crazy?"

"I don't know! I just..." I couldn't speak anymore. I was sobbing too hard.

"Oh, hell, Dale." He removed a handkerchief from his pocket and handed it to me. I wiped my face and blew my nose. But then it seemed weird to give it back to him, so I shifted it between my hands awkwardly. "Better?" he asked. I nodded.

He pulled something else out of his pocket: a cell phone. He offered it to me, and I took it with my good hand. "Isaac texted me before he died. We need to get rid of this phone before we go much farther, but I wanted to show you first."

I balanced the phone against my thigh, using my right hand to pull up the recent text messages on the touch screen. The messages John spoke of were easy to find; Isaac was the only sender.

I scrolled through the recent texts to the first one time-stamped for that day. It was when Isaac had found me at the park: *get up here asap. she called her friend. thrones may be on to us. we need to bug out.*

A minute after that: *too late. theyre already here.*

Two minutes later: *i have to do something stupid. im sorry, john. there are too many of them, but i have to try. my time is almost up anyway. i will do what i can.*

And then one last one, seconds after the previous: *tell dale shes a good egg. i love you, my friend. thank you for everything.*

Tears filled my eyes again. I picked up the phone in my good hand and threw it out the window as hard as I could. It hit the street beneath us and shattered into pieces. "I think we should go find my mother," I said.

CHAPTER

18

HALF AN HOUR AFTER WE got on the road, we stumbled upon an old service station that had closed for the evening. (I guess when you're in the middle of nowhere, you can close up at five.) We found another older model car that looked like nobody had claimed it in a while. John was able to hot wire it easily, abandoning the green Taurus with the broken back window in the vacated spot.

Several miles farther down the road we found a shopping center with a drug store. John ordered me to get into the back seat and lay my legs flat, if I could. He went inside and bought cold packs, elastic bandages, and a splint for my hand. He also, much to my relief, bought a T-shirt and a pair of sweatpants to replace my torn, bloody clothing. I'd left everything else at Isaac's.

When he got back to the car, I had already arranged myself—as much as I was able—in the back seat. My knees and left ankle were still swollen, but I thought they looked better than they had when we left the park. He probed them with his fingers. When he saw how much I cringed in pain, he broke three of the ice packs, one for each injury. "I'm fairly certain the

injuries to your legs are strictly soft tissue, not bone, so they should heal quickly as long as you keep them stabilized. After you've iced them for half an hour, wrap them up with the elastic bandages."

I grimaced. "That…might be difficult."

"I was afraid you'd say that. Let me see that hand." I held it out to him. It looked warped at this point, clenched into a fist-like position I couldn't move it out of. He poked at it and sighed. "This is going to hurt. Whatever you do, don't scream." I braced myself. John took my fingers with one of his hands and my wrist with the other. Then, he yanked my fingers forward into a "natural" position. I did not scream, but I moaned so loudly that I sounded like a dying elephant. He put the brace on my hand and secured it tightly. "At least two of your knuckles were broken, so it'll take longer to heal."

I nodded, holding back tears. He popped another cold pack—he must have bought every single one they had in the store—and gave it to me. "Keep this on it, too."

"Can I change clothes?" What I really wanted to do was run a hot bath and soak for hours, but I knew it wasn't an option.

"Give yourself a little time to heal first. I don't want you to move too much right now."

The tears I'd been fighting overflowed now. "Please. I just feel so…dirty."

John touched my cheek, wiping the tears away. "All right, don't cry. Lift your arms." I obeyed, and John carefully lifted my torn, bloody shirt over my head. I heard his sharp intake of breath, and I reached up to cover my damaged body and my ill-fitting sports bra. "No, don't move any more than you have to," he said. He stroked his finger along the snowflake marks on my shoulder and chest. "Hell, Dale, these are so close to your heart."

I shrugged, but the move hurt.

"Do they still hurt?" I shook my head. "You're lucky. The ElectraVolt is considered one of our 'crowd control' weapons, but it kills about one in eight supernaturals it's used on. It's the equivalent of being struck by a bolt of lightning."

He traced the marks, as if mesmerized by them. "Will they go away?" I asked.

He nodded. "You'll be just fine. In another day or two, it'll be like it never happened."

The image of Isaac's broken body reared up before me. My eyes flooded with tears. "It's my fault Isaac is dead. I called Nik, and the Thrones figured out where we were. Isaac is dead because of me. Why aren't you yelling at me or something?"

"You're tired, you're injured, and I doubt you can feel any worse than you do right now." More tears ran down my face. John swept them away with his fingers and then pulled me close to him, holding me tightly. "The Thrones shouldn't have been able to get there so quickly," he told me. "They must have already been watching the park. They traced us there before your phone call."

"But Isaac..."

"Isaac made a choice." John ran his fingers through my hair, the motion calming. "At least this way, he got to die on his own terms."

That just set off another wave of tears. John held me for a time. Once I was calm again, he got the shirt out of the bag. "Arms up," he said. I complied.

He pulled off the remnants of my tattered shirt and replaced it with the new one, being careful of my wounded hand. It was green, and it had that institutional big-box store smell. At least it didn't smell like blood. "Thank you," I said. It wasn't a hot bath or a cozy bed, but at least it was *something*.

"I'd like you to wait to put on the pants until your legs heal up a bit. Is that all right?" I nodded. I didn't think I had the dexterity right now to maneuver into the sweatpants on my own, and when I thought about John helping me out of my shorts, my face burned.

We got on the road again. John turned the radio to an AM news station. The calm, even voices soothed me, and I found myself drifting off to sleep. When I opened my eyes again it was dark outside, and we were on a deserted, two-lane highway with no other cars around. But it was the voice on the radio that had woken me, my years on the run having made me vigilant about anything that might necessitate me to go deeper into hiding.

"And out of Vermont, an accident has left eight people dead at the Funland Amusement Park near Newport. According to investigators, the incident was caused by faulty equipment during a scheduled laser light show. According to reports, one of the deceased may have been a park employee. Funland Park officials released a statement saying, 'Our hearts go out to the families of those killed in this tragic accident. We will continue to cooperate with investigators to get any and all relevant information to the victims' families.' In other news..."

John switched the radio off. "Is that it?" I asked. "Is that really what they're going with? An accident?"

John shrugged. "It's the easiest course of action. The Thrones have moles in the media, and in law enforcement, and they do this kind of thing all the time. They spun that massacre at the hospital into a gas leak."

"But anyone who was there will know that it wasn't an accident or part of some pre-planned show."

"It doesn't matter. The Thrones have people who can rewrite memories, do some tweaks to get the story they want out there. And those who can't be rewritten will be taken care of."

I couldn't see his face, because he was in the driver's seat and I was in the back. "You mean they're killed," I said.

"If necessary. But it usually doesn't come to that. People want to believe in things that seem sane and logical to them, things that make sense in their world. Attackers with rocket packs and zeppelins don't make sense. Angels and demons and being caught in the middle of a supernatural war don't make sense. But an accident during a show at an amusement park? That makes perfect sense. How tragic it is. They really ought to be more careful." His voice was flat, like he had told this story a thousand times and he was sick of hearing it. "A few well-timed hints from investigators, a few photographs or a fuzzy video, and you'd be amazed at how much people's memories change. It's actually a lot simpler than having to use our resources to rewrite everyone's memory."

"You said 'our.'" John didn't say anything. "When you were talking about the Thrones, you said 'our resources.' What was that supposed to mean?"

He dug into his pocket and fished out a Werther's candy. He unwrapped the gold foil with one hand and popped it into his mouth. His voice was quiet when he spoke again, and there was an edge of sorrow to it that I'd never heard from him before. "I was with them for a long time, Dale."

Shit. "I know. I'm sorry. I shouldn't have pushed you like that."

"Apology accepted."

We rode in silence for a while longer. The swelling around my knees and ankle subsided and my hand began to itch as the bones knit themselves together. The sensation was uncomfortable, and my neck was getting stiff from being propped against the door. Still, I drifted in and out of consciousness. About an hour later, John spoke again, rousing me from my stupor. "Here's what I don't understand," he said, as if we were already in the middle of a conversation, "when we worked together in training, you were barely able to hold your own. Yet on your way out of the park,

you killed four Thrones. These were men and women I trained. They were among the most disciplined, lethal warriors in the Thrones. But you killed them, with barely a scratch to show for it."

My voice was barely audible. "I'm sorry."

"Don't be. You would be dead if they'd gotten hold of you." His voice was even, unemotional—the voice of an assassin. Never mind that I had just slaughtered four of his protégées. "What I'm trying to figure out is how the hell you did it."

I hesitated. "Adrenaline?"

"Adrenaline. Hmm." I wished I could see his face, read his emotions. "Is that what happened on the night you killed the two women at the homeless shelter?"

"Fuck, John, I don't really want to talk about it." My head was beginning to hurt. I didn't know whether it was the remnants of an injury I'd received or just plain stress.

"If not now, then when?" He lowered his voice. "Dale, I want to trust you. You're not making that easy."

I rubbed my temples. In ten years, I had never told anyone about my Rages, never even hinted at them. John already knew about who I was and what I had done—and he had tried to protect me anyway. Even knowing I was responsible for Isaac's death, he was still trying to protect me. Still, my self-preservation instincts were strong. "What if—hypothetically—I were to tell you that I didn't remember why or how I'd killed those Thrones?"

John's response was slow, as if he were choosing his words carefully. "I would say that it's pretty common, after a traumatic experience, to have some memory gaps."

"Yeah, but what if it's more than just…gaps? What if…"

My breathing quickened, my body going into fight-or-flight mode. John pulled the car over into the shoulder and turned toward me. "Dale, are you…"

"Don't look at me! I can't tell you this if you look at me! So pull back on the road and just…listen, okay?"

Without another word, John turned back around and flipped on the left blinker to signal that he would be pulling back onto the road—completely unnecessary, since we hadn't seen another car for miles. As a distraction, though, it worked well: musing about the turn signal allowed my body to calm itself down enough that I could speak again. "I have these blackouts. I call them Rages."

And so I told him: how for the past ten years I'd been blacking out at random intervals and killing people; how I didn't know how to control or stop them; how I couldn't remember anything that happened when I blacked out; how I'd spent the last decade trying to evade punishment for crimes I didn't even remember. I also told him what had happened earlier: from the time I left the tunnels and made the phone call, until the time the Rage overcame me. "When I saw Isaac fall, I knew he was dead, but I had to stop and check. I couldn't just leave him, John."

"I know. I couldn't have left him, either."

"When the Throne leader approached us, she said something about dissecting his brain…and I just got so *angry*. I couldn't let them do that to him, not even if he was dead. And then I just…blacked out."

John hesitated. "You did protect him," he finally said. "The cops showed up right after we left. The Thrones had to retreat and leave all the bodies behind."

I sniffled. "It's not enough. I should have saved him."

"I know. I should have saved him, too. But he saved us instead."

I hesitated for a long time before speaking again. "Has anyone…I mean…have you ever heard of anything like this? Of other angels or demons having blackouts?"

"No. Nothing like that."

The answer was like a dagger through my chest. "Of course not." Once again, I wiped tears away from my face. "Stupid me. I was hoping it was like some kind of Incredible Hulk thing for demons or something."

"I didn't say it couldn't happen, just that I've never heard of it. I'm not an expert."

"No, but you've been around a really long time. Three hundred years, from what I've heard."

He shook his head. "You're trying to change the subject. It won't work. I think that your mother can answer a lot of your questions, maybe even help you figure out where these Rages are coming from."

We were silent for a long time. It was John who spoke first. "You didn't kill Brad Kinnard because you were jealous that he'd taken your friend to the prom, did you?"

"Jesus Christ, John." I rubbed my good hand through my hair, wincing when it got caught in some dried blood. "What the hell does that have to do with anything?"

"It's just something I've been thinking about." He tapped his hand against the steering wheel. "I spoke to people who knew you back in Pittsburgh—not just your aunt and the teachers you pissed off along the way, but people who really knew you. They said that you and Julie Wainwright were extremely close, and that you were very protective of her."

"Yeah, so?"

"If you were protective of her, why would you kill her sweetheart in a jealously-fueled blackout? The story has never made sense, and it makes even less sense now that I know you."

I leaned my head against the window and closed my eyes. "I wasn't jealous of Brad Kinnard. I found out he had slipped something into Julie's drink and taken her upstairs to a hotel room. I managed to get the room number and key from a desk clerk—I didn't realize it then, but I must have been using my powers—and I got into their room. She was unconscious, and he was on top of her. Next thing I remember, he was dead. Strangled. That was my first Rage." I shook my head. "You know, there was this moment when I thought 'maybe I didn't kill him.' I didn't remember doing it. But I was the only one there. Julie was still unconscious. And…there were marks on his neck, from the strangulation. I wore three rings that night, and I could match all of them to the marks on his neck. Pretty damn convincing evidence, right?"

"Julie never said it was rape—or if she did, it wasn't in any documentation I could find," he said.

I shrugged. "Who would have believed her? Brad was the class president, had a three-point-nine GPA, and came from one of the most influential families in Pittsburgh. Julie was drunk white trash and she wasn't a virgin. I know it's been a while since you've had to deal with it, but that's how things work in the human world."

"They might have believed it if you'd stuck around to corroborate the story."

I sighed. "Maybe. Maybe not. When I realized what I'd done, all I could hear was my aunt's voice, telling me what a fuck-up I was and how I was tainted on the inside. And at that moment, I realized…she was *right*. She'd always been right. I'd just killed someone. I *was* tainted."

"You tried to protect her."

"Hell of a lot of good it did."

"It was something, which was more than anyone else did."

I didn't reply. A few minutes later, John pulled off of the road into a gas station. Dawn hadn't arrived yet, but the sky was beginning to lighten. I opened the car door and put my feet on the ground, slowly easing weight onto my legs. Besides being a little stiff, they seemed completely back to normal. I stood up, and they held. My hand, on the other hand, still ached and itched, telling me that, as John had predicted, it would take longer to heal. "So where are we going?" I asked.

John shrugged. "Up to you, really. We're trying to find your mother. You probably have a better guess of where she would be than I do."

Unfortunately, I didn't. My mother had abandoned me—and I was still having a hard time accepting that, after all the years I'd spent believing she was dead. She hadn't exactly left a forwarding address. Hell, I'd never even seen a picture of her. The only person I knew who might have been able to tell me a little about her was my father, and he was long dead.

Except…he wasn't the only one. And the only other person I could talk to was the last person on Earth I wanted to see. I turned to John, knots forming in my stomach.

"We're going to Pittsburgh," I said.

CHAPTER

19

When we arrived at my Aunt Barbara's house, it was around seven in the morning. We'd stopped at a rest area outside of town, and I'd changed into the clean sweatpants and done my best to tame my hair. I'd washed my hands and face in the sink until they felt raw, and at least I felt marginally better. Not that any of it mattered. I could have shown up covered in diamonds with a bag full of money to give her, and it wouldn't have made her despise me any less.

We pulled into the driveway. I got out of the car and peered through the windows of the garage door. My aunt's silver Ford F-150 was parked in there, just as it was the day I left. I took a breath. "She's home."

"It's seven o'clock on a Saturday. Where would you expect her to be?"

I shrugged. "I don't know. Maybe I was just hoping."

John started toward the door, but I remained in the driveway, frozen. When John realized I wasn't right behind him, he turned around and came back to me. "I don't know if I can do this," I told him. "She'll call the police. I know she will. And if I have to use my power on her...I don't think I can."

He looked at me solemnly. "You can do this."

My breathing was getting shallower, my heart rate faster. "No, I don't think I can."

"You can." He took my hands in his. The shock of his touch, the electric zing through my system, was enough to shock me out of my panic…at least temporarily. "You are strong and brave and capable. And if you're not sure, think of that little girl who moved in here after her father died. Your aunt should have protected and taken care of you. But she didn't, did she?" I said nothing. "Think of the teenager who ran away and changed her whole identity after she killed Brad Kinnard. You were just trying to protect your friend, and if your aunt had loved you just a little, you might have come home. But you didn't, because you already knew what she'd do."

"What's your point?"

"The point is, your aunt was supposed to protect *you*. She failed. Whatever you do to her today, you won't be hurting her or incapacitating her in any way. But you will be enabling yourself to live a safer life— something she should have given you in the first place." He grasped my hands more firmly. "You are not doing anything wrong."

I wasn't sure whether I believed him, but his solid, steady voice calmed me down. I took a breath. "Okay. Let's go." Before I could talk myself out of it, I walked up to the door and rang the bell. Thirty seconds later, she opened it.

She looked older than I remembered, thinner; she was over seventy now, I realized. But, I had to admit—begrudgingly—she was still an attractive woman: slate gray hair, gray eyes, flawless skin that had only just begun to wrinkle. She reminded me of Nurse Ratched in *One Flew Over the Cuckoo's Nest*, but I wasn't sure whether it was because she actually looked like Louise Fletcher or because that's who I saw when I looked at her. There was a flash of surprise in her eyes when she recognized me, but she masked it almost instantly. "Oh, it's you," she said.

"I…I'd like to talk to you. Please?" Ten seconds in my aunt's presence, and I'd become a stuttering fool again. Ugh.

She shrugged. "As if I have any choice. Come in."

Well. No turning back now. I stepped through the doorway with John right behind me. As we stepped through the door, I thought I felt him tap my arm, the familiar tingle rushing through my skin. I turned to him. "What is it?" I asked.

He gave me a puzzled look. "I didn't say anything."

Hmmm.

I followed Aunt Barbara up the split-entry stairs to the living room, John trailing us both. One look in the living room told me that I had been right. Nothing had changed: not the beige shag carpet on the floor nor the plastic-covered furniture in the living room. The house still smelled like the rose potpourri she'd been buying as long as I could remember, and there wasn't a speck of dust to be found.

The only thing different about the house was the security system panel by the front door, but that didn't surprise me: Aunt Barbara had always been paranoid about being robbed. As if anyone would want to rob a split-level house in suburban Pittsburgh filled with knick-knacks that were forty years out of date.

I'd forgotten the pictures, though, a collage of framed images of her long-dead parents lining the wall at the top of the stars…and pictures of my long-dead father.

I eyed one of the pictures, an old, black-and-white photograph of my father riding a tricycle with my aunt trailing behind him. He was very young at the time, maybe only three or four. My aunt was already a young woman, pretty and vibrant, without the austere harshness I'd always associated with her. She'd been almost seventeen when he was born, already more a mother to him than a sister. My grandmother, their mother, had died of

cancer when my Dad was ten; his father had followed less than a year later. "He died of a broken heart," Dad told me. Even at five I thought a broken heart was a silly thing to die from, but less than a year later my dad was dead himself. It might have been a drunk driver that killed my father, but I wondered now—had he died of a broken heart, too? If Amara had stayed, would he have fought harder to pull back from the abyss?

Aunt Barbara cleared her throat, startling me. She sat down on the couch, causing the plastic cover to squeak. "What are you doing here, Karen?"

"That's not my name anymore," I said automatically, before realizing what a stupid idea it was to give my aunt any more information about my new life than I had to.

She shrugged. "I don't give a damn. What do you want?"

I turned away from her, back toward the picture. I may not have been that awkward seventeen-year-old who ran away from home because she couldn't face the consequences of her crime, but in the line of Aunt Barbara's harsh glare, I sure as hell felt like her. I remembered all the nights I spent here crying, desperately wishing to be taken away, dreaming of having my father back for just one more day to tell me he loved me, to tell me I was all right. "Dad looks so happy in this picture," I said.

She tightened her lips and nodded. "He was always happy. He was a happy little boy."

There was a hint of emotion in her voice, something I couldn't quite catch. I looked back at the picture. She was laughing; even in the faded, colorless print, her eyes were full of vivacity and life. I had never seen her look like that, not once. In the years that I'd lived with her, I never even remembered seeing her smile. How had I been so stupid, so self-absorbed, to miss what was right in front of my face? "You loved him, didn't you?"

She spoke in a flat voice. "He was my baby brother. Of course I loved him. Why are you here, Karen?"

I didn't remind her about my name again. She wouldn't have cared, and it's not like it really mattered much, anyway. Here, in my aunt's house, I would always be Karen Fowler, unwanted orphan and teenage hellion. "I came to find out whether you have any information about my mother."

She raised her eyebrows. "I'm not sure I should tell you."

I reached for her mind—I wasn't going to control her, not yet, but I just wanted to check—and I almost retreated in surprise. There she was, dear, sweet Aunt Barbara, the scourge of my childhood, and her mind was easier to breach than any of the others I'd encountered. It was like her walls were made of Swiss cheese.

I poked at the holes. They were jagged and pointy around the edges. Had I caused that? No, it wasn't possible. I felt when my power was activating, even when I hadn't known what it was. There's no way I could have done so much damage as a child and just not noticed. I didn't think so, anyway. So if I hadn't caused those holes, what had? Was her mind just naturally broken? Either way, it would be so easy to get into her mind—almost too easy. There was a part of me that was so tempted. She had caused me so much pain growing up, and it would have been so easy. "I can be very persuasive," I said finally, and then I almost rolled my own eyes. Really? I sounded like I belonged in some bad spy movie.

My aunt just rolled her eyes. "Yes. There is that." She sighed. "Let's just get this over with."

I sat down on the blue chair across from the couch. John remained by the stairs, standing sentry. I started with the softball questions. Maybe I was afraid to ask the real ones. "How did my parents meet?" I asked.

"I don't know. He never told me. Does it matter?"

No, I guess it didn't matter, not really. "Why did you tell me she was dead all those years?"

"I wanted him to tell you the truth from the beginning, but Steven thought otherwise. I would have told you everything after he died, but I couldn't go against his wishes, and I still won't. Not if I can help it."

It was the first time any trace of emotion had entered her voice. I looked at John desperately. "I don't want to do it," I said.

"She's the only one who might have information about your mother. Without her, where could we even begin?" he said.

This was true. But the thought of controlling her mind just made me feel icky inside. With her cratered mind and outdated furniture, Aunt Barbara had ceased to be scary. She was just...sad. Still, it didn't change the fact that my mother was alive, and she'd hidden that from me all those years.

I dug deep inside myself and found my anger, the anger of a teenage girl who had no choice but to run away after prom night, because she knew the only member of her family was looking for an excuse to get rid of her. I stoked the anger, let it grow. Then, with a deep breath, I pushed into her fracture mind. "You will answer all of our questions about my parents, and you won't call the police."

Most of the people I had mind controlled had gone glassy-eyed, but Aunt Barbara's remained clear and sharp. Her mind wasn't even putting up a token resistance. "The first time I met your mother was when your father brought her to Christmas dinner, about six months before they were married. Steven and I never talked about his dating life, so I hadn't even realized he was seeing anyone until she showed up at the door. You look like her."

It didn't sound like a compliment. "Well, I don't have any pictures of her, so I wouldn't know."

"You don't need any pictures. Just look in the mirror. It's uncanny."

I didn't know what to say to that. "So what happened?"

"What do you think? That night, he announced they were getting married. It was obvious he was crazy about her, but there was something strange about that woman, something I didn't like right from the beginning. I tried to tell him, but he wouldn't listen. Six months later I was sitting in a church, watching my baby brother make the worst mistake of his life. You were born about a year later."

I stiffened. Whatever might have happened between my parents, whatever she might have thought about my mother, *I* was the result of that pairing. John put his hand on my shoulder, just firmly enough for me to know that he was there. "How long after I was born did my mother disappear?"

She rubbed her temples with her fingers, like she had a headache. "About six months or so."

"So she just…vanished?"

Aunt Barbara furrowed her eyebrows in confusion. "No, of course not. She didn't vanish. We made her disappear."

I gaped at her, but she just continued to speak calmly. "Steven knocked on my door in the middle of the night, and he brought you with him. He told me that he had discovered Amy had ties to an organized crime family, and that people from her old life were after her. They were the type of people who wouldn't hesitate to use Steven—or even you—to get to her. I could tell he was lying, though—Steven was a horrible liar, even as a boy. So I pushed him. Then he told me some inarticulate nonsense about angels and demons. I didn't believe it, but I could tell he did."

"So what did you do?" I asked.

She shrugged. "I did what he asked me to do: I helped him make Amy disappear. He moved to another neighborhood where no one had known them and fabricated a story about her death. Cancer, we said. It was all very tragic. We even had an obituary placed in the newspaper. Afterward, I tried

to talk him into having some kind of psychiatric evaluation, but he refused. I didn't push because he had his hands full taking care of you, and because he seemed more stable once Amy was out of his life. You know the rest."

Yes. My father had spent the next six years telling me my mother was dead, until he'd been killed himself in a head-on collision with a drunk driver. I'd moved in with Aunt Barbara, who always made it very clear that she wanted nothing to do with me. Jesus. It sounded like some kind of soap opera. "Is this all true?"

She fixed me with a hard stare. "You know very well I can't lie to you right now."

Right, because she was under my mind-control power. Except that she'd said she didn't believe my dad when he'd told her about Amara and angels and demons. And now, she knew exactly what I was doing and how it affected her. And she had gigantic holes in her brain. "When did you see my mother again?"

Aunt Barbara looked right at me. "Right after your father died."

CHAPTER

THE ROOM SPUN.

The hot chocolate I'd grabbed on the road swirled in my stomach. The potpourri smell suddenly became overwhelming, like all the roses were dying at once. I ran to the bathroom.

I was flushing the toilet when I heard a tap on the door. "Are you okay?" John's voice.

"Fine. Great. Fantastic." I scrubbed my hands until they were red. Then I sat on the floor and rested my head against the cabinet. "She came back, John. My mother came back, and my aunt never told me."

"I know."

"She was alive all those years, and no one ever told me."

John came into the bathroom and sat down next to me on the floor. "I know this has been a lot for you," he said. "We can always come back tomorrow."

"No. I'm all right now." I stood up and splashed cold water on my face. "Let's go."

I don't know what John saw in my expression, but he nodded. We walked back into the living room together, where my aunt was still sitting on the couch. "You always did have a weak stomach," she said. "You got that much from your father, at least."

"I don't want to be here any more than you want me here, so let's cut to the chase. You saw my mother after Dad died."

She gave me a small smile. "I'm glad to see you've finally grown into your gumption, Karen. You need that, as a woman in this world. It was one of the things I admired about your mother. Amy always had gumption, too. I could have liked her, if she hadn't been ruining my brother. At least, before I knew what she was."

I clenched my teeth. "Quit the bullshit, Barbara. What happened after my father died? When did you see my mother again? What did she say to you?"

"She asked me to take care of you." A sharp intake of breath. "She made me take care of you."

She tapped her finger against the arm of the couch, her only betraying gesture, but she didn't say anything else. "You wouldn't have taken care of me just because I was your niece?"

She hesitated. "No."

It wasn't a surprise. I'd always known my aunt didn't like me. But to hear her just admit it like that. My eyes filled with tears in spite of myself. "Why not?"

She got up and went to the window, facing away from me. "Even after Amy left, your father was insistent that her story about demons and angels was true. And as you grew, I noticed things. You weren't...normal."

"What are you talking about? I was just a little kid!"

"A 'kid' who never so much as got the sniffles or scraped her knee. A 'kid' who had to be pulled out of gym class in first grade because you

were so much faster and stronger than the other kids. A 'kid' who could convince all the other kids to play hide-and-seek as soon as you got to the park, even if every last one of them was happily playing kickball beforehand. Your father insisted there was nothing wrong with you, that it was perfectly normal childhood behavior, but I heard him telling you, over and over again, to be nice to the other children and let them play their games if they wanted to."

God, I remembered those talks. "You have to stop telling the other kids what to do," he always said. But what he had told my aunt was right, in a sense. It's normal for a kid to want everyone else to do what they want. What's not normal is for a kid to be able to force the other kids to do it.

My dad knew. My dad knew I had these abilities, and he had been trying to help me control them. My head spun.

My aunt, not sensing (or not caring about) my distress, continued. "After I started to suspect what Steven had told me was true, I asked around. I wondered if, perhaps, an exorcism would be the proper route..."

"An exorcism? I'm not Linda Blair, for God's sake!"

"Yes, well, that's what I found out. There are people—scholars, let's say— who are well aware of the presence of demons and angels among us. They told me what I needed to know about who and what you were. I couldn't exorcise the demon inside you when it's part of your very makeup."

"I'm surprised you didn't try anyway." I pinched the bridge of my nose. "So this all happened before Dad died?" She nodded. "Did you tell him any of this?"

"I didn't tell him anything he didn't already know."

I sighed. "So what happened when my mother came?"

She was still staring out the window. I glanced outside, wondering whether she saw something I didn't—wondering whether, somehow, she'd managed to go against my compulsion and call the police—but all I saw was

a young girl riding her bicycle up and down the cul-de-sac. She couldn't have been much older than I was when I came to live with my aunt. "Two days after your father died, your mother showed up at my door. She asked me what my plans were for you, now that Steven had passed away. When I told her that I did not intend to take you in, she...commanded me to take care of you."

I heard the hitch in her voice when she said it, and I thought about the holes on the shell of her mind. Is that what I was doing to people every time I invaded their minds? I reached out for her mind again, touching the jagged edges of the holes and the hairline fractures splintering out from them. Aunt Barbara had known exactly what I was doing when I forced my way into her mind, and she hadn't fought it. Maybe she didn't have any fight left. "She probably should have just let me go to foster care."

"You wouldn't have gone to foster care." Her voice was hoarse. "The scholars I told you about? They said they had resources for children like you."

I glanced at John, wondering if he had any idea who these scholars were or what kind of "resources" they'd have for a half-demon child. He shrugged. "What kind of 'resources'?" I asked her.

"I don't know. I didn't ask. But I thought it would be better for you."

Better for me? She hadn't even bothered to ask what they planned to do, but she thought it would be better for me? I'd read *Flowers in the Attic* too many times to believe that people always had children's best interests at heart, even family. Maybe especially family. But she couldn't lie to me now, so some part of her must have believed it, and I was just too drained to work up the appropriate level of outrage. "Anything else? Did she ask to see me?"

"No, she never asked to see you. She just told me to raise you, and to do my best to take care of you. And I always did. Even the police assured me that it wasn't my fault that you got jealous and killed that boy."

"Do you know where she's living?"

"No."

There wasn't any wiggle room in that answer, but something told me to push a little harder. "Do you know where she was living when she came to see you that night?"

"Yes." She clenched her teeth, almost spitting out the words. "She was at Zamorski House."

Holy shit. Zamorski House was one of the most famous architectural landmarks in western Pennsylvania. The world-famous architect, Virgil Kaufmann, built it as a vacation home for the Zamorski family—who founded a chain of department stores—back in the thirties. The Zamorskis opened it up for school tours sometime later, when they stopped using it as a private residence. After the last Zamorski heir died in the eighties, the Pennsylvania Historical Society made an offer on the property, but they were outbid by a private buyer, who ended the tours completely.

Zamorski House was near Erie. My mother had been two hours away while I was growing up, and I had never even known it.

I got up. My throat felt dry. "That's all I needed."

I walked down the stairs, and John followed. When I got to the landing, I glanced up. My aunt had moved away from the window, and now she was staring at the wall of photographs I had observed on my way inside. If I had to guess, I would say she was looking at the same photo I had been captivated by, the one of her and my father. And then it just hit me: her entire family was gone. Her parents were long dead. Her brother was dead. He might have been my father, but he was also the boy she'd practically raised since infancy. Rightly or wrongly, she blamed my mother for his

death, and she couldn't blame my mother without blaming me, too. Maybe some people could have overlooked it and loved me anyway, but she just didn't have it in her. Maybe she just hated my mother too much. Or maybe she just loved my father too much. Whatever it was, I didn't think it had anything to do with me being a demon. "I miss him, too," I said.

She turned toward me, her hands on her hips. "You couldn't possibly remember him."

"Not enough. Not as much as I'd like." If things were different, I would have stayed and asked her about tricycle rides and Christmas dinners and all the memories I'd never have. But she wasn't that kind of aunt, and I hated her a little for that. Still, I was overcome by the urge to tell her something, to show her the true me. "I didn't kill Brad Kinnard because I was jealous," I said. "He...hurt Julie. I was trying to protect her."

"Oh, I know that. Not the details, but I knew it wasn't jealousy. I knew as soon as the police came to me with that cockamamie story that it wasn't what happened." She turned around and faced me. "Contrary to what you probably believe, I'm not stupid. You are many things, but you have never been malicious. What you are, though, is very, very dangerous. Whatever happened that night, whatever set you off, just proves that I was right to be worried. You're stronger than everyone else, faster than everyone else, and you can do things none of us humans could even imagine. You may not be malicious, and you may not be evil, but you do not belong among our kind. You never did."

The words stung more than I could have imagined. "Well, I guess that's it, then."

I reached for the doorknob, feeling a prickle on my skin as I crossed into the threshold. Suddenly, John grabbed my hand and pulled me away from the door. "Don't."

"I can't be here anymore."

"Wait," he commanded. He pulled back the curtains on the mini-window framing the door. The little girl riding her bicycle was gone, and the street was deserted—eerily so. No families heading off to breakfast, nobody running off to do their grocery shopping, no one jogging along the sidewalk or mowing their lawn before the day got too hot. I slid my gaze to my right, where the new security alarm panel was embedded into the wall. I hadn't noticed it much before, because it looked just like every other security system I'd ever seen. But now I took note of the brand name across the bottom: AziziCorp. Oh, hell. "Aunt Barbara, what did you do?"

But no answer came. I ran back up the stairs just in time to hear the back door slam. Seconds later, Barbara ran into the front with her hands over her head, screaming, "They're in there! They're in there."

A bang echoed through the air, loud enough to make the windows rattle. When we peered outside again, Aunt Barbara's body lay face down on the street, a puddle of blood growing beneath her.

I cried out, but John covered my mouth quickly and pulled me to the floor, beneath the line of sight of the windows. He crouched in front of me. "You have to be quiet now, all right?" I nodded, and he released my mouth. "Okay. Now we're going to peek out the window. Try not to ruffle the curtains or make any noise. We don't want them to know where we are."

I nodded. We rose to our knees slowly and peeked out the window by the door, John on one side and me on the other. The scene had changed. My aunt's body still lay on the pavement, but now the people who shot her were beginning to emerge from behind bushes and trees and the neighbors' cars. I counted two dozen of them before I stopped trying. They wore dark gray military-style fatigues, Kevlar vests, helmets, and sunglasses. But what really bothered me is that they each carried very large rifles, the kind you needed two hands to use, and they had strapped extra ammunition

across their chests like they were all Rambo or something. I got back on the ground. "These don't look like the Thrones we've seen before," I whispered.

"That's because they're not." John ran his fingers through his hair, nervous energy twitching through his body. "Back in the fifties, during the Red Scare, the government got wind that there were people out there who were *other,* not human, but living and acting like them. CIA, NSA, FBI, and all the military branches came together to investigate the 'supernatural menace.' They formed an interagency working group called the Zeta Coalition."

"They're the scholars my aunt talked about."

"Must be. Over the years they've become less an investigative group, and more a bunch of paramilitary nut-jobs."

I risked a peek out the window again. They still stood there, apparently oblivious to my aunt's body, waiting…for what, I didn't know. "So they're a government organization?"

"They used to be. Rumor has it they broke away from the government decades ago. I have no idea who they answer to anymore."

A man—they were all men, every last one of them—stepped to the edge of the driveway with a bullhorn in his hands. He was muscular and compact, the perfect model for one of those old G.I. Joe action figures. "We have the house surrounded. Come out with your hands up."

I looked at John desperately. "What the hell are we going to do?"

"I don't know. I need to think."

G.I. Joe spoke again. "If you come out right now, no one needs to get hurt."

Somebody's already been hurt, asshole. "I don't think we have time to think," I said.

"Just…a minute."

G.I. Joe's voice echoed through the air again. "If you don't come out, we will be forced to shoot at the house."

I grabbed John's arm and pulled us away from the windows, where we'd be less likely to be struck by glass. What I didn't know was whether the walls were strong enough to withstand bullets—particularly bullets that looked like they were designed to take down a rogue dinosaur. "John, we need to do something!"

"You're right," he said. And then he kissed me.

He tasted like butterscotch and a hint of coffee. The kiss was rough and desperate, his tongue sweeping against my mouth until I opened for him. His hand fisted in my hair, pulling me closer. I wrapped my legs around him and felt the bulge of his erection pressing against me. *Yes, yes!* I touched him all over, the tight muscles of his arms, the bristly stubble on his cheeks, that soft triangle of skin between his neck and shoulder. Whatever he asked, whatever he wanted…I would give it to him.

He broke the kiss first and we stared at each other for one desperate, crazy moment. Then, without warning, he jumped up and opened the door, his hands in the air. "I surrender!"

CHAPTER

TIME SLOWED.

I ran outside after John.

The Zeta Coalition aimed their guns, readying to shoot.

I seized their minds. "Stop!"

The men froze in place. They must have still been breathing, but you wouldn't have known it to look at them. They held so perfectly still that they could have been mannequins in a store window. Several of them already had their fingers on the trigger and their eyes lined with the sights, just one breath away from killing us both.

John gaped at me. "You have them? All of them?"

I peered into my mind. "It's like...I'm holding the strings to a bunch of helium balloons."

"Is it hurting you?"

I shook my head, strumming a mental finger along their strings. God, the power. "I could make them all dance."

"Dale?" When I didn't respond, he shook me by the shoulders. "Dale!" I met his eyes, still consumed by all the minds I had in my head. "How long can you hold them?"

"I don't know. Forever, maybe." I walked over to one of the men and punched him in the face. His nose crunched beneath my fist, and blood gushed down over his mouth and onto his pristine gray uniform. He didn't move. I laughed.

"Dale!" John shook me again. "How far is your range?"

"I don't know. Isaac and I were never able to test it." Pain lanced through me at the thought of Isaac, and I felt my control slip a little. I took a breath and grabbed on to the balloon strings again. I couldn't screw up. Not this time.

"Dale? Shit, hang on to them. We need to go. Now." John opened the car door, and I hopped into the passenger's seat. He ran around the car and got in the driver's side. "Just hang on to them as long as you can."

THE BALLOON STRINGS SNAPPED ABOUT half a mile away from my aunt's house, leaving me feeling strangely empty after having all those minds in my head. "They're gone," I said.

John glanced over at me, then back at the road. "You all right?"

"I don't know." I wrapped my arms around myself and shivered. "Is it cold? I feel cold?"

John turned the heater switch, filling the car with warm, stale air. "We need to find someplace to hide for a few hours."

"Won't they be looking for us?"

"They'll expect us to run. They'll be checking the roads out of the city. If we stay put for a few hours, it'll throw them off the trail."

I hesitated for a moment. "I know a place."

John followed my directions until we got to an access road, barely large enough to earn the name "road." We made a sharp turn and drove down it until we arrived at an old railway tunnel in the woods, dug deep into a hillside, far enough away from the street that no one could see or hear us. The walls of the tunnel were covered in graffiti. If there had ever been actual railroad tracks in the tunnel, they were long gone, the tunnel lingering only as a teenage make-out spot and a convenient place for the county to store rock salt in the winter. It had rained recently, and a narrow channel of water flowed through the tunnel into the dirt behind it.

"Flash your lights into the tunnel three times."

John furrowed his eyebrows. "Why?"

"Just do it."

John obeyed. When we received nothing in response, I said, "All right, pull in."

The tunnel was just wide enough and long enough for a single vehicle. But since there were only trees on the other side, this was the only way to drive in. If anyone else was going to join us, they'd be doing it on foot. "What is this place?" John asked.

"It's called the Faceless Tunnel. Years ago, an employee from the electric company was working on some downed power lines nearby. He picked up a live one, and he was electrocuted. When they found his body, his face had been completely burned off."

"Damn."

"They say he hasn't figured out he's dead, and he still roams to this day. The lights were the signal that the electric company used to use to signal other workers that they were okay. It's supposed to keep the Faceless Man at bay. I don't know if the whole 'ghost' thing is true, but if it is, and if the lights give him some comfort...can't hurt, right?"

"I hunt demons for a living, and I find that story terrifying," he said.

"Well, you're welcome, I guess." I got out of the car and slammed the door so hard it hurt my hand. I walked over to the wall and stared at the graffiti. Names of lovers long gone; cheers for the Steelers and the Penguins; random designs, some of which actually resembled art. One brave soul wrote "Faceless Man was here, 1988." Yeah. If the legendary tunnel haunt had really shown up, I'm sure some random teenage chucklehead would have stuck around to document it. In spray paint, no less.

I kicked the wall. Then I kicked it again and again, over and over, until my foot throbbed. "Fuck!"

"Dale..."

"What?" My scream echoed through the tunnel and faded into nothingness. All I could hear was flowing water, and the sound of my own breathing. John didn't speak. He just stared at me, watching, waiting. "All this time, my mother was *alive*, living two hours away, and no one ever bothered to tell me. What the *fuck* am I supposed to think about that?"

"I don't know." His voice was raspy.

I shook my head. "So what good are you, then?"

John didn't respond. I took several shaky breaths before I spoke again. "I can't do this anymore."

"We're almost there. Can't you..."

"Isaac is dead, John, because of me. My aunt is dead, because of me. If I had just left New York and gone on the run again, they'd still be alive."

"What about the Rages?" John asked. "Your mother might be the only person who can help you control them and live a more normal life."

I turned toward him. "What the hell do they *matter*, John? In case you've forgotten, I'm still a serial killer. Regardless of whether my mother can help me control the Rages or not, I've got a trail of bodies behind me a mile long."

"Don't say that."

"Yesterday you said that Nik and Chaz weren't really my friends, that they didn't know anything about me. And you were right. But that's all I have." My eyes filled with tears. "Those pretend lives and pretend friendships, that's all I get. Otherwise...I'm alone, John. I'm always alone."

John gave me a sad look and took a step closer to me. I put my hands up, stopping him. "No, don't you dare feel sorry for me! Don't you fucking dare! I don't need it, and I don't deserve it."

"Dale..." his voice was barely more than a whisper. He took a step closer.

The tears that had been threatening spilled over my cheeks. He touched my face, wiping them away. "I'm always alone, too."

He kissed me.

He kissed like a man who was about to be executed, like a man who knew it was going to be his last minutes on Earth but was still desperately clinging to every last breath, desperately hoping for one last hour. I could feel his touch vibrating in my skin, like electricity running through my veins. It was the same as other times we had touched, but *more*. And more was all I wanted. I wrapped my arms around him and thrust my tongue into his mouth.

He groaned and twirled us around, pushing us against the car, bracing us there for support. He reached behind us and opened the back door. We tumbled into the seat, him on top of me, never bothering to stop touching one another.

He ripped my shirt over my head, but he had some trouble with my too-small, blood-crusted sports bra. When he finally got it, he threw the stretchy fabric to the floor of the car and took my nipple between his teeth. A rush of arousal ran through my body.

I took off his shirt and ran my fingernails down his taut chest. He inhaled sharply and kissed me again, his lips bruising against mine. He had

trouble getting my shorts and underwear down, so I wriggled to help him along. "Arch up to me," he said, his voice rough. I did, and he grabbed my hips, steadying me, before he found my core with his tongue.

I cried out and tried to thrust against his touch. But the harder I moved, the harder his fingers dug into my side, stopping me. His assault was merciless, overloading my senses. It was like he had a psychic connection with my body. When I would get close, he'd pull back, leaving me aching. "John..." I gasped finally.

He met my stare. His cheeks were flushed, and he had a wild look in his eyes. Taking my clit into his mouth, he bit gently. I exploded, wrapping my legs around him as my body shook.

I wanted more, needed more. I unzipped his pants and took his penis in my hands. He groaned. "You're killing me, Dale."

"Good." I positioned him at my entrance and rubbed against him. "Now, John."

"Are you sure?" he asked. His hands were shaking.

"I am so sure."

He kissed me, softer and gentler than before. "Brace your legs against the seats," he said when he broke away. I did so, and he pushed inside of me.

It hurt, and it was wonderful. I wanted skin, I wanted to touch his body and know whether his golden tan was as warm as it looked. I wanted to lick him all over and find out if he tasted as good as he smelled. I leaned up to kiss him, and he used the opportunity to grab my hips and thrust deeper. Another orgasm began to build.

It was all too much, and I couldn't think, couldn't speak, couldn't breathe. All I could do was dig my nails into his shoulders, pull him toward me, and gasp one word into his ear: *more.*

He thrusted harder and faster then, and that was enough to send me over the edge, my body clenching around him. He whispered my name

into my ear as his rhythm grew erratic. I held on tighter and looked into his eyes. He shuddered and pulled out before he came, spilling onto my skin.

I closed my eyes and let myself feel him, the tingle of his skin on mine, the warm butterscotch smell of his skin. I felt him reach up into the front seat, heard the pop of the glove compartment opening. Seconds later, there were tissues on my stomach, wiping away the semen. "Are you okay?" he asked.

I smiled without opening my eyes. "I'm great."

"I should throw these away."

John got up and left the car, and I felt chilly without his body heat nearby. I shut the door, and managed to wriggle into my sweatpants and T-shirt. By the time John returned, I had curled up on the back seat and nearly fallen asleep. "That's not a safe position to be in while the car is moving," he said.

"So don't move the car." I cracked my eyes and looked at him.

"We still need to find your mother."

"Don't wanna. We've been running and running and running, and I'm tired. So let's just...not do anything for a while."

"All right. Just for a little while."

John popped the trunk open and exited the car. A minute or so later, he returned with one of those metallic blankets you often find in roadside emergency kits. He covered me with it, tucking the ends around my body, and kissed my forehead softly. "Forgive me, my Little Demon," he whispered, holding my body tight against his. I wasn't sure what he was apologizing for, but by that time my eyes had closed again, and I was drifting off to sleep. My last thought before unconsciousness was, *Don't call me Little Demon.*

I DON'T KNOW HOW LONG I slept. It must have been a while, because the late afternoon sun was shining in through the back window, heating the car to uncomfortable temperatures. I sat up and rubbed my eyes. The car was empty, and I didn't see anyone nearby. I stepped out of the car and looked around. "John?" I called as loudly as I dared. If those Zeta Coalition assholes had managed to track us down, I didn't want to give myself away.

Nothing.

I walked up the hill closer to the street and called his name again. Still nothing. A car approached, and I folded my arms across my chest self-consciously. I hadn't bothered to put a bra on before I left the car, and now I felt naked. But the car drove past me without even slowing down. I walked back down toward the car, hoping I'd see John there, maybe with some doughnuts and hot chocolate.

And…nothing.

What if the Zeta Coalition had gotten him? Or the Thrones?

But that didn't make sense. My years on the run had made me a light sleeper, and I hadn't heard anything out of the ordinary. No yelling, no fighting, not even any unusual animal noises. Furthermore, if the Zeta Coalition or the Thrones had found him here, why hadn't they taken me, too? I had been alone, asleep, and barely dressed—not my brightest move, considering we were hiding from people who were trying to kill us. But instead, John was gone, and I'd been left in the car alone and undisturbed.

Suddenly I remembered his last words before I fell asleep. *Forgive me, Dale.* I'd been too out of it at the time to process what it meant, but could it be…he *knew* he was leaving?

No. I wouldn't accept that. John and I had been through so much together in the last few weeks. He wouldn't just pick up and leave.

So I waited.

By the time it got dark, a few things became clear.

John wasn't coming back.

There was still a part of me that worried that maybe he'd been taken, wondered whether I should mount a rescue campaign. But I was a pragmatist. That wasn't what was going on here. John had left. He had known he was going to leave, and that's why he asked for my forgiveness after we'd had sex. Maybe all the running and fearing for his life had finally gotten to him. Or maybe he just didn't find me that attractive and was afraid I'd get all clingy after sex. Maybe if I'd been just a little more…no, I wasn't going to do that, wasn't going to beat myself up over some guy, especially when I wasn't even sure why he'd left!

But he was gone. That fact, at least, I couldn't argue with.

So what the hell was I going to do now?

Before my visit with Aunt Barbara, before I'd had sex with John and screwed everything up, I knew what my plan was: I was going to go find my mother, because I hoped she could give me some insight into my Rages and how to control them. I didn't want to kill people anymore, to leave dead bodies behind everywhere I went. I had told John the truth. For ten years, I'd always been alone. But something had happened to me recently. I wanted more than that. And maybe it had started in New York, with having Nik and Chaz—people who actually considered me a "friend" rather than just someone passing through their lives—but being around John had solidified it. He knew who I was and what I was and what I had done, and he still treated me like a regular person. Like someone who mattered. When we were on the run together, it was the first time in more than a decade I'd felt like myself. I didn't have to think about how this version of

me would dress or what kind of food she'd eat or what her mother's maiden name was. I was just me, even if I didn't know who that was most of the time anymore.

My eyes filled with tears, not of sadness but of anger. I would *not* let John take that away from me with his disappearing act. I got into the car and started the engine.

It was about a two and a half hour drive from the Faceless Tunnel to Erie up I-79, and I spent the whole time blasting eighties power-girl rock, Joan Jett and Blondie and Pat Benatar. When I got to the driveway of Zamorski House, it was blocked by a guard station that looked more like it belonged at a military compound than a private residence. A man wearing the uniform of a security company, a gun at each hip, approached the car and motioned for me to roll down the window. He had to shout over the sound of the stereo. "State your name and business."

I didn't bother. I seized his mind. His face slackened like a balloon deflating, and his eyes glazed over. "Let me in," I said. He pushed a button and the metal gate opened.

Zamorski House was one of those places you couldn't help but know about if you went to school in Western Pennsylvania, mainly because every art teacher *and* every history teacher you ever had would spend hours lamenting that it wasn't open for tours like it had been in the seventies. I remembered hearing that it was next to a waterfall. But it wasn't next to the waterfall so much as *over* the waterfall, large terraces cantilevered so that it looked like the waterfall was flowing out from under the building to the stream beneath. Wall-to-wall windows covered the building, and the brownish-gray stone that comprised its walls and foundation blended in perfectly to the trees and rocks that surrounded it, making it appear that the house had grown out of the valley rather than being built here. The landscape itself acted as a natural barrier, bordered by the stream and

waterfall on one side and a rocky outcropping on the other. A thick forest surrounded the compound, making it seem like the trees were large, silent sentinels. Lights built into the roof completed the effect, illuminating the waterfall as much as the house.

I pulled the car up the windy driveway and parked near the entrance. When I got out of the car, I felt a dozen pairs of eyes on me. I looked up. The trees weren't the only things protecting the house. The perimeter of the roof was lined with snipers, at least a dozen that I could see, armed with rifles you'd normally see members of a SWAT team carrying. Every last one of them had their guns up and ready, aiming at my chest.

I reached for their minds. They all had shields around their minds, but nowhere near as strong as John's. Someone had taught them to protect themselves, but not from me. They were concrete, but I was a jackhammer. One by one, they each relaxed their stances and sat down on the roof, their legs dangling over the edge—a touch of whimsy for my entertainment. Why had I ever thought this was difficult? Maybe something inside me had shifted when I had controlled those Zeta Coalition men at my aunt's. Or maybe it was easier because I recognized that this was a necessary evil, so as not to get shot in the chest. More likely, I was mad as hell and all out of fucks to give.

I marched up to the front door and rang the bell.

A frail, white-haired old man in a suit answered the door. When he saw me, his jaw dropped. "Dear God..."

"Good evening. Allow me to introduce myself. My name used to be Karen Fowler. I'd like to see my mother."

CHAPTER

THE BUTLER— WHOSE NAME, I HAD decided, was Eustace, for no other reason than he looked like a Eustace—led me to a large, open room, lined with windows and a set of sliding glass doors leading out to the terrace. The floor was made of stone, although much of it was covered with plush, white area rugs, the kind that looked like they would stain if you even looked at them wrong. A skylight spanned the center of the ceiling; it must have been almost unbearably bright during the day. The perimeter of the skylight was lined with LEDs, illuminating the room with a warm, yellow glow. The furniture was pristine and modern: sleek, solid-colored couches and cushioned seats set low to the floor. It was as if someone had decided to mix the aesthetics of a Japanese temple and an Ikea store just to see what would happen. The room smelled of the water running through the waterfall beneath it. I wondered what the utility bills must have been to keep a place like this comfortable in July.

The centerpiece of the room was a sandstone fireplace that stretched from floor to ceiling. It wasn't lit—even in northwestern Pennsylvania, a lit fireplace in midsummer would be a bit much—but it was still an impressive

sight. It was at least five feet wide, and there were no glass doors or metal screens blocking the doors, just a small, step-up hearth made of the same stone as the floor. I imagined the witch from *Hansel and Gretel* must have had a fireplace like that. *Walk right in, little children. It's nice and warm.*

I shivered.

Eustace pointed to one of the couches. "Please, have a seat." I did, and it was as firm and uncomfortable as it looked. Someone needed to teach Amara about the wonder of leather couches and overstuffed chairs.

I expected Eustace to offer me something to drink, because that's what butlers did in all the movies. But instead, he just said, "Wait here," with an almost imperceptible glare in his eyes. I guess mindfucking his mistress's guards and immobilizing her snipers didn't go over too well.

Eustace left the room, and I waited, chewing on a hangnail nervously. It felt like a museum, all pristine furniture and not a speck of dust to be found, and I worried that my slept-in clothes and my bloody shoes were going to soil the place. There was also not a single photograph anywhere to be seen. I don't know what I expected. A portrait of my father in a place of honor above the mantle? A collage of my awkward school pictures, with my God-awful haircuts and ridiculous outfits, marring the immaculate coffee table? Yeah, right.

I heard footsteps coming toward me. I stood up as a woman entered the room. We both stared at each other. I had never met her before, but I would have known her anywhere.

She was exactly my height and had the same curvy body that I had despised since I was fifteen. Her hair was darker than mine, a rich chestnut shade, and hung down about halfway down her back. She wore a long, white summery dress, the kind you expect women to wear during moonlight walks on the beach, and she was barefoot. No wonder my aunt had said

we looked alike. I stared into the same face in the mirror every day. With a little bit of makeup and hair dye, we could have passed for identical twins.

I knew she was thousands of years old but, physically at least, she looked no older than I did. I don't know why I didn't expect that. She was immortal, and immortals seemed to stop aging once they reached full maturity. John had certainly been proof of that. But in my imagination, I'd always expected her to look more *motherly*, middle-aged with graying hair and home perms, maybe some appliqué sweatshirts tossed in for good measure. Only her eyes gave her away. They were the same color and shape as mine—light blue, fringed with dark eyelashes—but there was something there I'd never seen in my own. Even when she looked right at me, it was like she was staring at something thousands of years away.

She spoke first. "You have freckles."

Uhhh... "Only on my face."

"Your father had freckles. And auburn hair like yours. You look so much like him."

"Funny...everyone else seems to think I look like you." Including, apparently, me.

She sat down on one of the low, padded seats perpendicular to me. "You caused an uproar with my staff tonight." Her words were perfect, but her voice had an odd cadence, as if she were a foreign actor trying to mimic an American accent: the words too precise, the consonants too enunciated. "I taught them how to defend their minds from intrusion, but you penetrated their shields. They are quite displeased."

I shifted uncomfortably. "You taught them how to shield their mind from intrusion from other people, but not from *you*."

"Naturally." Her lips turned up at the corners, the first hint of a smile I'd seen from her. "But that bit of information is my secret."

AMARA LED ME THROUGH A small hallway out onto another terrace, and then down a set of steps to a man-made pond, illuminated with blue lights, with colorful fish swimming in it. She dipped her feet into the water. The fish scattered at the intrusion, and then resumed swimming as if her feet had always been there. She closed her eyes. "This reminds me of Rome," she said. "He took me dancing on the shore of the Tiber one night. I waded in, and the fish tickled my toes."

I sat down next to her. "Dad?" I didn't even know my father had ever been to Rome, let alone danced along the Tiber River.

"Yes...no...yes." She paused. "Lucius was so strong, the perfect soldier. But he was kind, too, and warm. We never had much time because of the wars. Hannibal, it was then, I think, but I can never remember. Still, I'll never forget the look on Lucius's face the first time he touched my skin." She wrapped her arms around herself, lost in the memory.

"M—uh, Amara?" I waited for her to focus on me. "*Steven* was my father. Steven Fowler."

She smiled. "Oh, yes. Yes, I know. But Steven *was* Lucius. As soon as I saw him, I knew. Those eyes...that smile. They were just the same." She paused for a moment, her expression turning serious. "Do you believe that people can be reborn, that human souls can come back again in another vessel?"

"You mean reincarnation? I don't know. I've never really thought about it."

"I think it's true. I hope it's true. Otherwise, humans would lead such sad, small lives." She ran her fingers through the water. "Don't fall in love

with a human, Kare-bear. They're like butterflies. They're beautiful, and they bring so much joy...but they die so fast."

"Don't call me Kare-bear. Only Dad got to call me that."

She stopped stroking the water and stared at me. "What shall I call you, then?"

"Call me Dale. That's my name now."

"That's not a name, it's topography."

"Well, it's my name now, and I like it." I stood up. "Hey, I have an idea. Maybe you should call me by your dead kid's name. How about that? I'm probably just a reincarnation of him, right?"

"Ka—Dale..."

"Look, if you manage to track down a Ouija board, let me know, and we'll sort this all out. In the meantime, I need to take a shower, and I'd really like to get a nap before I say anything I'll regret."

I walked inside the house, slamming the door behind me. Eustace rushed out from whatever he was doing in the main room—probably scotch guarding the couch in case I ever sat there again—and glared at me. I ignored him and climbed up the steps. I opened several doors until I found a guest bedroom that obviously wasn't being used. I flopped down on the bed and sighed.

"That went well," I said.

ABOUT TEN MINUTES AFTER I ran away from Amara, I heard a knock on the bedroom door. I opened it and found Eustace standing there. "The mistress instructed me to ensure you were comfortable. Is there anything I can do for you?"

He still wasn't going to be winning the Friendliness Olympics, but it was a long way from the barely disguised glares I was getting earlier. I wondered if Amara had whammied him. "I don't know. Some clothes, maybe. I kind of left in a hurry, so I don't have anything else. But right now, I pretty much just want to take a shower and sleep until next Christmas."

"The bathroom is behind you. You should find it well stocked with towels and toiletries."

"Thank you..." I was about to call him Eustace, but then I stopped. "What's your name?"

The old man raised his eyebrows. "John, ma'am."

Of *course* it was. "What's your last name?"

"Covington, ma'am."

Covington, huh? I could live with that. It fit him even better than Eustace. "Thank you, Covington."

He hesitated in the doorway. "Before you do anything rash, keep in mind that your mother is not always..."

"Sane?" I suggested.

"Well. She is not always well." He lowered his eyes. "I think it must be difficult, to remember so much, to have been alive so long. She has lost a lot in her life. Maybe too much."

I didn't know how to respond. "The car I brought with me is stolen," I said finally. "I didn't want to steal it, but it was kind of a necessary evil. Maybe you could try to get it back to its owner. At least get rid of it so that no one comes to arrest me."

"I will have it taken care of." The old man left, and I shut the door behind him.

The bathroom was small—surprising, on a house this big and luxurious—but what it lacked in space, it more than made up for in amenities. A basket on the vanity was filled with shampoos, conditioners,

body lotions, aromatherapy bath beads, hydrating oils, and—to my surprise—toothpaste and toothbrushes. The one toiletry every hotel neglects is the one that everyone uses every night. What's the logic in that? The linen closet was filled with soft, fluffy towels in every color imaginable. I took one out and opened it. It was the biggest towel I had ever seen, large enough to wrap around myself twice with room to spare. Forget the bed; I wanted to wrap myself in this thing and take a nap on the bathroom floor.

But in the end, I climbed into the old-fashioned claw foot tub and started the shower, turning it up as hot as I could stand. Days' worth of dust and dirt flowed toward the drain, staining the tub that looked like it had never been used. I wondered if Covington would be angry about it.

I closed my eyes and sighed. "This sucks."

You haven't given it much of a chance.

Of course it would be John's voice responding in my mind. He'd abandoned me, left me to face my mother on my own, but he was still in my head, the bastard. But I couldn't help myself. I was all alone in this big house with unfriendly butlers and snipers on the roof, and it was nice to have someone to talk to—even if that someone was a figment of my imagination. "She's crazy."

Maybe.

"She only married my father because she thought he was the reincarnation of some Roman soldier she fucked thousands of years ago."

Maybe he was.

"Yeah, and maybe the only reason she let me in is because she thinks I'm the reincarnation of her dead baby."

Even if that's true, it doesn't matter. You're you, and that's what counts. And you're wonderful.

I turned off the water. "Don't say things you don't mean." I wrapped the gigantic towel around myself and returned to the bedroom.

When I came out, there was a pile of clothes waiting for me on the bed. I hoped Covington had at least found a female servant to do it rather than come in here himself when I was naked and showering just feet away. Judging by the style—mostly long, pale-colored dresses—I was guessing they were Amara's. They weren't anything I would normally wear, but considering otherwise I'd be stuck in dirty clothes, I didn't have much of a choice. Besides, it would be nice to have *something* that fit into my mother's spotless world.

I found the least fussy items in the pile: a pair of cropped white pants and a soft blue T-shirt. I kept my old, bloody shoes, because Amara's serfs hadn't included shoes in their offerings. But they had at least thought to bring new underwear, still unopened in their plastic packaging. I grabbed a pair—white, of course—and put them on. I'd wash the other few pairs, but given the choice between the underwear I'd had on for the last two days or the industrial processing chemicals that may or may not be on the new pair, I'd take my chances.

By the time I dried my hair, I was feeling much better about myself and the situation. John was gone, but I could deal. I'd survived on my own for ten years; I could do it again. I'd go elsewhere, change my name again, find a job, whatever. Amara was the one variable in this situation. Like it or not, she was my mother. A blind person couldn't miss the resemblance between us. Yet she was the one variable in this situation, the one X-factor, the one thing I didn't yet feel comfortable with or sure about.

Which meant, of course, that when I opened the bedroom door, she was standing there. "May I come in?" she asked.

I opened the door wider, and she stepped inside. She sat down on the edge of the bed, which was covered by a thick duvet. Like the bathroom, the bedroom didn't give much space to spread out, so I leaned back against the wall and waited. After a few moments of awkward silence, Amara gestured

toward the sliding glass door leading out to the terrace. "Would you like to go outside? I think we'll be more comfortable out there."

Without waiting for an answer, Amara stood up and went outside. I followed. To my surprise, it was like Amara had a whole other living room out there: two rounded wicker sectionals, covered in green and white cushions, surrounded by a stone fire pit that matched the surrounding walls. There were wicker end tables on the sides of each of the sectionals. A large canopy covered the furniture, with tiki torches at each corner. If you ignored the four snipers facing the exterior of the balcony, it was almost cozy.

Amara and I sat across from one another. Less than thirty seconds later, an attractive, well-muscled servant emerged from one of the other doors with a drink in each of his hands, a rose-colored liquid with a paper umbrella perched near the top of the glass. He sat one glass by Amara, and the other by me. I took a sip, expecting something alcoholic, and I froze at the tart, sweet taste. "Pink lemonade?"

Amara nodded. "My reaction to alcohol is...more sensitive than most, even compared to other demons. I suspect yours is, as well."

It was. But I wasn't going to tell her that. "How did he know to bring us drinks so fast? Do you have a buzzer or something?"

"He's clairvoyant. His range is limited, both geographically and in terms of how far into the future he can see. He can't predict a financial collapse or foretell your enemy's next move in war. But in domestic situations, he's proven quite useful." She took the umbrella out, tucked it behind her ear, and sipped her lemonade. "He also services me in other ways, too, when necessary. His ability provides him with some extra advantages there, as well."

My jaw dropped. Was my previously presumed dead mother talking about having sex with her psychic manservant? "Okay. I'm just going to

pretend I didn't hear that for now, and then tonight I'm going to pour some bleach into my ears and hope it hits my brain."

She frowned. "I wouldn't recommend that. You'd likely survive, but I think it would be quite uncomfortable."

Oh, God, I really had entered the Twilight Zone. "I was being sarcastic."

"Ah, I see." Her lips turned up at the corners, a faraway look in her eyes. "Your father used to do that, too. It was frustrating for me, because I'd often miss the tenor of the conversation. He'd tease me about it, and we'd laugh."

"Which one, Lucius the Roman soldier or Steven the accountant from Pittsburgh?"

"Steven." She set down her lemonade and closed her eyes. A long sigh rolled out of her before she looked up and said, "I wanted to apologize for earlier. I didn't mean to upset you. It can be difficult for my mind to stay in the present sometimes."

"Do you really believe they were the same person? Lucius and my dad?"

"Sometimes. Does it matter? I loved them both."

Long before I knew Amara was alive, long before I even knew I was a demon, I had this fairy tale image in my head of my parents' relationship. I may not have had a picture of her, but my dad had always spoken of her lovingly. I imagined them up in Heaven, together and in love, even long after I no longer believed it. Even after I found out Amara was still alive, I clung to this idea that she and my father had been very much in love. He'd protected her all that time, weaving the fantasy of the mother who'd loved me very much and died too young, a loss so painful for him that he couldn't even stand to have pictures of her around. But now my mother was *here*, talking about reincarnated Roman soldiers and clairvoyant manservants. "No, it doesn't matter," I lied. What else was I going to say? It *shouldn't* have mattered. I couldn't have expected that my dad would be the only

person she'd love for all those years, and he had been dead for over twenty years now.

Amara pulled her legs up onto the sectional and wrapped her arms around her knees. "How long...I mean...how much time...how old are you now?"

"I'm twenty-seven."

"Still so young." She leaned forward like she was going to reach out and touch me, thought better of it, and then reclined back in her seat. "Though I guess it doesn't seem so to you."

A cool breeze blew toward us from the nearby hills. It made me think about John and about the nights we'd spent on the road together, driving through abandoned sections of countryside with the windows down. But John was gone, and Amara was here, and there was so much between her and me that needed to be addressed.

I took a breath and decided to get the first elephant in the room out of the way. "Dad's dead," I said.

"I know. I came to his funeral. I stayed in the back where no one could see me, and I left right after the service, but I was there."

"You used your powers to force Aunt Barbara to take care of me."

She braced her head against her hand. "I thought it would be better for you to stay with family. Perhaps that wasn't the best idea, in retrospect."

"Why didn't you stay? Why didn't you take care of me?"

She put her feet down, crossing them at the ankles. "How did you find me?"

"That doesn't answer my..."

"I *will* answer your question." There was a violent gleam in her eyes, a warrior in her rigid posture. *This* was the woman who had single-handedly caused a civil war, who was feared even by her own kind. Now I could finally see it. "Answer my question first."

"Aunt Barbara told me. She didn't want to, but I guessed. She's dead now, too." I swallowed, squashing the unexpected emotion I felt when I talked about her. "An anti-supernatural group called the Zeta Coalition got her."

"Good riddance." She gave a one-shouldered shrug. "But does anyone else know where I am? Anyone at all?"

There was the edge of a knife in her voice. I had been just about to tell her about John. Why shouldn't I? He had left me behind. But still... something stopped me. Some misplaced loyalty to the guy who had gotten me here. "No. I came on my own."

She smiled. "Good. Very good." She paused, taking a sip of her lemonade. Her face became grim. "How much do you know about us, the demons? About our history?"

"Just the basics, I guess. I know about the War of Purity. I know it started because Zaphkiel and his followers killed a baby—*your* baby."

"*Your* brother." She leaned back in her seat. "Zaphkiel is long dead. I killed him, watched the worm bleed out, and I regret nothing. He doesn't matter anymore, except to one...but that's another tale for another day. But I've come to believe that Zaphkiel was merely a figurehead, masking the actions of the true villain. What do you know about Gabriel?"

I know that he nearly killed John right in front of me. I know that he's still after me, right at this very moment. "He's the leader of the Thrones."

"Yes." She got up and walked to the wall of the terrace. She looked out toward the forest. "He's also my husband."

CHAPTER

M Y HEAD HURT. "YOU MEAN in the past tense, right? You're divorced now. Aren't you?"

"There's no such thing as divorce among our kind."

I got up and began pacing the length of the terrace. One of the snipers glanced over at me, a good-looking, dark-skinned man about my age. I glared at him and he turned away. "So you're saying that asshole is my *stepfather*?"

"Yes, I believe that is the common term for it now." She must have seen the look on my face, because she froze. "What's wrong?"

"I'm waiting for Darth Vader to come along and cut off my hand."

She furrowed her eyebrows. "I don't understand."

"Don't worry about it." I said. "What about Lucas, or Luscious, or whatever the fuck his name was? What about *Dad*?"

"I never married Lucius, so it's irrelevant. As for your father, he was human, and marriages to humans have never been valid among the angels. From an angelic perspective, your father would have been a mere

plaything—and we were never discouraged from taking outside lovers. Forever is a long time to remain with one partner."

"You said marriages to humans were invalid to angels. But you're a demon."

"But I was an angel once. We were all angels once."

A breeze blew in from toward the forest, ruffling her hair. She took out a matchbook and lit the fire pit. "I loved Gabriel once, back when humans were young and we were younger. He was strong and handsome and brave. And he loved me more than anything. He called me his world, and maybe for a while I was." She leaned back into her seat, gazing into the flames. "I was reckless with his feelings, though. So many among us considered our lives a curse. But I thought this world was novel and exciting, and I wanted to experience all of it. The more time I spent away from him, the angrier Gabriel became. I drew away from him, took human lovers. Gabriel became jealous."

"And then you got pregnant."

"Yes." She started to laugh. "I didn't understand what was wrong with me until the baby was nearly birthed. An angel had never conceived a child before. Gabriel was furious. We had been apart for too long for him to be the father..."

"And purebloods can't conceive among themselves, anyway," I interrupted.

"Yes, but we didn't know that at the time. Everything was new then. We had no idea of our limits." The wind blew again, and she ran her hands through her unruly hair. "Gabriel always disliked humans, felt they were barbarians and beneath us. Even as they helped us acclimate to the world, he resented their presence. His anti-human sentiment increased after I began to take human lovers. But Gabriel did not have the influence or the charisma to lead a rebellion. Zaphkiel did. I believe Gabriel convinced Zaphkiel and his Thrones to turn against me. They cut the babe out of my

stomach and killed it. Their next atrocity, however, wasn't directed at my child—but solely at me."

She unbuttoned the front of her dress. Raised white scars crossed her stomach and chest, crossing down beneath the cup of her bra. She must have been cut dozens of times. Even all these centuries later, the scars still looked brutal. I sat down again and lowered my head between my knees, breathing deeply, trying to stop the nausea that was overwhelming my body. She buttoned her dress, hiding the scars once again. "When I recovered, I led a rebellion against those who had attacked me and killed my child. We won the war, but it led to a permanent schism between the two factions: the angels and the demons."

"That's a horrible story," I said when I finally felt like I could sit up without puking, "but that happened thousands of years ago. The war ended. You won. What does any of this have to do with anything?"

She sighed. "As I said, Gabriel is my husband. He has not been my lover or companion for millennia now, but by our laws, he is still my husband. And I am his one weakness. After all these years, he has never struck against me directly. But he does not hesitate to go after those I love."

I gasped. "Dad..."

She shook her head. "No. *You.* Gabriel came after you. That's why I left. I'd already lost one of my children to him. I wouldn't lose another."

My jaw dropped. When I didn't say anything, she continued. "Gabriel found me shortly after you were born. He threatened me. He said if I did not leave you and your father, he would kill you both. I told your father what was happening. I loved him too much to do otherwise. He helped me disappear. I was rather ill-equipped for dealing with the modern world's nuances, I'm afraid."

"Is that why Dad died? Because Gabriel killed him?"

"No." Her tone didn't allow for argument. "After your father was killed, my people and I checked and rechecked every source I could think of. Your father's death was nothing more than an accident caused by a human man who had consumed too much alcohol. If Gabriel had violated our agreement, I would have retaliated. He knows that."

I didn't know whether to be happy or sad that my father's death had been caused by mere human stupidity, and not by renegade angels. Was that better or worse? "What was your agreement with Gabriel?"

"That I would leave you and your father. I was never to contact Steven again. With you, I negotiated for the estrangement to be temporary, so that I could introduce you to the demonic world and train you in your abilities, should you manifest any. Gabriel agreed that I could contact you after your eighteenth birthday, but that his concession not to hurt you would also end on that date. Your eighteenth birthday arrived..."

"...but I was already gone," I filled in.

She nodded. "I tried to find you. But your ability to hide went beyond my ability to track."

Of course it did. I had managed to elude the Bloodhound for ten years, and he was the best hunter and assassin in the Thrones. We all have our skills. Running and hiding were mine. "So now I'm an adult, and Gabriel can kill me any time he wants?"

She shrugged. "True, but it shouldn't cause you much worry. Gabriel's main focus has always been me, not you. He used my affection for you as a means of getting to me. You were an inconvenience to him, nothing more."

Maybe that had been the case, before I turned his best assassin against him and killed several of his people. Something told me it had become personal to him somewhere along the way. The fact that I was his very much unwanted stepdaughter probably didn't help matters any. "So what does he want now? Is he still in love with you, or is he trying to get revenge?"

"Nothing so simple." She crossed the terrace and sat down on the sectional again. "Gabriel loved me once, as much as he could. I believe that. I have always believed that. But his true love was always for power, for control. It was one of the things that drove us apart."

"So you think he's going to try to take control of the demons again?"

She shook her head. "I don't think he'll bother. I think he's going to try to take over the world."

I stared at her. She calmly took another sip of her lemonade. "Gabriel has always looked for long-term gains. After the War of Purity ended, the angels had neither the strength nor the numbers to challenge us, or to force humans to worship and follow them. So he has spent the last several thousand years building up the angel's strength, growing the Thrones to be a strong, powerful military force. I suspect Gabriel was the architect behind the Thrones' breeding program. Why else would angels procreate with humans when they fought an entire war to prevent it? Every war needs foot soldiers, and their part-breeds have always been expendable."

It was the same thing Isaac had said. "Do you think he can do it? Does he have that kind of power?"

"Possibly. The Thrones are a powerful and formidable group and have become even more so under Gabriel's leadership. But I think before he did anything like that, he would find me first."

My heart started to pound. "Why would you think that?"

"I am his weakness, his primary vulnerability. He cared about me once. He may care about me still. But more importantly, I am a symbol: the traitor, the defector. Demons rallied behind me during the War of Purity. Should I ask it, they would rally behind me again. But without me, the demons would not have the structure or the organization to mount a defense against him. I never tried to organize them into a cohesive force

like the Thrones. I never wanted them to be my militia." She sighed. "One should never live long enough to see oneself become a legend."

I picked up my lemonade glass with a shaking hand, trying to get rid of the dryness in my throat. I could barely swallow. "Gabriel is already coming after you."

She raised one eyebrow. "Is he?"

"Yes. The Thrones sent an assassin after me, because they thought they could use me to get to you. That's how I found out I was part demon, and that's what made me decide to come find you myself."

She froze for a moment, her back rigid. But then, just as suddenly, she relaxed. "Well then," she said, "I suppose it's likely that Gabriel does have the power and the resources to stage a coup against the human leaders after all. Or at least he thinks he does."

I began to pace again, thoughts whirling through my head. "But now that we know, we can do something about it! You're still this feared, badass name in the demon world. We can track down some of your former allies, organize our own counter-response. I know of a bar in New York City that might be a good place to start..."

"No."

Amara still sat on the sectional, her hands clasped in her lap. I turned to face her. "What do you mean no?"

"This is not my fight."

"Of course it's your fight. It's everyone's fight. Gabriel's a megalomaniac who doesn't care who he hurts to get what he wants. I saw..." I stopped myself, still unwilling to tell Amara about John—in spite of the fact that I still didn't know where the asshole had gone or why he'd left. "I mean, I've heard stories about him killing his own people when they don't do what he wants them to do. You know what he did to you, and who knows what he'll do to humans? This is a race whose entire history has been dedicated

to their own superiority. Do you think he's just going to let humans live in love and harmony? I kind of doubt it."

"Do you think I don't know that?" Her voice was cold and flat. "I know exactly what my husband is capable of. Gabriel stole my child from me, not once, but *twice*."

I sat down next to Amara and took her hand. It felt cold in mine. "I know. And I'm sorry. But I'm back now...Mom."

She snatched her hand away. "The baby I left behind had three teeth and fat cheeks. She smiled all the time, and her favorite toy was a brown teddy bear that had once belonged to her father. You left home at seventeen because you murdered a schoolmate, and I don't imagine he's the only one you've killed. Several of my best guards had to be dismissed today because they were compromised when you manipulated your way into their minds. I also know there's more to the story of how you got here and why than you're saying, but you don't trust me enough yet to confide in me. Maybe it would have been different if I hadn't left, or if your father hadn't died. I don't know. I have no doubts that you are my daughter...but you are *not* my baby."

I felt like I'd been punched in the chest. I stood up. "It's been a long night for me. I think I should go to bed," I said.

"I think that's for the best."

CHAPTER

I LEFT THE HOUSE. I WAS half tempted to get in the car, say "fuck this," and get back on the road. But Covington had apparently already gotten rid of the stolen car, and unlike John, I didn't know how to hot wire a vehicle. I was twenty miles from the middle of nowhere. Erie was the closest city, but even that was nearly half an hour's drive away.

I was stuck.

I circled around to the back of the house. I couldn't get too close to the structure from this side, because of the waterfall that flowed beneath it. Beyond the water, the ground was rugged, leading back into the thick forest that carried through into the hills. Amara had chosen her fortress wisely. The natural boundaries on all sides would make an attack difficult.

I sat down against a large tree and watched the water flow from beneath the house down into the stream. I closed my eyes and listened to the whooshing of the water over the rocks. I took several deep breaths and tried to re-center myself again.

Maybe I had been too hard on Amara. She had been around for millennia. She'd seen eras come and go. She'd seen dynasties rise and fall

and rise again. She'd seen wars. Many, many, many wars. She'd even started one and caused a schism among her own people as a result.

She'd lost both her children. She was right: I wasn't the chubby-cheeked baby she'd left behind. I'd seen too much, *done* too much. I understood why she mourned that baby, and I shouldn't begrudge her right to do so. But it had felt like all the air was being sucked out of my chest when she said it.

She'd also lost the men she loved. Lucius, the Roman soldier. My father, who may or may not have been a reincarnated version of Lucius.

Gabriel.

Gabriel was my stepfather. What was I supposed to do with that bit of information?

Amara was broken. It didn't take a genius to figure that out. But maybe she could still be brought back into the world. Maybe I could convince her that the world was still worth fighting for. I was still her daughter, and that had to mean something...right?

Plus, I was realizing, I really wanted to know her, and I had the feeling I was going about it all wrong.

I heard some leaves rustle nearby. I jumped to my feet, ready for a fight. A man approached me with his hands in a placating, "I come in peace" position. "Don't worry. I'm not here to hurt you."

He had dark skin and eyes so brown the pupil got lost in them. He was taller than me, though shorter than John had been. Lean muscles rippled his body, and he wore a polo shirt and khakis, both of which looked like they'd been pressed recently. Basically, he was hot. Too bad I had no idea where he'd come from. "Who are you?"

His voice was deep and rich. "My name's Travis. I'm one of Lady Amara's guards. I saw you on the terrace with her earlier. My shift ended, and I wanted to check on you to see if you were all right."

Lady Amara? Did she really make her servants call her Lady Amara? Ugh. "You were one of the snipers?"

"Lady Amara prefers 'guards,' but yes."

It took me a moment to place him. "I glared at you when I was talking to my mother, didn't I?"

He smiled. "Yeah, that was me."

"Sorry about that. I'm not usually so rude. At least not openly."

"No worries. I've been through worse. I have three sisters. At least I didn't get fired like the guards earlier tonight."

Christ. I could feel a tension headache coming on. "This has really not been my day."

"You did meet your mother, so that's something."

"I guess." I leaned back against the tree, the rough bark rubbing against my skin. "I just thought...shouldn't it be simpler than this?"

"Family is never simple. But maybe it'll be worth it in the end."

He put his hand against my arm—a sweet, totally innocent gesture. But I looked up into his eyes, and I saw something there. I took a step forward and touched his face. When he didn't object, I stood on my tiptoes and kissed him.

He wrapped his arms around my body and kissed me back. His lips were warm and soft, and he tasted minty, like he'd sucked on an Altoid. It made me wonder whether he had *intended* this, whether he came down here purposely figuring I would be emotional and unsteady, hoping that he would get a little something out of it. But honestly...did it matter?

He backed me up against the tree, and I let him. I opened my mouth, and he slipped in his tongue. I felt his erection pushing against my leg through his pants. It was nice. He was a good kisser, not too drooly or gropey, and he had good breath because of the mints he may or may not have consumed in hopes of making out with me. He didn't send me into

the stratosphere like John had, didn't send my nerve endings buzzing at his very touch. He didn't smell like warm butterscotch, and I didn't want to just wrap my arms around him and bury into his bulk all night long. No, it wasn't like being with John, but he had abandoned me, and he didn't matter, anyway.

A tear ran down my cheek. I pulled away from Travis and wiped it away. "I can't do this."

"What's wrong?" He looked genuinely concerned. "If it's too fast, I'm sorry. We don't have to..."

"No, it's not that. It's just that...I'm in love with someone else."

And as soon as I said it, I realized it was true. I was in love with John. I was in love with John, and that asshole was gone.

I DECIDED TO WAIT UNTIL the next morning to seek out Amara again. Even though I understood—kind of—why Amara had said the things she did, I was still having trouble controlling my temper. The encounter in the woods with Travis didn't help things any. It would be good for both of us to take the night to cool off a bit.

I took a shower, and I changed into a T-shirt and a pair of yoga pants I managed to find in the pile of stuff Covington had left me the night before. They were super-soft and smelled like vanilla, and I felt more like myself than I had in days. I found Amara in the kitchen—which had the same stone walls and floor as the living room—sitting at a large table, drinking a cup of coffee. She was wearing another long summer dress, beige with flowers on it, and her feet were bare. If they were cold against that floor, she didn't show it. I cleared my throat, and she looked up at me. "Do you mind if I sit down?" I asked.

She gestured toward an empty chair across from her, and I took it. "I'm surprised you're still here," she said.

"Yeah, well, I wanted to apologize for what happened yesterday. I know you've been through a lot through the years, and it wasn't fair of me to jump on you the way I did."

Amara wrapped her hands around the coffee cup, not meeting my eyes. "I accept your apology. I also offer my own apology. I said some hurtful things yesterday. I regret them."

"Thank you. I appreciate that."

She finally looked up at me, the blue eyes that looked so much like the ones I saw in the mirror every day meeting my own. "I cannot decide if you are not enough like me...or too much."

"Well, I guess for now I'll be like myself, and we'll just figure it out as we go along."

"That seems reasonable."

Amara didn't say anything else, just continued to sip her coffee. If there were guards or snipers planted inside the house, I didn't see them, though a quick glance out the sliding glass door revealed two on the terrace just within my line of sight. Neither of them was Travis, to my relief. "So, I was thinking that today we could..."

My stomach growled loudly, and Amara jumped out of her seat. "Oh! You need food!" The sexy servant who had brought us our lemonade on the terrace yesterday appeared. Amara pointed to the stove. "Raoul, prepare breakfast for my daughter. Kar—er, Dale, what would you like? He could make pancakes, or bacon, or omelets, or sausage, or waffles, or..."

"Whatever you have is fine."

Raoul, who was already removing pans from the cabinets, winked at me lasciviously. "I can do whatever you like."

Jesus Christ. What the hell kind of place was Amara running here? Had she actually *sent* Travis to me the day before? "I think I'll just stick to cereal then, thanks."

I sat back down at the table and eyed Amara. "Raoul likes to be accommodating," she said.

"Clearly," I replied, not wanting to upset the fragile balance we'd just established by elaborating further. "So, uh, I was actually hoping that maybe we could...train together today?" Amara didn't respond immediately, and I rushed to fill the silence. "I don't want to impose on you or anything. But I didn't find out I was half demon until the Thrones came after me. I'm still learning how to use my ability, and I really don't know how to control it yet. And there are...other things I wanted to ask you about, too. So what I mean is, I really need your help. If you don't mind."

She didn't speak for a moment, and I readied myself to start babbling and backtracking some more. But then she nodded. "I wouldn't mind that."

WE STOOD ON YET ANOTHER terrace, even larger than the one off of my bedroom. At Covington's direction, Raoul and some of the other servants had moved the furniture inside, leaving us with an empty platform. The sun was high in the sky, but the waterfall rushing beneath us and a gentle breeze cooled the air enough to be bearable.

I had expected Amara to change into athletic clothes the way John always had, but instead she stood before me in the same long dress she'd worn to breakfast. She was still barefoot. My God, didn't that woman *ever* wear shoes? Stone floors and bare feet just did *not* go together, in my opinion, but Amara didn't seem to notice or care. She stood about five feet

away, facing me. "You have the ability to control people's minds, as do I," she said.

"Yes."

"Did anyone show you how to use it?"

I lied. "I met another demon after I figured out what I was. He also had a mental ability, and he helped me a lot. He taught me how to reach out to other minds, how to penetrate shields, and how to shield myself. I have no problem with any of that. But when I actually try to influence people, I'm not always consistent."

"And you hadn't used your gift before you met the other demon?"

I hesitated, scraping my sneakers against the stone floor of the terrace. "I kind of think I've been using it all along. I just didn't realize what I was doing before."

She tucked a lock of thick brown hair behind her ear and sighed. "I always hoped this wouldn't be necessary," she said. "After you disappeared, I hoped you would be fully absorbed into the human world, and you wouldn't have to worry about angels or demons. You wouldn't have to be part of *this*."

"Don't you think I would have noticed when everyone else around me was getting older and I was staying the same age?"

"How long would that have taken? Another ten years? Twenty years? More, perhaps? At first you'd just assume you were aging remarkably well. And then...a rare disease, perhaps, or an odd genetic mutation? Humans have a remarkable ability to rationalize what they don't understand, and in that, my daughter, you are very much human."

I sighed, because I was getting really tired of this cryptic "I'm so much smarter than you because I've lived forever" bullshit she had the tendency to spew. But I guess if I were counting my age in epochs, I'd be holier-than-thou, too. "So how do we get started here?"

Amara walked around me in a circle. "Can you sense the minds of the four guards on the corners of the terrace?"

I reached out with my awareness. "Yes."

"How do they feel?"

"Solid and dense, like there's a wall around them."

"Could you break them?"

I probed against them, testing them for weaknesses. "It might be difficult, but I think maybe I could eventually."

"I don't know how difficult it would be for you, daughter. Yesterday you felled several of my guards in very little time. Was it difficult then?"

"Is this a trick question?"

Amara took a step closer to me. "What was the difference between yesterday and now?"

"I don't know, I just...really, really wanted to get to the house."

She grinned. It lit up her face, made her look like a giddy teenager. It was so weird to stare at a face that looked so much like mine. "Exactly!" She paced around me, as if trying to gather her thoughts. "When your tutor explained your ability, he probably talked about shielding, yes? That anyone can build a shield around their minds to keep you out." I nodded. "Shielding is a useful metaphor, but it's not precisely accurate. It's more like...a battle of wills, you see. Human are usually very easy to manipulate because they don't know how to use their minds, their *will*, to keep you out. Most of them don't even know we exist, so why would they? Other demons and angels can use their wills against you, build 'shields' so to speak. Some are more skilled at it than others. But the trick is, your will has to be greater than theirs. You have to want it more. Once you remember that, your ability will never fail."

She snapped her fingers. The sniper to the right of me, at the front end of the terrace, turned to her. She approached him. "Give me your weapon."

His eyes glazed over as he gave her his rifle. She handled it gingerly, but her unease didn't show on her face. "Now climb atop the wall."

He did. I glanced over the edge of the terrace. It was a good fifty feet or so to the ground—not a deadly distance necessarily, until you consider the fact that there was nothing to land on but rocks and the rushing water of the falls. "Amara..."

"Now dive off," she said.

The sniper dove.

CHAPTER

I SCREAMED...AND THEN I STOPPED. THE sniper hovered in front of me, suspended in midair, his head pointing toward the jagged rocks below. I stared at Amara. "What the fuck?"

She gestured to one of the other snipers, a female standing at the corner opposite us. "Elena is a telekinetic, a very powerful one. Before this demonstration, I asked her to watch out for her fellow guards should anything happen." Amara looked at Elena. "You may put him back now."

The floating sniper drifted back over the terrace and landed on his feet, exactly where he had been before my mother ordered him to take a swan dive into a waterfall. He blinked rapidly as Amara handed him his rifle. "What happened?" he asked.

"I just asked to inspect your weapon. I feared it might be malfunctioning. But I was mistaken."

"Of course, that's right." His pupils came back into focus, and he looked at my mother. "Do you need anything else, Lady Amara?"

"No, that's all. Thank you, Hayden. You are dismissed for the day."

The guard, Hayden, left through the glass doors without another word. My mother turned back around and focused on me. I gaped at her. None of the other snipers had moved, had even *blinked* to suggest that anything was out of the ordinary. "*That* was a demonstration. Every living creature had the will to live. It is the most powerful impulse we possess. If you can overcome that, you can overcome anything. You just have to want it more than the other person."

"If the other sniper hadn't caught him, you would have just let him die."

"He *deserved* to die. And I would have killed her, too, for failing to protect her comrade," she snapped. "My desire to give you a training demonstration outweighed his desire to live, so what use is he, anyway?"

"That's the most fucked up thing I've ever heard."

"That's the world we live in." She stood across from me, her shoulders squared, her spine straight, her hair blowing in the breeze. "I know you think you can convince me to join your fight against Gabriel and the Thrones, but you're wrong. I'm done with this world. But if you're determined to face them, you need to understand what you're fighting. I did not give up everything to protect you so that you could make a martyr of yourself!"

"I don't want to make a martyr of myself! That's why I need you."

I sat on the ground and held my face in my hands. We were talking across each other, and arguing wasn't going to get anything accomplished. Her will was stronger than mine, as she would say.

Which made me wonder... "Can I touch your mind?" I asked.

She frowned, still standing above me. "I'm not sure. No one has ever tried before. Or if they have, they weren't alive afterward to discuss it with me."

"Would you mind if I tried?"

She waited. I reached toward her with my mental awareness...and found nothing but darkness, sucking in all the light around it. I sent a

tentative probe toward the darkness. It bounced back off like a superball and came back to me, smacking me like a punch rattling around in my brain. Something dripped down my face. I touched my cheek and wiped away blood. My temples throbbed.

The sliding glass door opened, and Raoul emerged with a box of tissues. I grabbed the box from him and began wiping off my face. Prognosticating rent-boy sure made for an odd job description, but he certainly performed at least the first part of his duties well. "This must be what it feels like to stick Q-Tips in your ears too deeply," I said.

Amara sat down on one of the chairs that had been pushed to the side with an expectant look on her face. "Well," she said, "were you able to touch it?"

"I touched something, all right."

"Could you break it?"

I shook my head. "I don't think so."

"Not surprising. My will has had a much longer time to develop than yours, and I'd be in poor shape if I couldn't protect myself from my own power." She stood up. "I believe that's enough for now. You have blood dripping out of your nose onto your clothes. You should probably take a shower."

Looking down, I saw that blood had dripped down from my face onto my formerly clean and sweet-smelling T-shirt. When I looked up, Amara was gone. "Goddammit."

I COULDN'T SLEEP THAT NIGHT. I walked out onto the terrace and found Amara sitting there. The night was cool, and the fire pit was lit again, illuminating the terrace with an eerie orange glow. Amara wore a long

nightgown and had her legs tucked to her chest, her bare feet resting against the cushions. She looked so young then, maybe even younger than me. "Aren't you cold?" I asked.

"No. It's warm here by the fire."

She patted the seat next to her. I sat down and gazed up into the sky. In spite of the fire, I could still see the stars. "Do you know anything about the stars?" She asked me.

"Not really."

"I know the name of every star in the night sky." She rested her head against her knees. "There are a lot of stars up there, and even more that we can't see with our eyes. But they're easy to learn when you have nothing but time."

I stared at Amara. In the flickering firelight, she looked so sad. "Are you all right?" I asked her.

She looked over at me, surprise on her face. "I was just thinking about things. About your father, and you. Your father was one of the only two people I've ever met, human or otherwise, who could block my abilities instinctively. I could have broken him eventually, of course. But then I realized I didn't want to."

"His will was stronger than yours," I said.

"Always." She smiled at me. "I suppose you inherited that from both of us."

"Who was the other—" I stopped, realizing the answer was right in front of me. "The Roman soldier, Lucius. The father of your first child. That's why you think Dad was his reincarnation."

She rocked back on her heels. "I don't know. It's a silly story, a romantic story. Maybe it's just easier to imagine everything has a pattern, easier to believe it all has meaning. One husband lives, one husband dies. One baby

dies, one baby lives." She paused. "Though the longer I live, the easier it is to see how everything seems to come around in circles."

I had lost the direction of what she was talking about, so I didn't say anything. Amara reached out and touched my hair. It felt nice, comforting, so I closed my eyes and leaned into the sectional cushions. "When you were a baby, you had almost no hair. Just this springy, little curl that would pop up on the top of your head. Sometimes you'd wake up during the night, and I'd go into your room and stroke that little baby curl just like this. You used to love it."

I opened my eyes. "I'm sorry I'm not that baby anymore."

She kept stroking my hair. "You're alive. You're safe. You're *here*. I couldn't have asked for anything more."

I let her stroke my hair for a few more minutes, relaxing into the feel of it, imagining how things would have turned out differently if Amara had stayed, if I'd been with her all along. But that wasn't the reality, and no amount of wishing would change it. I opened my eyes again. "There's something else I wanted to ask you about. I have these blackouts." I took a deep breath. It was so hard for me to talk about this, even now. "You heard about how I killed Brad Kinnard the night of the prom?" She nodded. "Well, it wasn't because I was jealous. It was because he had raped my best friend. I got into the hotel room and I saw them together and the world just...stopped. My vision turned red, and that's the last thing I remember. When I woke up, Brad was dead. I knew Aunt Barbara wouldn't help me, so I just ran." I wiped snot off of my face. "I changed my name, changed my identity, and I thought that would be the end of it. About six months later, I was living at a homeless shelter, and these two women attacked an old lady..."

I told her all of it, every person I'd killed in my years on the run, and how I couldn't remember anything afterward. I spared myself nothing,

except for the one detail I'd been keeping from her all along: John. I *wanted* to trust her, felt an almost compulsive *need* to tell her everything, but a little voice inside my head was still holding me back, still wanting to protect John in spite of his disappearance. "Do you have anything like that? Or have you ever heard of anything like that, even?"

She shook her head. "No, never."

It was what I'd been expecting, at this point, but I was still hoping for a magical cure. My eyes filled with tears again. "So there's no hope? I'm always going to be like this, always just randomly killing people?"

She rocked back and forth for several minutes, saying nothing, while I kept sniffling. I had dried my eyes when she finally spoke again. "Have you considered the possibility that your Rages are psychological, not physiological?"

I frowned. "I don't understand."

"Well, we know they're not triggered by your demonic abilities. You have the same abilities as me, and yet I've never had anything like that happen. I've also never heard of something similar happening to another demon. I have, however, heard of humans going into fugue states."

I tucked my knees to my chest and wrapped my arms around them. "So I'm crazy."

"No, I don't think you are. But you have spent your life being pulled between two different worlds. You were brought up among humans, who have very different laws and mores than we do. But I'm guessing that, deep in your heart, you always knew you were different from them."

I felt chilly all of a sudden. I moved myself closer to the fire, dangling my feet as close as I dared. "Aunt Barbara said the same thing."

"She spent the most time with you, so she should know." Amara sat back down next to me. "Tell me again about that night at the prom. You walked into that hotel room, and you discovered your closest friend being

violated by someone she should have been able to trust. How did you feel? What were you thinking in those seconds after you opened the door?"

"I wanted to kill him."

"Exactly. You wanted to kill him, and subconsciously you knew you had the capability to do so. But you were still a seventeen-year-old girl. I suspect your brain may have just blocked those memories, because it knew you weren't capable of handling what you were about to do."

I was shaking, and I couldn't seem to stop myself. "I don't understand."

"Every time you've had one of these Rages, it's been in defense of someone or something. You're a protector. But according to the human world, who you are and what you do is wrong. Immoral, even. So your brain has been trying to shield you from it all these years. But you're no longer a seventeen-year-old girl. You have a choice. If you embrace who you are, what you are, I believe the Rages will likely cease on their own. I doubt you need them anymore."

"But I didn't want to kill all those people."

She gave me a hard look. "Some part of you *did* want to kill those people, otherwise we wouldn't be having this conversation right now. What you just said—that's your human half talking."

I waited for several long moments. A cool breeze blew in again. It felt like it was going to rain. "But what about Andrew Seymour?" I asked finally, my voice barely audible. "I killed him during a Rage. I chopped off his head with a fucking kitchen knife. And I don't remember anything triggering it."

She shook her head. "He was the outlier. Don't worry about him right now. I suspect if you start digging, though, you *will* find the trigger there. But if you look at all the others, the pattern is consistent."

I leaned back against the loveseat, watching orange sparks shoot into the sky. "So now what?"

"You've spent your life being pulled between two worlds. Now you have to decide where you belong. You have to decide which part of you will dominate: the human or the demon?"

"What does that even mean? We all live in the same world, right?"

"I suppose that's an argument that can be made. But we're not of this world. Not really."

I hesitated. "So…where *do* we come from, then? Are all of those religious stories true?"

She frowned. "I don't remember. The first thing I recall is being here with the other angels, many thousands of years ago. Humans were still in their prehistoric era, running around in animal skins and dying by the age of thirty." She placed her hands in front of the fire, warming them, as if the talk of that time was making her cold in the here and now. "Sometimes if I think very hard, I can remember…warmth, love. A feeling of safety. Of home. But it's foggy."

"The book I read said that the angels were cast out of Heaven by God as punishment. Is that true?"

"I don't know. I don't think anyone knows anymore. Humans invented much of our history through the years. They prefer to think that the universe revolves around them, that we exist for their edification." She paused for a moment. "If it was a punishment, I would think it would have been more successful if we could remember. Then again, maybe that was part of it. The punishment of seeing the world pass by, of feeling that sense of loss but never really knowing what you're missing, of falling in love and losing *everything*, only to do it all over again."

"So do you think there's a God?"

She shook her head. "I don't think it matters. If there is one, I think he forgot about us a very long time ago."

She sounded so sad, and I wanted nothing more than to comfort her. "Maybe this was never a punishment, and we were never divine outcasts. Maybe it's more like we're just different types of humans, like X-Men or something. And so you have this life, and you just have to do the best you can with it like everyone else. Sometimes you'll love, and sometimes you'll lose that love, and it's not a punishment, but it's just the way life is. But it's better to put your heart out there than never to do so at all, because otherwise, what are you doing here?"

She didn't speak for a long time. When she did, her voice was hushed. "You're so like your father."

"I don't think that's a bad thing."

"No, it's not." She folded her hands into her lap and gave me a sad smile. "You're not strong enough for this world yet. But you'll learn. And I'm sorry for you when you do."

She stood up, picked up a glass of water that was sitting on the end table, and poured it over the flame in the fire pit. The fire sizzled, and then died. "On that note, I should be going in now. Raoul has been growing quite restless over these last few hours. It's going to be a long night."

She walked to the sliding glass door that connected to her own room. At the door, she hesitated and turned back toward me. "Goodnight, Kare-bear."

I didn't bother to correct her this time, thinking of the baby I'd once been with the lonely curl on my head. "Goodnight, Mom."

Hours later, I awoke suddenly to find someone in my room. I tried to scream, but a hand was clamped over my mouth.

Oh, no. The Thrones found us.

CHAPTER

I STRUGGLED AGAINST THE BODY THAT was pressing against mine, but a familiar voice said, "Dale, shhh. It's all right." He switched on the light. "John?"

I reached out and touched him. He was cold and shivering, his clothes and hair drenched. That only served to convince me that this wasn't a mirage. "Where the hell have you been?"

"I'm sorry, I don't have time to explain." He opened the bedroom door and peeked out. When he didn't see anything, he closed it and turned on the lamp. He was armed to the teeth, guns holstered on his hips and both legs and a rifle strapped to his back. "You have to leave. Now."

"What? What are you talking about?"

He pressed a set of keys into my hand. "If you go down past the driveway, out onto the main street, there's a black Hummer parked about a block up. I want you to take it and drive away. Get as far from here as you can."

"I don't understand."

He grasped my shoulders. "The Thrones are here. They've found Amara, and if you don't leave, they'll find you, too."

I gaped at him. "What? How?"

"You said you didn't want to meet Amara anymore. I didn't think you would come here."

I was still half asleep, and my brain was foggy, so it took a second for his words to penetrate. That's when I noticed what he was wearing: dark body armor with a flaming angel insignia on the arm. "You brought them here."

He hesitated, just slightly. A crease appeared between his eyebrows. "I promised to protect you, Dale. That's what I'm trying to do. Please just leave, before they find you."

"I can't do that. I won't."

I pushed John out of the way and ran out onto the terrace, which was connected to my room on one side, and Amara's on the other. It was raining, causing my T-shirt to cling to my skin. I tripped on a large object laying a few feet in front of the sliding glass door. I looked down to see what it was. The light from my bedroom illuminated the terrace just enough.

It was a person. One of the snipers.

I crouched down and rolled him over, but his eyes were glazed over and sightless, his mouth forming an "O" shape, as if he was surprised that this was happening. I recognized him immediately: Travis, the guard who had kissed me. Oh, God.

Three other bodies littered the terrace. I didn't bother to check on them. If any one of them had been alive, they would have been protecting Amara. They hadn't even made it as far as the bedroom door. This was really bad.

I ran into the master suite, not bothering to close the door behind me. The lamp had been knocked to the floor, and several of the crystal figurines Amara collected had been shattered on the dresser. But Amara was not here.

Red tinged the edges of my vision, and I fought for control. I could not have a Rage, not now. I needed to think.

I heard a noise, and I followed the sound. To the right of the bed, hidden from the door, was a man. A silver knife protruded from his chest, but he was not dead. Instead, he made desperate croaking noises as he lay there like a dying whale. I didn't recognize him as one of Amara's people, so I probed his mind. I couldn't see what she had done, but there was a gaping hole in his mind where a solid shell should be. It was probably what prevented him from taking the knife from his chest and healing. Judging by the pool of blood underneath him, it was too late now.

The *humane* thing would be to kill him, pull the knife out of his chest and end his suffering. But I couldn't bring myself to do it. So I stepped over him and picked up Amara's bedside phone. Covington's crisp voice answered. "Get everyone you can over here. We're being attacked."

I hung up before Covington could reply, scrambling desperately to pull together my thoughts. There had been an attack here, clearly, but this guy's presence made it clear that Amara had made it out of this room alive. If I were her, I'd head for the nearest exit.

I tiptoed down the stairs and peeked around the corner into the entryway. Two people in Thrones uniforms, a man and a woman, blocked my path to the front door. The man didn't notice, but the woman saw me. "Hostile, six o'clock!" she called.

The man turned. They both carried large rifles with bayonets attached to the end. I seized their minds, and they dropped the guns and fell to the ground. But three more Thrones came in, all armed with the same bayonet rifles that the first two had. I tried to grab their minds, but one of them managed to throw a small black ball toward the wall first. I thought it might have been a bomb of some kind. I braced myself, covering my head.

That's when I heard the skittering of tiny legs running across the stone floor.

Mechanical spiders. Fuck.

The spiders crawled toward me. *They're not real,* I kept telling myself. But it didn't matter, especially not when the first one touched my foot and burned off the skin. I couldn't pluck the spiders off of my skin and hold the Thrones at the same time. I lost my grip on their minds.

The female Throne who had first spotted me grabbed her rifle again. I kicked her legs out from under her, sending her crashing face-first to the ground, but not before she stabbed me in the stomach. Blood oozed out of the wound. But what I didn't expect was the burning sensation surging through my body and the growing weakness in my limbs. The female Throne looked up at me, her face and teeth covered in blood. "Injectable silver, bitch. It's inside you now."

The other Thrones grabbed me, leaving me unable to move my arms or legs. Fire surged through my body, and spiders still crawled up my legs. The first Throne stepped back and aimed her rifle at my chest, a smug smile on her face.

I reached out with my mind and *pushed*, breaking through the shields of their minds as if they were made of straw, clenching them in my mental grip. They all fell to the ground, unconscious.

I ran into the living room. There was blood everywhere. Bodies lined the floor. The few remaining alive were bad off. They no longer fought because they *couldn't*.

I heard someone moan. Fearing it was my mother, I went toward the noise. Laying on the floor, his neck bent at an angle it should have never been bent, was Raoul.

He opened his eyes. Dear God, he was *alive*. He gave me a weak smile, his teeth covered in blood. "I saw this. Told Amara. She ordered everyone home, except the guards. But I stayed with her. Told her I wouldn't leave her."

"Don't try to talk, okay? And don't try to move. I think you might have a neck injury."

"Sssokay. Can't feel anything, anyway."

I didn't know anything about medicine, but I knew that, and the way he was wheezing for breath, was a bad sign. I also knew there was nothing I could do to help him. "Where's Amara?" I asked him.

"Roof," he gasped.

"All right. I'm gonna try to find her. Just stay here, and don't try to move. Help is coming soon, okay?" I had no idea whether I was lying or not, but it seemed like the right thing to say. I ran outside. The carnage continued, bodies lining the walkway to the door. I didn't bother to check to see if they were dead or alive.

All the terraces had staircases on each side connecting them to one another, and then up to the roof, making the house vaguely resemble an M.C. Escher painting. But unlike the terraces, there was no wall around the roof, making it an incredibly dangerous and stupid place to have a confrontation.

I hesitated before I went up to the roof. I was alone, unarmed, in my pajamas, and had no idea what I was facing up there. I crept up the rest of the way, bracing against the wind and the rain, and peered over the edge.

There were normally two snipers stationed on the roof at opposite corners from one another. Both of them lay dead. I could see the one closest to me had been shot through the forehead.

One of the people on the roof was Amara; though I could not see her face, the long dress and billowy hair gave her away. The other was a man, thin, dark skinned, and taller than anyone I'd ever seen outside of a basketball court. He wore a long, hooded cloak, and I'd recognize him anywhere. *Gabriel.*

I climbed over the top, grabbed the rifle away from the dead sniper, and pointed it at Gabriel. "Get the fuck away from my mother."

The rifle was heavier than I thought it would be. My hands were shaking, and I had no idea how to shoot it. Gabriel, meanwhile, just smiled at me. A knife gleamed in his hands. "Ah, the daughter. I was wondering when I would meet you."

I dropped the gun and lunged at him. Red colored the edges of my vision, but this time I went with it, allowing my mind to turn *with* the Rage rather than against it. My vision grew darker and darker…until everything snapped into sharper, clearer focus. The pain I felt from the bayonet wound and the silver running through my blood was gone. I felt invincible.

Gabriel rolled me back against the concrete. I kicked up with my legs. It got him off of me, but he jumped up to his feet again. He pulled something that looked like a pen out of his pocket and hit a button. The pen made a high-pitched squeal, and a strobe light flashed into my eyes. But I remembered the weapon from before. I pushed my way through the pain in my head and grabbed his arm and sunk my fingernails into the fleshy part of his arm. The shock of pain must have startled him, and he dropped the pen. It shut off, and the pain in my head immediately went away.

Gabriel lunged for me. I punched him in the throat. While he was struggling for air, I kicked out his knee from the side. The move caused him to stumble and fall to his knees. He retained his balance, but it put us at a more even height.

I tried to punch him again, but before I could, he disappeared. I felt a warm breeze blow past me. I turned, and Gabriel rematerialized in front of me. "You don't understand what's happening here."

I grunted. I wasn't capable of speech at that point. Instead of talking, I launched at him again.

This time, he was ready for me. He slashed at me with his knife. I deflected the blow with my arm, but the burning sensation running through my body flared. More silver. Shit. I punched him with the heel of

my good hand. I heard bones crunch, and when I pulled back, blood was dripping from his nose.

I heard voices yelling behind me. I ignored them, focusing all of my attention on Gabriel. I swept his leg out from under him. He collapsed. I grabbed his knife and jumped on top of him.

He vanished into thin air. Seconds later, he reappeared on my back. His weight was too much for me, and I collapsed. But I still had the knife in my hand. I reached behind me and stabbed blindly.

Gabriel grunted and rolled off of me. His neck was bleeding now, blood dripping down into the collar of his cloak. But I hadn't hit anything major, apparently. I got to my feet, and we faced each other. I found his mind. It was a solid wall, like John's had been, but I knew my will was stronger. "You will not kill my mother."

I didn't get the reaction I was expecting: no resistance, no blowback. But I didn't get a chance to ponder what that meant, because Gabriel tackled me. I tumbled backward, the knife falling out of my hands, the upper half of my body dangling off the roof. Gabriel grabbed my feet and held me there, the only thing keeping me from crashing to the rocks below. "You don't understand," he said through gritted teeth, "I don't want to kill her!"

"So why the fuck are you here?"

"I am not your enemy! I've never been your enemy!"

A gun fired.

Gabriel screamed, and then he vanished. I slipped toward the ground. Somehow I managed to hook my foot over the edge of the roof. I dangled there for a minute, with nothing but my right foot holding me to the side of the building. Directly below me, water rushed over jagged rocks toward the waterfall that was Zamorski House's focal point. If I hit them head first, I wouldn't survive.

I arched myself toward the building slowly, until the left side of my body hit the edge of the building. I got my other foot over the edge of the roof and hoisted myself back up. If I made it out of this alive, I would be doing more sit-ups in the future.

There were two people on the roof: Gabriel and John. Gabriel was crouching down beside what looked like a crumpled pile of clothes, crying. John had a gun in his hands—an old-fashioned, flintlock pistol just like the one Gabriel had shot him with weeks ago—and it was aimed directly at Gabriel. There was blood splattered across John's face and hands.

I looked at the pile front of Gabriel. Maybe I was just in denial, or my mind refused to process what I was seeing, because I just couldn't figure out why someone left dirty laundry on the roof in the rain. But then everything came together and the sight made sense. I just didn't want it to.

Amara lay on the roof, her eyes glazed over and sightless. I ran over and crouched down beside her. There was a bullet hole in the front of her dress, blood splattered across the front. Another flintlock pistol lay discarded to the side, as if it had just been thrown away after she was killed. She had been shot with the same fractal bullets that had almost killed John. But unlike that night on the subway, the shooter hadn't missed. The wound was perfectly aligned with her heart. The organ had probably already exploded inside of her, shredding as the fractal bullets splintered.

No, this wasn't right.

Gabriel stood up and spoke, his voice hard. "John, you knew your orders."

John's voice was cold, colder than I had ever heard it. "I am not your puppet. I have never been your puppet."

"But Amara was…"

"You *know* what she did to my parents, Gabriel."

I didn't understand. This was wrong. It had to be wrong. But then things started to click into place.

John had spent the last three hundred years trying to avenge his parents' death.

His father had once been leader of the Thrones.

Zaphkiel had been leader of the Thrones...and then Amara had killed him.

My mother killed John's parents. And John had been using me to get to her.

Gabriel glanced down at Amara's body, and then back at John. "You don't have to do this, John."

"Yes, I do." Then John fired.

Gabriel collapsed, falling on top of Amara so quickly that I had to jump out of the way. His body spasmed a few times, and then it was still.

I stood and stared him down. "You killed her."

"Yes."

"Was that your plan all along? To use me to get to my mother?"

His breath hitched. "Yes." He could barely get out the word.

"Are you going to kill me, too?"

"No." He dropped the pistol he'd used to shoot Gabriel. Then, he stripped himself of all other weapons—the rifle on his back, the knives in his belt, two more modern-looking handguns holstered to his thighs—and dropped them as well. He stood with his arms outstretched, his defenses gone. "Dale, I'm so..."

I grabbed his mind.

You have to want it more, Amara had said. At that moment, I wanted more than anything to hurt John. I imagined my mental reach as talons, crushing his shields and then sinking deep into his brain. Blood poured out of his ears and nose. I stepped closer to him. "Dale...don't," he rasped.

"She was my *mother*, John!"

I crushed his mind harder, and John's knees buckled, sending him to the ground. He recovered and got up quickly, then took another step away from me. "Listen to me, Dale. Gabriel is gone now. I'll be taking charge of the Thrones, just as I always should have. They won't be after you anymore. I'll make it better for people like you...and for people like Isaac."

It was the mention of Isaac that sent me over the edge. All this time, I'd been blaming myself for his death. "Isaac would still be alive if it weren't for you!"

I twisted my grip on his mind. Blood began to leak from the corners of his eyes, running down his face like tears. "Dale...I'm sorry."

I kept twisting. He stumbled backward, toward the edge of the roof, and fell over the edge.

A second later, I heard a crash. I ran up to the edge of the roof. John lay face down on the rocks, arms and legs akimbo. "No..."

Something trickled down the side of my face. Tears? No, blood. It was coming out of my ears and nose, too. A stabbing pain hit my head. I crumpled to my knees. My brain imploded.

Black.

CHAPTER

M Y EYES FELT LIKE THERE were weights attached to the lids. I forced them open. Blinked.

I was in a hospital room. An IV filled with a clear solution dripped into my hand, and the steady *beep, beep, beep* of my heartbeat filled the room. My head throbbed.

There was a man sitting in the chair next to my bed, rigid-backed and stern. He was wearing khaki pants with a crease pressed down the center and a polo shirt. Damn. I'd never seen him in anything except tuxedos. He was still clean shaven, but his hair was a little unkempt, which showed me just how bad off he was. Now I knew what "roughing it" looked like for a butler. "Hello, Covington."

He smiled at me. To my surprise, it seemed genuine. "Hello, Dale."

THE DOCTORS WHO CAME IN and out stared at me like I had a second head. I didn't, but I *had* almost died.

When I was admitted to the hospital, an MRI revealed massive bleeding inside my brain, as if several blood vessels had decided to burst at the same time. I had been in a coma for six days. The doctors had figured I would have permanent brain damage, if I awoke at all. Yet here I was, awake and aware and talking to the nursing staff as if nothing had ever happened.

The silver poisoning was a trickier issue. My body couldn't expel the poison on its own, and the doctors in the human hospital didn't understand the necessity of over-saturating me with fluids. Thankfully, Covington was able to pull a few strings, and the amount of fluids I received was quadrupled. It had been enough to flush out the worst of the silver. But when I looked at my arm and my stomach, they still had an unsightly gray pallor. When I told Covington, he promptly bought me a Gatorade from the hospital cafeteria and told me to keep drinking extra fluids for at least the next forty-eight hours.

How had I managed to survive twenty-seven years without a butler?

Amara was dead. Covington had found her body himself. She was being stored…somewhere. Covington didn't elaborate on where, and I didn't really want him to. He asked me if I wanted to have a funeral or some kind of memorial service. "I already thought she was dead for years. What does it matter now?"

"You didn't know her before. Now you do. And you're her next of kin."

I shook my head. "I think you were more her next of kin than anyone. So just do whatever you want. Whatever's easiest for you. It doesn't matter to me."

All in all, thirteen of Amara's people had died that night. Not a bad count, until you consider that Amara evacuated everyone she could before the attack. The guards had been slaughtered. They were outnumbered, and outgunned, and they never had a chance. Raoul, Covington told me, had

died before medical help could get there. Telling me Amara was on the roof was probably the last thing he did.

Out of Amara's people who had been at the house that night, I was the only one who survived. "I don't understand. Why wouldn't Amara have brought in *more* guards if she knew she was going to be attacked?" I asked.

Covington sat down on the edge of my bed, being careful not to jostle the wires and tubes that were still attached to my body. "I think sometimes, the older ones just give up. After a few millennia, ennui sets in, and then what? When you live forever, you have nothing to look forward to. Amara's great loves were dead. She had no hope of ever reconciling with Gabriel. She was only living for one thing: to find you one day. Once she did that, there was nothing else left."

"There was still me," I whispered, but I'm not sure if he heard me.

The Thrones had cleared out their dead before Covington arrived. The only evidence that they'd ever been there at all were the video feeds from the various security cameras in the house. "The Thrones disabled most of the cameras, but they missed the ones that were not linked in to the house's main security feed." He paused. "You should be proud of yourself. You fought well that night." Proud. Ha. That was about the last word I'd use to describe my state of mind. But Covington continued, oblivious to my internal conflict. "I only regret that the man who killed Amara got away."

Wait, what? "Got away? How? I saw him fall off the roof myself."

Covington reached into his bag and pulled out a laptop computer. After a few keystrokes, he turned it toward me. "This was taken a few hours after the attack, after we'd all gone. The footage is grainy, and the coverage isn't great on that side of the house, but...you'll see."

On the screen was a long shot of the east side of Zamorski House, where John had fallen. Everything was still. Then, a few seconds into the video, something dashed across the screen. I rewound the video and slowed it

down at the appropriate spot. The footage was too grainy to see what—or who—had run across the camera, but it was definitely human-shaped. A ray of hope swelled in my heart, even as I tried to squash it. John had survived! But it didn't change anything. He had lied to me, betrayed me, violated everything I thought we had.

I checked myself out against medical advice around midnight that night. I didn't want to risk the (presumably more awake and engaged) day-shift doctors coming back on shift and starting to ask too many questions. "There was nothing abnormal about my case," I said to the doctor who discharged me. "You will investigate no further."

"I really must advise against this, Miss Highland. Two days ago you were...oh, your nose is bleeding."

Damn. I pulled a tissue out of the box beside the hospital bed and wiped the blood away. My head ached worse than it had before, and obviously whatever attempts I'd made at manipulating the doctor's mind had failed. But maybe it wasn't a bad thing. You shouldn't be able to go through life getting people to do whenever you want, anyway.

I looked at the doctor and tried my best to look dignified—in spite of the fact that I was still wearing an open-back hospital gown and I probably had blood smeared on my face. "Nonetheless, I will be checking myself out." And the hospital couldn't get very far investigating a miraculous patient recovery without a patient to investigate.

I was trying to figure out the problem of what to wear out of the hospital when there was a knock on the door. Covington stood there with two shopping bags full of clothes in his hands. I peered inside. Skirts and sundresses, ugh. But at least I would have something other than my bloody, sliced-up T-shirt to wear.

I managed to get dressed in the bathroom. I was more than a little shaky on my feet, and my head still felt like it had been pounded with a

sledgehammer, but the grab bars along the walls and on the side of the toilet helped considerably. I didn't know whether asking one of the nurses or orderlies for help would give the hospital cause to detain me longer, but I wasn't going to find out, and I'd be damned before I'd let Covington help me change.

An orderly rolled me out of the hospital in a wheelchair, Covington by my side. A limousine waited for us in front of the entryway. Covington opened the back door for me, and I got inside. He got into the driver's seat, reached over, and handed me a manila envelope. "What's this?" I asked.

"Amara told me about your legal predicaments. She asked me to work on this before she died."

I opened the envelope and poured the contents onto the seat. A driver's license. A birth certificate. A Social Security card. Even a passport. All of them with the name "Dale Annette Highland" on them. "Everything will pass legal inspection," he said as he pulled out of the hospital parking lot. "You can go anywhere and get any kind of employment."

It was the very thing I'd wanted my entire adult life: freedom. The chance to live like a normal person. But now that I had it, I wasn't sure it mattered anymore. "Thank you, Covington. This is amazing."

"So where would you like to go?" he asked.

There was one thing I needed to do as Dale Highland, a couple of loose ends I needed to tie up. I owed them that much.

"New York City," I said.

Covington nodded and flipped on the turn signal. I pushed the button to raise the privacy glass. Then, I crumpled into the plush leather seats and sobbed until my head hurt.

CHAPTER

I HADN'T SPOKEN TO NIK OR Chaz since that ill-fated phone call at Isaac's, but I knew I needed to before I could do anything else. They were put in the line of fire because of me. They were interrogated by the Thrones because of me. Who knew what else had happened since I was gone? I had to make things right.

I'd called Nik when we were about thirty minutes outside of the city. She told me on the phone that she'd moved in with Chaz, because she couldn't afford the rent after I left, and because the "big guys with the dark clothes" had freaked her out so badly that she couldn't sleep while she was alone. She said it nonchalantly, as if it was no big deal that I'd contributed to her Post-Traumatic Stress Disorder, which only made me feel worse.

Covington dropped me off in front of Chaz's apartment in Hoboken. Even after all that sleep, I still felt woozy, though my head ached less.

Chaz opened his apartment door. Both of his eyes were blackened, his lip was split, and there was a stitched-up cut running from his cheekbone to his mouth. Three of his fingers on his right hand were splinted and wrapped with white tape. "Jesus, Chaz, what did they do to you?"

He glowered at me. "What do you think they did?"

"What do the doctors think about your hand? Will you recover full use of those fingers? Will your art suffer?"

"That really isn't any of your business, is it?" But he stepped aside and let me in.

The apartment was more cluttered than I'd ever seen it, littered with the debris of Nik's life as well as Chaz's. I wondered if they were suffering from a lack of room, or if neither had bothered to clean it.

Nik was sitting on the couch, wearing a tank top and pajama bottoms, her dreadlocks loose around her face. Unlike Chaz, she appeared to be uninjured—at least physically. When she saw me, she ran up and gave me a hug, almost knocking me over with her body weight. "I'm so glad you back, and you're safe. Aren't you glad she's safe, Chaz?"

Chaz scowled some more, and Nik just hugged me tighter.

God. These weren't the two people I had left behind. Less than a month had passed since I'd jumped onto that subway platform, but everything had changed.

"I have something to tell you both," I said.

Nik sat back down on the couch. Chaz leaned against the kitchen pass-through, folding his arms across his chest. I sat in his reclining chair, knowing he probably didn't want me to, but also knowing that I didn't have the energy to stand up to tell what would inevitably be a very long story. But they were part of this now, and they deserved to know the truth. Besides: I was free now. And that meant I could start showing people some of the real me.

"About a month ago, I found out I was half demon..."

And so it began.

I TOLD THEM HOW JOHN had found me and led me to the truth about my heritage. I told them how I rescued him. I told them about the Thrones, about why they wanted me, about why they'd interrogated Nik and Chaz for my whereabouts. I told them how we'd gone on the run together, and how I'd fallen in love with him.

I told them how he betrayed me.

I told them about my mother, and how she died.

I told them about everything except for the Rages. There was no reason they needed to know about Karen Fowler killing her best friend's prom date, or the man whose head I'd cut off for some reason I could not remember, or any of the rest of it. Maybe I was afraid it would change the way they looked at me. I'd only trusted two people with those secrets. One of them was dead. The other had killed her. My track record wasn't looking very good on that one.

When I was done, Nik had tears running down her face. Chaz rolled his eyes. "I can't believe you're buying this bullshit," he said. "She could have just told you that unicorns had flown her around the moon, and you would have believed it."

She wiped her face and looked at him defiantly. "I'm not as naïve as you think I am. But you said yourself the people who tortured you weren't *normal*, that they could do things that weren't humanly possible. Maybe this is it. Maybe this is the answer."

When Chaz didn't respond, I stood up, balancing myself on the back of the chair. "I'm so sorry for what happened to both of you. I never thought they'd connect you to me, and I never thought they'd come after you."

"Yeah, well, doesn't do us much good now, does it? Guess that road to hell is a little bit shorter when you're already a demon." He stormed off to his room, slamming the door behind him.

Nik sighed. "I'm sorry, Dale. He's been having a hard time over these past few weeks. His fingers were badly broken—compound fractures, you know? The doctors don't know if he'll ever get full use of the hand back, or if it'll ever be good enough for him to draw again."

Chaz's art was his life. If he didn't get that back, I didn't know what he'd do. "Jesus, Nik, I'm so sorry. For all of it."

"It's not your fault. I know you didn't mean for any of this to happen." She tried to smile, though the effort was wobbly. "So what are you going to do now?"

I sighed. "I'm going to do what I do best."

THE GREAT THING ABOUT INTERSTATE buses is that, unlike an airplane or train, if you print your ticket at home, you don't need to present identification to get on. It was a security loophole that, despite the world's growing paranoia, had somehow been overlooked. Or maybe the powers that be just figured it wasn't worth it to secure buses, since bus travelers were already on the lowest rung of decent society, anyway. Whatever the reason, it worked out for me. I bought my ticket under another assumed name and printed it out on Chaz's computer. Once I got where I was going, I would get new identification. But I wouldn't be Dale Highland anymore. The identification documents Covington gave me were perfect, amazing, but I didn't want to be Dale Highland anymore. I *couldn't* be Dale Highland anymore.

Nik waited for my bus with me at the Port Authority Terminal. "If this John guy is anything like you say he is, he'll want to know where you are," she said. "He'll probably find Chaz and me."

I shrugged. "So tell him." I was on a 10:15 p.m. bus to Chicago, but I'd only be staying there long enough to dump out my Dale Highland clothes and get yet another ID. After that...west maybe, or south? It didn't really matter. Would John be able to find me? Would he even bother? I didn't know, and I didn't really care anymore. I'd just keep on running. I didn't know how to do anything else.

Nik took off her backpack and opened it. She pulled out a cardboard tube and handed it to me. "I know you probably won't be able to keep this after you change identities, but I want you to have it, anyway."

I opened the tube and unrolled the sheet of paper inside. On the paper was the drawing of a woman, dressed in a tight red jumpsuit that accentuated her large breasts, a matching cape blowing behind her. Her short, coppery hair stuck up in all directions. But it was her face that really got me. Fair skin, dotted with light freckles, a small, roundish nose, and bright blue, unmistakable eyes. "Nik, is this me?" She nodded. "Are my boobs really this big?"

"You're a superhero. Big boobs are a prerequisite. Although..." Nik looked me up and down, "your boobs are up to the challenge."

I punched her lightly in the arm, and she grinned. I rolled the drawing back up and returned it to the tube. "I love it. I'll keep it no matter what. But Nik...I'm anything but a superhero."

"You've got these amazing abilities. You're super strong, and you kick ass. You saved John, even though he turned out to be an ass, and you tried to save your mother even though it almost killed you. That makes you a superhero in my book."

An announcement for my bus came over the intercom. "That's me," I said to Nik.

We hugged. I held on longer than I should have, letting tears fall on her shoulder. "I'll miss you," she whispered, which made me cry harder. "Be safe."

I sniffled and pulled away. "You, too."

Wiping my tears on the sleeve of my coat, I picked up my duffel bag and went out to board the bus.

AN OLDER WOMAN SAT NEXT to me, her dark skin wrinkled and salt-and-pepper hair peeking out from beneath a felt hat. One look at her, and I knew she would want to talk. "I'm Norma," she said as we were crossing through the Lincoln Tunnel.

"I'm Rose." At least, that's what it said on my bus ticket. I had read *Romeo and Juliet* back in high school, when I wasn't a killer and everything was easy. A famous quote bubbled up from my memory:

That which we call a rose by any other name would smell as sweet.

Maybe that was why I picked it, or maybe not. I didn't know anymore. It was a name, and I needed a name, and it was the first one that came to mind.

The woman smiled at me. "I'm so excited. This is the first time I've been to Chicago. My daughter and son-in-law moved there a few months ago. I'm hoping we'll get there early enough tomorrow that I'll have a chance to sightsee. What about you?"

Once upon a time, I would have taken the opportunity to fill in all the details of Rose's life. Where she was born. Where she had gone to school. Why she was going to Chicago. It would be good practice for when I got to

wherever I was going. I had long known it was the little details that make a person.

But I didn't. "I'm sorry, but I'm really tired. If you don't mind, I think I'm going to go to sleep now."

"Oh. Of course, dear." She couldn't hide her disappointment. But I couldn't manage to care.

I itched to take my MP3 player out of my bag, to use the music to drown out the quiet. But I couldn't do that either. Each song was a memory, a place I would never return to, a person I would never see again. The thought made me ache even more, threatened to bring back the tears I'd been fighting.

So instead I closed my eyes. Morning rain pounded on the roof. Tires swished on the pavement. As the roar of New York City faded behind me, I fought the urge to cry, holding my breath until it passed. Those tears had no business here. They belonged to Dale Highland.

And Dale Highland didn't exist anymore.

ACKNOWLEDGMENTS

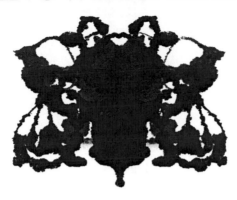

N O BOOK EVER HAPPENS IN a vacuum, and there are a lot of people I need to thank for helping me write and publish my first book. First of all, I'd like to thank my parents, Diane and Walt Woodward, without whom I would (literally) not be here. They have both passed away now, but I know this book would not have happened without their influence. When I was a kid, my father used to let me take over his computer to write my stories, and then he'd take the finished products into his office to brag about me to his coworkers. He died when I was thirteen, but this early encouragement is still one of the most vivid memories I have of him. Even after his death, my mom continued to encourage my writing dreams, even when everyone else seemed to think I should just settle into a practical "adult" job and forget about writing. *The Demon Within* was the last work of mine that she read before she died, so it's fitting that it's the first one that got published.

To Robert Peterson and the entire California Coldblood/Rare Bird Books team: thank you for taking a chance on an unknown, unproven writer. Bob, you in particular deserve so much credit for pushing me to be a better writer and to take chances I wasn't always comfortable with. This process

wasn't an easy one, and I know I probably wasn't the easiest person to deal with at times. I thank you for continuing to persevere and for putting up with me. This book is better because of you.

Jean Russell and the entire Thursday night Writer's Harbor crew: this book only exists because of all of you. Once upon a time, *The Demon Within* was only going to be a short fiction piece about a woman who had blackouts and murdered people. I brought the short story into the group, and everyone asked, "Well, why does she murder people?" A discussion began, and an idea was born. You guys were there at the genesis of this story, and I hope you like the final product.

My early beta readers, Tara Tadlock and Phoebe Schlesinger: thank you for taking the time to read an early draft of the story and offer your unbiased critiques. It could not have been easy to be both a critic and a friend, and I owe you so much for helping me iron out those initial kinks before I got on the road to publication.

And finally, to my fiancé, Jason: thank you for encouraging me, for cheering me on when I need it, and for always being in my corner. You are the best thing that has ever happened to me, and I am so lucky to have you in my life.

ABOUT THE AUTHOR

BETH WOODWARD has always had a love for the dark, the mysterious, and all things macabre. At twelve, she discovered the wonders of science fiction and fantasy when she read *A Wrinkle in Time,* which remains the most influential book of her life. Growing up, she was Meg Murray with a dash of Oscar the Grouch. She's been writing fiction since she was six years old; as a cantankerous kid whose family moved often, the fictional characters she created became her friends. As an adult, she's slightly more well adjusted, but she still withdraws into her head more often than is probably healthy.

When she's not writing, Beth enjoys traveling, going to sci-fi and fantasy conventions, watching movies, and reading voraciously. She is a rabid *Doctor Who* fan and spends a lot of time with the two cats whose household she shares. She currently lives in the Washington, DC area.

CPSIA information can be obtained at www.ICGtesting.com
Printed in the USA
LVOW07s0911020316

477448LV00003B/5/P